GHOSTS
FROM THE LIBRARY

It is said that books are written to bring sunshine into our
dull, grey lives—to show us places we want to escape to, lives
we want to live, people we want to love. But there are also
stories that can be found only in the deepest, darkest corners
of the library—about the unexplained, of lost souls, of things
that go bump before the silence. Before the screaming.

And some stories just disappear. Printed in old newspapers,
broadcast live on the wireless, sometimes not even published
at all—these are the stories you cannot find on even the
dustiest of library shelves. Until now.

Ghosts from the Library resurrects forgotten tales of the
supernatural by some of the most acclaimed mystery authors
of all time. From Arthur Conan Doyle and John Dickson
Carr to Agatha Christie and Daphne du Maurier, this
spine-chilling anthology brings together thirteen uncollected
tales of terror, plus some additional surprises.

*For more information about the Golden Age of Detective Fiction
and the conference that inspired this collection, visit:*
bodiesfromthelibrary.com

GHOSTS FROM THE LIBRARY

Lost Tales of Terror
and the Supernatural

Selected and introduced by

TONY MEDAWAR

COLLINS
CRIME
CLUB

COLLINS CRIME CLUB
An imprint of HarperCollins*Publishers*
1 London Bridge Street
London SE1 9GF
www.harpercollins.co.uk

HarperCollins*Publishers*
Macken House, 39/40 Mayor Street Upper,
Dublin 1, D01 C9W8, Ireland

This paperback edition 2023
2

First published by Collins Crime Club 2022

Selection, introduction and notes © Tony Medawar 2022
For copyright acknowledgments, see page 275.

These stories were mostly written in the first half of the twentieth century and characters sometimes use offensive language or otherwise are described or behave in ways that reflect the prejudices and insensitivities of the period.

A catalogue record for this book
is available from the British Library

ISBN 978-0-00-851484-6

Typeset in Minion Pro 11/15 pt by
Palimpsest Book Production Ltd, Falkirk, Stirlingshire

Printed and bound in the UK using 100% renewable electricity
at CPI Group (UK)

	MIX
FSC www.fsc.org	Paper | Supporting responsible forestry FSC™ C007454

This book is produced from independently certified FSC™ paper
to ensure responsible forest management.

For more information visit: www.harpercollins.co.uk/green

CONTENTS

INTRODUCTION

'Some people can't see the colour red.
That doesn't mean it isn't there.'
Sue Grafton, *M is for Malice*

Bodies from the Library, the Collins Crime Club's annual anthology of unknown and rarely seen short fiction, has to date focused on crime and detection. In five volumes, so far, we have brought to light uncollected stories by Agatha Christie and more than 50 other writers of the Golden Age of crime and detective fiction, as well as stories and scripts never previously published including novellas and short stories by Edmund Crispin, Christianna Brand, Dorothy L. Sayers and Ngaio Marsh. However, Christie and her contemporaries *also* wrote stories of the supernatural and many of these too have not been published before or have appeared only in obscure periodicals or anthologies.

Stories of the supernatural are very different from crime and detective fiction. After all, the art of detective fiction is *to explain*. There are some crime stories that fail in this precept, most notably Raymond Chandler's *The Big Sleep* (1939), in which a chauffeur appears to have been murdered but no one—not even the author—can explain how it happened. Such oddities aside, with a detective story, a thriller or a mystery, the reader can be reasonably certain that *everything* will be explained and that order will be restored, even in the most baffling of circumstances. The art of supernatural fiction is the exact opposite. In these, there are some things that will not—*cannot*—be explained, and when the sunlight hits the room, a little darkness always remains . . .

Like stories of detection, stories featuring the supernatural have been around a long time. A *very* long time. While the Quran holds that ghosts—as such—do not exist, a ghost does appear in the Bible's Book of Samuel, and in the New Testament there are several occasions when Jesus Christ is mistaken for a ghost by his disciples. Across the centuries throughout the world, there have been stories of ghosts that are vengeful or loving or penitent—ghosts that are benign and ghosts that are evil. While stories of ghosts and other supernatural happenings became popular as a form of entertainment in the medieval period, at least in Europe and Asia, the popularity of the genre in Britain was probably at its zenith in the late eighteenth century, the heyday of the Gothic novel. By the nineteenth century, the ghost was becoming more domesticated. In 1843, the firm of Chapman & Hall published *A Christmas Carol*, with illustrations by John Leech. Charles Dickens' tale of hauntings and redemption is probably the greatest supernatural story, and its success almost certainly influenced the editors of the countless magazines and newspapers of the period to publish festive 'spook stories' annually. And many—if not most—crime and detective story writers responded to the challenge, producing at least one supernatural tale, sometimes unsettling and sometimes amusing but always entertaining.

Today, though there are some notable exceptions, few crime writers write stories of the supernatural. Nonetheless, the genre remains extremely popular. There are novels of the new Gothic like Stacey Halls' *The Familiars* (2019) and the work of Laura Purcell, most recently *Something Wicked* (2022), as well as contemporary scarers like *This Is Not a Ghost Story* (2021) by Andrea Portes. In London's West End, Danny Robins' play *2.22*

A Ghost Story is entering its third season while Stephen Mallatratt's 1987 adaptation of Susan Hill's *The Woman in Black* (1983) is soon to mark its 35th anniversary. In the cinema the supernatural is less common but it is a staple of the streaming channels, and on the small screen, Mark Gatiss has successfully reimagined the BBC's 1970s series *A Ghost Story for Christmas*, while his fellow members of *The League of Gentlemen*, Reece Shearsmith and Steve Pemberton, pepper their award-winning anthology series *Inside No. 9* with tropes of the supernatural and horror fiction.

Welcome, then, to the thirteen stories that comprise *Ghosts from the Library*. Here you will find ghosts aplenty as well as a haunted house, courtesy of Sir Arthur Conan Doyle, a haunted— or is it haunting?—dress, provided by Anthony Berkeley. Christianna Brand tells a sinister story of a witch, and there is a radio play by Agatha Christie in which . . . but that would be telling! There are lost stories by—among others—Daphne du Maurier, Josephine Tey and Margery Allingham, as well as the horrific final case of Q Patrick's Lieutenant Timothy Trant, which foreshadows by more than 30 years one of the most infamous horror novels of all time. And as bonuses, we are reprinting a rare essay by G. K. Chesterton, and Dorothy L. Sayers provides an unusual coda to one of M. R. James' most famous tales.

Now, please, find a comfortable chair by a well-banked fire. Settle down to read. And if there is a noise somewhere in the room behind you, an unfamiliar sound of something scraping at the door or swishing across the carpet, *don't* look round . . .

Tony Medawar
March 2022

GHOST STORIES

G. K. Chesterton

I can claim to be tolerably detached on the subject of ghost stories. I do not depend upon them in any way; not even in the sordid professional way, in which I have at some periods depended upon murder stories. I do not much mind whether they are true or not. I am not, like a Spiritualist, a man whose whole philosophy may be said to consist entirely of ghosts. But I am not like a Materialist, a man whose whole philosophy is exploded and blasted and blown to pieces by the most feeble and timid intrusion of the most thin and third-rate ghost. I am quite ready to believe that a great number of ghosts were merely turnip ghosts elaborately prepared to deceive the village idiot. But I am not at all certain that they succeeded even in that; and I suspect that their greatest successes were elsewhere. For it is my experience that the village idiot is very much less credulous than the town lunatic. On the other hand, when the merely sceptical school asks us to believe that every sort of ghost has been a turnip ghost, I think such sceptics rather exaggerate the variety and vivacity and theatrical talent of turnips.

There is no particular difficulty about the artistic problem of the ghost story as distinct from the spiritual problem of the ghost. All that is required of this literary form, as of any other, is that it shall observe the laws and limits of its form. Nothing is more fatal, for instance, than mixing up the convention of the ghost story with the convention of the crime story. In the solid and profitable matter of murder, I do not hesitate to say that the artist must be a materialist. I do not say he must accept the dogma that dead men tell no tales; for, after all, he whole art of a detective story is the art of getting tales out of dead men. But I do say that the dead men must be dead; and no mystical transcendental spiritual immortal nonsense about it. Every art has in it something of the quality of a sport. The rules of a sport have nothing to do with reality; but they have a real element of loyalty. Literature is only a game; but it is not even literature unless we keep the rules of the game. Just as the pugilist must not hit below the belt, so the crime novelist must not hit above the body. His business is to present to his reader a nice, fresh, fascinating, suggestive, satisfactory body. He may happen himself to believe in the survival of the soul, an eccentricity which has actually occurred in many cases, including my own; but he has no right to bring in the higher mysteries of immortality to illuminate the lower mysteries of detection. He has no right to do it because it is not playing the game; it is like looking out the answer to a riddle or using a crib in an examination. Even the village idiot can solve the village murder, if he receives private information from the ghost of the murdered man.

Whether there is any historical truth in such a notion of a ghost I have not the ghost of a notion. Roughly speaking, I should say that the probabilities are in its favour. For where there is a very great amount of gossip, there is generally some groundwork for the gossip; even if the ground is the graveyard. It is doubtless easy to make very uncharitable use of the proverb that where there is smoke there is fire; but that is because the more puritanical moralists of the village are rather prone to twist it into a totally different proverb; that where there is fire there is hell-fire. I do not suggest any such savour of brimstone, or any extreme evil or terror, as necessarily clinging either to the dead or to the living in this matter; and it is no business of mine to suggest either that the village ghost came from the lower regions, or that the village prodigal is going there. But just as such a village character, while perhaps not so black as he is painted, may he of the sort that is seldom successfully white-washed, so I think it difficult for the sceptic to seal so hermetically all the whited sepulchres of a rationalised model village as to hide all the hints there have been in history of such spectres sometimes escaping from such sepulchres. There is too large a mass of tradition for there not to be some small nucleus of truth; but beyond that very general impression, which is indeed the common sense of mankind. I have neither will nor power to dogmatise in the matter. But I am quite certain that when such things are used merely as symbols, by an artist, the emblematical figures should be of one definite decorative style; or the sepulchres, so to speak, of the same school of monumental architecture, I mean that we must not mix up the ghost story, which is a story about a ghost, with some other technical type of tale, such as a story about a corpse. The ideas are on two different planes, and one will always suffer from the presence of the other. Either the spiritual story will be much too thin, or the blood and bones story will be a bit too thick. Ghosts, in short, may wander about in real life, if they like, because truth is stranger than fiction; but in the refined world of fiction we must be a little more exclusive and fastidious in our selection of ghosts. They must be family ghosts, in the sense of ghosts of good family; or only living (like the dear old butler) with the best. A mere mob of phantoms, for all I know, may march like an army up the high road of history; but we must know more about the particular ghost before we allow him to appear in so serious a thing as a novel.

I happened recently to pick up and re-read *The Hound of the Baskervilles*; which is something of a curiosity of literature, because its author afterwards became an ardent Spiritualist, having written this full-length mystery novel from the stand-point of a complete materialist. And here, more than anywhere, appears this impression the incompatibility of the two types of imagination. It is not merely that the two explanations of the ghostly hound cannot co-exist as theories; they cannot co-exist even as hypotheses. The materialistic detective cannot use a ghost even as a guess. It cannot rank as one of the theories which he abandons at the end; he is obliged to abandon it at the beginning. We must start with the assumption that a dog cannot really be a demon; and yet the whole story has to be haunted like any ghost-story with a demon dog. There is evidence that Sir Arthur Conan Doyle took more trouble than usual with the atmosphere of this drama; even if it is rather the atmosphere of a melodrama. He took a wider canvas; he lavished much on scene-painting the landscape of Dartmoor; he went into details of topography and physical geography which would naturally have been too big a background for argumentative anecdotes of Baker Street; the whole panorama seems to be unrolled before us like a scroll of mystery and symbolism, solely to suggest a half-belief in the hell-hound we have already been forbidden to believe in at all. The result is that the Hound of Baskerville and the Hound of Baker Street are looking for each other in two different worlds; they cannot be said to be hunting each other, for they are racing on two different levels. I know not at what stage of Conan Doyle's conversion the book was concluded; but, even if he had already become a Spiritualist, I must congratulate him as an artist on leaving Sherlock Holmes a materialist. The same author, writing as a Spiritualist, later gave a rather lurid description of the conversion of a material-istic doctor to Spiritualism.

But the difference is not between the different opinions either of the author or the character, at different times of their lives. The difference is that not only was the character then a different sort of character, but the author was a different sort of author.

The materialistic medical gentleman was a melodramatic character; and his conversion to ghosts was melodramatic. But Sherlock Holmes was a comedy character; and I cannot call up any picture of what a real interview between him and a real ghost would be like. Sherlock Holmes, having the kind of cleverness that belongs to a comedy character, has also the kind of stupidity, or at least the kind of limitation, that belongs to a man who could never have had a chat with a ghost. For instance, if I remember right, he begins his review of the possibilities with a well-known sceptical sneer, of the sort that is very familiar and really very shallow, to the effect that it is a strange sort of spirit hound who leaves material traces, such as footprints. If he were living for one instant in the tradition of the great ghost stories, he would be more likely to say that it would be a very unusual spirit hound who did *not* leave material traces; or make some imprint in some way on the material world. Nobody would be particularly frightened of a *completely* immaterial hound; a metaphysical and mathematical abstract hound; a hound in intellectual solution. The power in every preternatural story, as in every supernatural belief, is in some suggestion of what is mystical communicating with what is material. But there is no thrill either in blood and thunder or theology that has not that touch of materialisation; even the tale about a skeleton is in a manner the word made flesh; and the ghost is but a shadow of the resurrection of the body.

G. K. CHESTERTON

Gilbert Keith Chesterton was born on 29 May 1874 at Campden Hill, Kensington in London, the son of Edward and Marie Louise Chesterton. He attended St Paul's School, excelling in everything and winning the school's Milton Prize at eighteen for his recitation of 'St Francis Xavier, Apostle of the Indies'—perhaps a surprising choice given that Chesterton had been baptised into the Church of England, but less surprising given his eventual conversion to Catholicism. On leaving St Paul's he attended classes at the Slade School of Fine Art and he began reviewing books, first for *The Bookman* and then for *The Speaker*, a prestigious weekly review to which he also contributed poetry. In 1896, Chesterton's first published short story, 'A Picture of Tuesday', appeared in *The Quarto*, and he wrote on a freelance basis for various other publications while working for a London publisher.

In 1902, Chesterton joined the staff of the *Daily News*, where he would become a leader writer and one of the newspaper's chief literary critics. In the letters' column he jousted on political issues with the likes of George Bernard Shaw, while the newspaper's editor was light-heartedly implored by one correspondent to stop Chesterton's 'reckless practice of making old-established and highly respected proverbs stand on their heads', a facility which will be very familiar to readers of Chesterton's Father Brown stories. Styled 'the prince of paradox', he also reviewed books for the paper and contributed to other leading literary periodicals like *Pall Mall Magazine*, *Echo* and the *Illustrated London News*, for which he wrote a weekly column for over thirty years. He also excelled as an artist—illustrating *The Wonderful History of Dunder Van Haeden* (1901), a children's book by his father, and a book of nonsense verse by Cosmo Monkhouse, whose obituary Chesterton had written for the *Daily News* a few months earlier. He even found time for romance, marrying Frances Alice Blogg, a poet and dramatist whose organisational skills—and patience—provided the stability needed by her extraordinary husband.

Chesterton's journalism led to success as an essayist, with confidently opinionated publications on an extraordinary variety of subjects, including *The Conspiracy of Journalism* (1902), and he wrote several biographies. He became prominent as a political thinker with speaking engagements on subjects like 'Patriotism', 'The Future of Liberalism' and 'Why socialists and radicals should co-operate'. For the rest of his life, he juggled journalism and fiction, while also championing the church, for which Pope Pius XI made him a Knight Commander with Star in the Order of St Gregory the Great, editing *GK's Weekly* and much else besides. Today, almost a century after his death, he is perhaps best remembered for *The Man Who Was Thursday* (1908)—a thriller parodied by Agatha Christie in *The Seven Dials Mystery* (1929)—and for the long series of stories featuring Father Brown, a shrewd and self-effacing Catholic priest. Father Brown is among the immortals of the genre and Chesterton's wordplay and ingenuity inspired many other Golden Age writers, most obviously John Dickson Carr whose *modus operandi* owes much to Chesterton, the model for Carr's main character, Gideon Fell. And when in the late 1920s Anthony Berkeley Cox and Dorothy L. Sayers were considering who should become the first President of the newly formed Detection Club, Chesterton was the obvious choice.

A giant in so many ways, G. K. Chesterton died of heart failure on 14 June 1936 at 'Top Meadow', his home in Buckinghamshire where, at Bekonscot Model Village and Railway, a church dedicated in Chesterton's memory stands to this day.

'Ghost Stories' was published in the *Illustrated London News* on 30 May 1936 as an untitled edition of the long-running feature 'Our Notebook'.

DEBORAH

Josephine Tey

It was on our way home after a few days at the coast that we found it—the cottage, I mean. We had made a detour in order to inspect the new racecourse at Pontbridge, and it was in the, to us, unexplored country between there and Dorking that we came across it. It stood on a knoll about three hundred yards outside as pretty a village as you'll find in Sussex, and it looked like a picture in a fairy-tale book. I had an impression of white lilac, and a laburnum tree at the gate.

I heard Lizbeth gasp, and she twisted in the seat at my side and craned her neck till she couldn't see it any more. We were in the village street before she suggested going back for a closer inspection, and I had to point out that we were late as it was. I have never really liked driving in the dark since I used to skate round shell holes on two wheels with intermittent illumination on the Bethune road.

'Besides,' I said, 'the board you're talking about probably reads "W. Higson, Sweep", and has nothing to do with letting the place.'

She said, 'All right, George, I expect you do need dinner rather badly. Did you notice the lilacs?'

We were nearly home before she spoke again. 'There was an illustration in my Grimm like that. Hansel and Gretel, I think it was.' And at dinner, apropos apparently of bottled peas, she said, 'There were little crooked apple-trees at the side.'

At intervals through the week I remembered the place—or rather I had occasional pictures of it at the back of my mind when I was thinking of totally different matters—and yet when Lizbeth said next Saturday morning at breakfast, 'We are going to start early today and go round by that cottage,' something made me say, 'What cottage?'

'*You* know,' she said. And I had a queer feeling of being found out.

When we pulled up at the little green gate in the hedge, Lizbeth clicked her tongue the way she always does when she has scored off me, for the notice-board, planted drunkenly at one corner of the garden, read 'To Let'. There the information ended. There was no 'Apply to' or 'at'. We went back to the village and in a thatched post office got the information we wanted. The cottage was most certainly to let and the key was to be had at Halkett's. Halkett's was the farm on the slope behind the cottage. The cottage had belonged to an old woman, a childless widow. She had died about eight years ago come June. The present owner was a grandnephew of the old woman, who lived in New Zealand and had never seen the place. He was sort of sentimental about the cottage, though, and wouldn't sell it. It was only to let, and the Halketts looked after it.

We took ourselves to Halkett's, where a large damsel in blue gingham, her enormous arms bare to the elbow and still damp, announced that she would 'fetch Miss Halkett to us', and clattered down the cool tiled passage with the threat still on her lips.

Miss Halkett proved to be a replica of her maid, perhaps a pound or two less, and a shade lighter on her feet—a pleasant, practical girl. She fetched the key and accompanied us down the field path to the cottage. We should have preferred to explore it alone, but could not very well refuse her chaperonage. She preceded us into the living-room and drew aside the curtains that hung across the latticed windows.

'Why,' said Lizbeth, 'it's furnished!'

'Yes, the nephew I was telling you of said that it was to stay just the way it was when old Deborah died and tenants were to be taken only on that condition. We look after it when it isn't let.'

In spite of the emptiness of the wide hearth the room had a pleasant look, very welcoming. It was, moreover, an authentic cottage interior. There were no Liberty cretonnes, no rush mats, no colour scheme. The curtains, as Lizbeth remarked afterwards, were made of flowered chintz at a few pence a yard, and the possibly valuable bits of china on the mantelpiece were cheek by jowl with the kind of tea-caddy a grocer gives away at Christmas and souvenirs of half a dozen watering-places. Nothing in the room had been placed there for its effect. Each article was there because of its value to the owner. And yet in spite of that—or perhaps because of it—the room had a charm that no arranged room in my experience ever had. And the rest of the house was the same.

We moved out of doors and stood looking at the place in a sort of speechless satisfaction. On one side the garden was bounded by a row of white lilac trees, heavy with bloom. At the back, rather close to the house, were aspen poplars—the kind that make a sound like rain when the lightest wind comes— and on the grass at the other side were Lizbeth's crooked little apple-trees. By the road ran a very low hedge of box. A narrow brick path went up to the door, but not round the house. There was no back door, and the grass, unbroken by any flower-beds, grew close up to the walls. It was no show place, inside or out, but it had a most definite charm. All buildings have an atmosphere of some kind or other. 'Laburnum Cottage'—for that was its prosaic name— had an air of primness. It wasn't smug—not even complacent. But there was a happy well-orderedness about it. It both deprecated and disowned the tipsy notice-board. The unmown grass had the incongruous effect of dishevelled hair on a carefully dressed woman. And yet it wasn't in its physical peculiarities that the primness lay. You can get an ordered effect with poplars or cypress or trimmed box. But lilacs are not exactly prim, and the laburnum at the gate was positively wanton. The primness hung in the atmosphere itself, somehow.

As we came back to the living-room Lizbeth said, 'You keep it beautifully, Miss Halkett. We shall have something to live up to.'

Facial expression is the subtlest thing on earth. What is the difference between a pleased blush and an uncomfortable flush? Something too indefinite for words, isn't it?—and yet as definite as daylight. It was certainly an uncomfortable flush that showed in Miss Halkett's honest visage at the moment, and she turned with obvious relief to follow Lizbeth, who had been examining a piece of lustreware, to a second inspection of the kitchen.

Now, why?

We left the place some ten minutes later its accepted tenants, and Lizbeth's parting words to Miss Halkett were, 'And do take down the board at once, won't you? It's a—a blot!'

All the way to the coast she was jubilant, the burden of her song being 'that it should be our luck to get it, when country cottages were at a premium'.

'Perhaps there is a snag somewhere,' I suggested. 'Don't let's crow too soon.'

'George! You unbearable wet blanket!' she said. 'I won't be damped by you. I just won't. If you want to be liverish on a glorious spring morning on your way to the sea through a country reeking of lilac, you'll have to do it without my hitherto unfailing sympathy.'

And certainly it would be difficult to find a snag in the perfect days we spent at the cottage. We would let the Halketts know when we were coming down and they had the place open, clean, and aired for us. They supplied us with milk, butter and eggs, chickens, ducks, and salads. The weather all the summer was the kind that leaves one in no doubt. We spent the long, brilliant days in the garden on the little patch of shaved turf, I working in a deck chair, Lizbeth supine in a hammock slung from the lilac trees. Little flaws of wind ran in a whispering patter through the aspen poplars and ceased abruptly as if afraid of being overheard. Our flowered Chintz flapped lazily at the yawning windows. Over the tops of the trees across the road the blue Sussex distances shimmered in the sun. In July, when London was a blazing furnace, we migrated altogether to Laburnum Cottage. It was then that the change in Lizbeth began. She grew listless and nervy. I blamed the long heatwave and wished that I could take her for a sea voyage, but a country cottage was the best we could do. She woke to animation sometimes when Mary Halkett would look in in passing, and would discuss with every appearance of interest our predecessors in the role of tenant, especially the former owner. I had the impression that the Halkett girl was not quite at her ease at these moments, and I wondered which of the tenants had been the undesirable one. But she was frank enough and showed no disposition to avoid us. She remembered old Mrs Margetts only vaguely, but such recollection as she had was evidently pleasant.

'Everyone liked her,' she said. 'She was a sweet old woman.'

'Was she house-proud?' asked Lizbeth surprisingly.

'She was awfully fond of her cottage, if that's what you mean.'

Later on Lizbeth said, 'How is it that none of the other tenants wanted to hang on to a little heaven like this?' It was a question we had often asked each other, and we both turned to our visitor. On Mary Halkett's face was the expression of one who sees a step just in time. It was gone even as I turned, and she said evenly:

'Well, it's a very lonely spot, and once summer's gone, not so very attractive. Most of the tenants were the kind who like to go to a different place every year.'

Which seemed a reasonable enough explanation.

But when we were left alone again, Lizbeth would sink back to her strange rapt listlessness. And she grew more and more queer in her fads. She gave up the hammock because it 'didn't belong', apparently, was 'out of the picture', and took to sitting at the door in a hard wooden chair with a thin turkey-red cushion as the only mitigant of its penitential qualities.

And then one evening at the end of July, after a grey, dusty day, sultry and full of the promise of storm, we arrived back from a short walk along the parched lanes. Lizbeth had gone in front of me through the open door and was standing apparently gazing down at the table where the evening meal was set.

'Oh, I don't *like* it!' she said suddenly with such passion that it took my breath away.

The chicken salad on the table was one of her favourite dishes, but the best course was to humour her, I thought.

'There's some cold beef in the larder,' I said. 'Shall I get you that?'

To my surprise she turned with a little shaky laugh.

'You prosaic darling!' she said. Then her smile died away. She came close up to me and peered half-searchingly, half-confidingly into my face. 'Have you never noticed the queer thing about the house?' And as I struggled for words in my astonishment, she added, 'No, I suppose a man wouldn't notice. Well, look at the room. There has been a wind all day and clouds of dust have been drifting over the garden. The doors and the windows have been open since morning, *and there isn't a speck of dust in the room!* And it's *always* like that!' Her voice rose hysterically. 'No dust anywhere!'

It sounded perilously like an anticlimax to her dramatic question. But less so when I searched round in my brain for an explanation that might meet the situation. There didn't seem to be one at hand somehow. And the longer I searched, the more at sea I became. To my unbounded relief, however, Lizbeth lapsed suddenly from the borders of hysteria to her normal calm. She sat down at the table and began to serve, and I followed her example. It was rather a silent meal.

'You know,' I said at last, 'there must be a perfectly ordinary explanation. A draught that acts as a vacuum cleaner, or something of that sort. Some quite reasonable explanation.'

She was silent, crumbling her bread. Then she said rather absently, ' Oh, perfectly reasonable!'

But I had a feeling that she did not mean exactly what I did. We dropped the subject. And next morning the weather broke and we went back to town.

For a month I was so busy that we had no chance of getting away even at the weekends. And then, quite unexpectedly, I had a free Saturday and Sunday. It was hot and very much the fag-end of August in town, and I tentatively suggested the cottage. To my surprise Lizbeth, who had quite recovered her good spirits, seemed not only willing, but glad. I heard her humming as we packed, and I called through to her, 'There won't be time to let the Halketts know, but I don't expect we shall starve.'

It wasn't a pleasant journey down. The whole countryside was crying aloud for water, the wind was blustering, and pillars of dust that looked as high as the Nelson monument would rise in front of us and just as we reached their base would, deliberately it seemed, collapse on us. The hedge and the trees outside Laburnum Cottage were grey with dust and the grass looked shabby. Lizbeth went up to Halkett's for the key while I tinkered with the engine before consigning it to the mercies of the garage-late-blacksmith in the village.

'There was no one to be seen at Halkett's,' she said when she came back, 'so I just took the key off the nail.'

I joined her at the door and went into the living-room with her.

Do you know the feeling you have sometimes on entering a room that it has just that moment been vacated? You didn't see or hear a door closing, but you have the impression that someone went out as you came in. Well, there wasn't another door to the living-room at Laburnum Cottage, but I most distinctly had that feeling.

Lizbeth was examining the shining spick-and-span room with interest.

'I just wanted to be sure,' she said inconsequently.

'The Halketts must have cleaned up on the chance of our coming,' I said, ignoring her remark and its possible application.

'No,' she said. Just like that. As if she knew all about it.

'Look here,' I said, exasperated, 'come up to Halkett's with me. I'll lay you fifty to one in pounds that they have been here either today or yesterday.'

'All right,' she said.

We walked up to the farm in silence, I feeling ridiculous and rather angry, Lizbeth apparently serene. We met Mary Halkett by the barn. If one glance at her face was enough for us, I think her glance at us must have been equally enlightening.

'You didn't expect us?' said Lizbeth. I have never heard a more conventional question. It had the unaccented tone of one discussing the weather.

'No,' said Miss Halkett. 'No, or I'd have—No—'

'It doesn't matter,' said Lizbeth. 'We're not staying. We looked in on our way to Bognor to collect some things. We're leaving the cottage to Deborah.'

Mary Halkett put down the can she was carrying, as if suddenly incapable of bearing its weight. 'Oh, I'm so sorry!' she cried. 'So sorry! You've been the nicest people we've ever— You liked the place so much that I thought she might—But I was afraid back in July that you'd noticed. And she wouldn't let up. You're not angry, are you? There's no harm in the cottage. Only the—the queerness.'

'No,' said Lizbeth, still in the same serene way. 'Not a bit angry. For myself I'm rather glad to have known the place. And you see, I have a sympathy with Deborah. I'm awfully attached to sticks and stones myself. We'd be quite happy to think that Deborah had the cottage all to herself until the end of our lease. Wouldn't we, George?'

'Yes,' I said, making with difficulty my sole contribution to this incredible conversation.

Miss Halkett then offered us something to eat at the farm, which we refused. But we each had a glass of milk—just to show that there was no ill-will, as Lizbeth said afterwards.

I drove down to Bognor in a dazed condition. As we sighted the sea, Lizbeth seemed to wake up from a trance. She gave a little amused snort and said, 'Isn't it ludicrous that in these days of shortage of labour we refuse to have anything to do with a cottage that dusts itself!'

It *is* ludicrous, isn't it? But we are going down to the coast next weekend. And I owe Lizbeth a cool fifty, which I'm hoping she won't remember. And worst of all, something I don't understand keeps me from saying, 'I told you so!'

JOSEPHINE TEY

'Josephine Tey' was one of the pen names of the novelist and playwright Elizabeth MacKintosh who was born on 25 July 1896 in Inverness, Scotland. The eldest of three sisters, her parents were Josephine and Colin MacKintosh who ran a fruit and vegetable shop in the city. She studied at the Inverness Royal Academy and later at Anstey Physical Training College in Birmingham where in 1916 she also studied anatomy at the city's university. Between 1918 and 1919, she taught physical education at Lilley & Stone's Girls' High School, an experience she drew on for the play *The Staff Room* (1956), and she went on to teach at other schools in Nottinghamshire, Sussex and Kent.

However, in the early 1920s, MacKintosh gave up teaching to look after her mother at their home, Crown Cottage, near Loch Ness, where after her mother's death she decided to stay and keep house for her father. She had always enjoyed writing and in 1926 she was published for the first time with stories appearing under the name 'Gordon Daviot'. It has been suggested that the pseudonym combined her favourite male forename with the name of a village near the river Nairn where she had holidayed as a child. 'Daviot' was a regular entrant in the weekly 'Problems and Prizes' competition run by the *Westminster Gazette* and she was often among the prize-winners. In February 1926, she came second with 'The Last Straw', a stinging little anecdote that ends with a devastating twist; in March of the same year, her story 'Canis Major' came second in one competition, while the satirical 'True Gratitude' won a prize in another; and the humorous 'The Modern Pirate' was also a prize-winner in April. The newspaper also published several charming pen portraits by 'Daviot' of Perthshire children, stories such as 'Pat Wears His Second-Best Kilt' and 'Janet', as well as her account of the 1927 Highland Games and poems that included 'The Song of Racing' and 'The Song of Stations', which concerned the journey from London to Inverness.

In the late 1920s, she began work on a novel. The result, *Kif* (1929), was Dickensian in concept but distinctly more compact, recounting the 'unvarnished history' of an ex-soldier who finds peace harder than war, drifting into petty crime and worse. At the same time, the publisher Methuen had announced a detective story competition, judged by A. A. Milne, H. C. Bailey and Father Ronald Knox. She did not win, but while few reviewers were convinced by the merits of the story that did—by N. A. Temple Ellis—her entry was widely praised on publication. As required by the competition's rules, *The Man in the Queue* (1929) is very much a detective novel, complete with a realistic but memorable detective, Alan Grant of Scotland Yard. However, despite the positive response to the book, MacKintosh parked the idea of writing detective fiction and her next novel, *The Expensive Halo* (1931), was a light but rather slow romantic comedy about two contrasting London families.

During her periodic visits to her sister in London, she regularly went to the theatre and in the early 1930s she decided to become a playwright. Ambitiously, she began by retelling the life of a Shakespearean king and, with *Richard of Bordeaux* (1932), produced by and starring John Gielgud, 'Gordon Daviot' exploded into the theatre. While working on the follow-up, *Queen of Scots* (1934), MacKintosh scripted a film, *Youthful Folly* (1934), originally titled *Intermezzo* and based on *The Expensive Halo*; this led to her signing a contract to write for Universal Pictures but this seems to have led to little other than some uncredited work on the script for *Next Time We Love* (1936).

Her next play to be produced was a tragic romance that she said had been 'suggested' by the lives and love of the sculptor Henri Gaudier and the writer Sophia Brzeska. *The Laughing Woman* (1934), was not well received but with *Queen of Scots* (1934) she consolidated the reputation of 'Gordon Daviot'. Like *Richard of Bordeaux,* the first production starred Gwen ffrangcon-Davies and it was also produced by John Gielgud. As well as providing a rounded portrait of the doomed queen, MacKintosh focused on the question of Mary's guilt as an accessory to the murder of Lord Darnley, anticipating the historical investigation to be undertaken by Alan Grant in *The Daughter of Time* (1951); Darnley's murder fascinated MacKintosh and she revised the relevant scenes in *Queen of Scots* to produce a one act play, *Kirk o' Field* (1940).

As 'Daviot', MacKintosh continued to write plays for the stage and radio, her last being the posthumously produced *Dickon* (1955), about Shakespeare's 'villain' king, Richard III. In later years MacKintosh adopted a third pen name, 'F. Craigie Howe', named for a Scottish ancient monument and adopted to separate the work in question, a relatively weak stage play, from the works of 'Gordon Daviot'.

In the mid-1930s, to supplement her income as a playwright without affecting her reputation, MacKintosh decided to write another detective story and to bring back Alan Grant. Although *The Man in the Queue* had been written by 'Gordon Daviot', the reputation that that name had garnered meant that a new pseudonym was needed and so Bess MacKintosh became 'Josephine Tey', combining her mother's forename with a phonetic rendering of the name of Scotland's longest river. An immediate success, *A Shilling for Candles* (1936) was optioned by Alfred Hitchcock and released the following year in Britain as *Young and Innocent* (1937) and in America as *The Girl Was Young*.

Perhaps surprisingly—and certainly disappointingly—MacKintosh decided to concentrate on her career as a playwright, publishing only one book in the next ten years and then as 'Gordon Daviot'. *Claverhouse* (1937) is a revisionist hagiography of John Graham, the first of the Jacobites. 'Josephine Tey' did not return until *Miss Pym Disposes* (1947), whose setting owes something to Anstey Physical Training College where MacKintosh had trained 25 years earlier. Fortunately, 'Tey' was now back for good. *The Franchise Affair* (1948) reimagines the eighteenth-century case of Elizabeth Canning, while disappearances are also at the centre of *Brat Farrar* (1949) and *To Love and Be Wise* (1950). In 1949, MacKintosh was invited to join the Detection Club. She accepted but as she never attended a formal meeting she was never enrolled as a member. Grant's penultimate case, *The Daughter of Time* (1951), is surely MacKintosh's best, a bed-bound investigation into a crime that took place 500 years earlier, the disappearance of two royal princes, the sons of King Edward IV and Elizabeth Woodville in 1483. The novel is a perfect combination of the writer's two great passions—history and mystery—and in 1990 the Crime Writers' Association voted it the greatest crime novel of all time. MacKintosh's final novel as 'Gordon Daviot' was *The Privateer* (1952), a romance about the pirate Henry Morgan, and the final 'Josephine Tey', *The Singing Sands* (1952), appeared posthumously.

In comparison with some of the best-known writers of crime fiction, Josephine Tey wrote very few books and, like her contemporary Christianna Brand, this has tended to undermine her status. However, for her ability to present a sensational plot in a realistic manner and her elegant, economical prose, MacKintosh is deserving of a status among the very best.

Around 1950, Bess MacKintosh was diagnosed with cancer. She moved in with her sister who looked after her at her home in Streatham until MacKintosh's death in February 1952. She left her estate to the National Trust.

'Deborah' was published in *The English Review* in March 1929 as by 'Gordon Daviot'.

THE RED BALLOON

Q Patrick

The receptionist at the Braeside County Hospital was decidedly snooty. Nor did she condescend to remove her high hat even when I showed my press card from the *Sentinel Courier*. She had orders, she said.

I had orders, too, said I, and I fingered in my pocket the Colt .32 which I always carried when calling on any case which had the least whiff of homicide. Finally I told her that if I couldn't see either Lieutenant Trant or Dr Beardsley quick, pronto, *tout de suite*, there'd be an explosion which—

So she said she'd see.

The explosion, as it happened, had occurred two hours earlier, and I had, quite unwittingly, heard of it first from my young daughter Barbara, when I fetched her from a special Sunday School Class, around noon. She had simply said, 'Something awfully happened to the two Greiser kids when we came out of school just now. Miss Bedford shooed us away, but there was a red balloon, and well, Ellie Spence said that the Greiser kids were hurt or something.'

I had not given the matter another thought until the middle of our Sunday dinner, when the telephone started shrilling like mad. It was the Big Boss himself, so I knew it was important. Howard Greiser's two daughters had—well he didn't know what, but I was to get myself to the Braeside County Hospital

at once and ask for either Dr Beardsley or Trant. And since
Trant's name was synonymous with Homicide, I presumed the
Greiser children had been murdered, or at best kidnapped.
Anyhow, it must have been something pretty sensational to
get the Big Boss so excited on a Sunday. Hence my belligerency
and the gun.

Meanwhile the receptionist had been 'seeing'—and finally a
female appeared and beckoned. I followed her along subterra-
nean corridors until we reached a room which, from its smell
of formaldehyde, I knew to be the morgue. It was full of doctors,
arguing, discussing or merely staring. Amongst them was my
celebrated uncle, Professor Edgar Saltus.

The attention of them all was fixed on two small figures lying
on marble slabs. I took one glimpse, and that was enough. The
things—for one could scarcely call them human bodies—were
shrivelled and shrunken like two little old monkeys, or like
corpses deep-buried centuries ago.

They were, I presumed—and presumed rightly—the remains
of the two Greiser children to whom, as Barbara had put it,
'something awfully funny' had happened that noon. Quickly,
fearfully, I dismissed the shuddering thought that one of those
'things' might have been Barbara herself.

I was glad when Tim Trant detached himself from the
medicos and came over to me. Though a traditional terror to
the malefactor, Trant was as pleasant a fellow as one could wish
to meet. We had been friends at Princeton and he gave the
Sentinel Courier a break whenever possible.

'Let's get out of here,' he suggested, much to my relief. In the
passage we lit cigarettes and inhaled deeply.

'When I first heard about it,' he said, 'it sounded like another
of those darn flying saucer scares. But—' He shrugged—
'you've seen for yourself. And there's no need for me to tell
you who or what Howard Greiser is. He could break you and

me, the *Sentinel Courier,* the whole New York Police Force if he wanted to.'

Then Dr Beardsley came out too, and between them they gave me the facts as they were known to date. And I report them as they later appeared in the evening edition of the *Sentinel Courier.*

SUNDAY SCHOOL TRAGEDY

A strange and, as yet, unexplained tragedy occurred today at the well-known Braeside School for Girls, when Mary (Minnie) and Eveline (Evie) Greiser, aged 9 and 10 respectively, lost their lives. The two children—daughters of Howard Greiser, widely known as a manufacturer and philanthropist—were taken to the school as usual by the old family chauffeur. Both were in excellent spirits and perfect health. The car waited outside the school gates—a little longer than usual, since the junior girls had been rehearsing Nativity Play for the Christmas Festival, and there was also a short presentation of seasonal gifts by the school authorities. Shortly after noon the chauffeur (Joe Williams, 56) saw the children emerging, and opened the door of the car ready for Minnie and Evie. Snow was falling lightly at the time. The younger girl came alone to the car and, while waiting for her sister, remarked on the fact that there was a red balloon in the air, just by a low group of bushes, not fifteen feet from the school gates.

The chauffeur, as well as Miss Ethel Bedford, a Braeside teacher, and several children saw what they described as an ordinary, child's balloon. They paid no attention to it, thinking it had perhaps broken loose from one of the many Christmas trees that line the Braeside roads. Anyhow, Evie remarked to the chauffeur: 'Someone's balloon is flying away. It's not very high, I'll go and catch it.'

Impulsively, she ran cross the snow-covered grass and disappeared behind the bushes. The chauffeur waited a few minutes, and then went to investigate. To his horror he found what seemed to be the lifeless bodies of Minnie and Evie, lying in the snow a few feet from each other. His cries brought the school porter and several staff members, who soon summoned aid from both doctors and police.

All this took place within the space of less than five minutes.

Who or what had been lurking behind those bushes to deal such swift and terrible destruction to two innocent children?

No intruder had been seen on the school grounds, and the Police have no theory to offer, since the falling snow had covered any potential footprints. There was no signs of violence and no visible wounds, external or internal, to account for the deaths.

The medical experts are equally baffled, since the disease — if disease it was — had struck so suddenly, and presented post-mortem symptoms unfamiliar to our pathologists. Mention was made of a type of galloping anaemia, sometimes concomitant with certain oriental maladies, but no case has ever been reported in this hemisphere.

That death was instantaneous and probably painless seems to be proved by the fact that numbers of children passed within a few yards of the fatal spot, and none of them heard a cry or even a faint moan.

Miss Ethel Bedford, the teacher who presented the gifts to the children, states that they were of a religious nature and certainly comprised no balloons, red or otherwise.

The bereaved parents are offering a reward of $10,000 for information leading to the arrest of any person or persons responsible for what must, we feel, be classed as a cruel and motiveless crime.

Such was the story I phoned in from the hospital. Trant was waiting for me at the receptionist's desk.

'It's all very well for you,' he said gloomily. 'You journalists can spin out yarns on vampires, murderous balloons, flying saucers, little men, unknown poisons, impossible maladies—anything your readers will swallow. But what am I to report to *my* hard-boiled chief on the Homicide Squad? He wants real facts to chew on.'

'You might suggest that he start chewing on the works of Charles Fort.' A familiar, rather squeaky voice sounded from behind me. 'And perhaps even my own popular articles in the *Sentinel Courier*.'

My uncle, Professor Edgar Saltus, had moved noiselessly towards us and was staring at Trant over an antiquated pair of spectacles. He was an elfish, wizened little man with a large, baldish head, and clothes that looked as though he slept in them. I had adored him as a child, and now despite the crankiness that accompanied his increasing age, I respected him and enjoyed his company inordinately.

He had turned now and was addressing me severely.

'And as for you, Edgar James, you should tell that boss of yours to read his correspondence more carefully. I've written to him every day this week. I've warned him to have his correspondents all over the world on the look-out for something of this sort. I knew it would happen, and I told him so. Of course, I couldn't guess that it would happen here—right in our own back yard, but—'

'You mean, you knew—?' I asked excitedly.

'Of course I knew; but those old fogies wouldn't understand if I told them.' A contemptuous thumb designated the specialists—some of them really famous—whom I had seen in the morgue. 'But if you *young* men really want to hear, you can come along with me to my laboratory.'

Having left the necessary instructions with the now less-snooty receptionist, both Trant and I accepted the offer with delight.

*

My uncle was one of the most colourful and certainly the most controversial figure in the scientific world. The letters after his name might have circled one of the astral spheres which he tossed about so lightly.

Some called him a charlatan, despite the fact that he had won the Nobel Prize before he was forty and held an honorary Chair in four or five of the world's greatest Universities. He had been distinguished as a biologist, pharmacologist, physicist and many other things in his time, shifting his interest as soon as he felt he had exhausted the possibilities of the science in question. I had often heard him say—and modesty was not one of his cardinal virtues—that he was the only man living who could talk intelligently with Einstein on his particular subject. But there was *no* man living who could talk to him, Professor Saltus, on all his numerous specialties. Recently he had chosen to style himself as the world's greatest astronomer.

And I was not the man to prove him wrong.

One great gift he had which is rare among great scientists. He could talk and write on the most recondite subjects accurately and scientifically, and yet so simply that an intelligent boy of fifteen could understand him. This gift, being usually considered incompatible with really expert scientific knowledge, had made him an outcast among his lesser contemporaries. But it had made him a fortune, and had, incidentally, tripled the circulation of the *Sentinel Courier's* Sunday supplement, where, in kindness to me, he had contributed such famous articles as: *And Why not Life on Venus?*, *The 'Lost' Planet*, *Out Goes Our Sun*, and many others. Although I was his normal heir, he was, as he often told me, leaving his money to increase in an enormous trust fund, to be used at some distant date when men would dare really to think for themselves, and when a trip to the moon would be no more than a one-block ride in a bus.

*

We drove to his so-called laboratory in a nearby New York suburb. It was an enormous room, whose walls were so thickly lined with books that no self-respecting fly could have found sufficient wall-space. There were no intricate machines, no telescopes, microscopes or other paraphernalia such as one might expect in a scientist's laboratory. The only sign of his astronomical interests was a ticker-tape which was connected with Mount Palomar in California.

He sat us down, side by side like school children, and handed us a scrapbook containing newspaper clippings, either actual or as photostatic copies. These were in many languages, but in each case the English translation was typed neatly below.

While we studied them, he made fussy little preparations—for he had a childlike desire always to put on a good show, with himself 'playing teacher'—and at last mounted a small rostrum between two screens.

He began a trifle bombastically:

'You are neither of you much over thirty, and you have witnessed today what seems to you an unpredictable and utterly unprecedented event. It is my intention to try and prove that it is neither unprecedented nor inexplicable—in fact it was perhaps predictable and certainly precedented.'

He pointed to the scrapbook on our knees.

'You can hardly have taker proper cognizance of that first item, since it occurred in Finland, and at a time when you were probably in your cradles. Perhaps you'd give me the highlights, Edgar James.'

I read: 'Strange malady epidemic among school-children in Trjon, a small village in Finland. Bloodless corpses found—mostly children—vampirism suspected. No marks on throat or body.'

'And the next,' said my uncle, 'is from Nova Scotia, I believe, about the time I was in my cradle.'

It was the same story again, and the next time in Colombo,

Ceylon. Then, much earlier, a clipping from the Cape of Good
Hope; another, dating back to the 18th century, from Turkey.
They all told of sudden, unexplained deaths among children;
and each one, allowing for changing styles of journalism, might
have been the same story as was even then on the *Sentinel
Courier's* presses for the midnight edition.

'My attention was drawn to these gruesome little incidents
by my late and very much-lamented friend Mr Charles Fort.
All similar, of course, but—I wonder if you notice any other
point of similarity?'

My uncle screwed up his puckered little face and stared at
us like a hopeful school-teacher.

'Well, they seem to be about thirty years apart,' put in Trant.

'Good boy.' My uncle beamed. 'Actually it's twenty-eight of
our years and forty-seven weeks: very good. That's what put me
on the track. You've read, of course, my article on what the
Sentinel Courier was pleased to misname *The "Lost" Planet*?'

Had I read it? Had I not had to defend it against not only
my own better judgment but against that of scientist and layman
alike? Had I not—or well—anyhow, I suppose my uncle saw
disbelief in our faces.

'And, of course, you don't believe it. You wouldn't because I
could not prove it—at least, not with any figures that our modern
scientists could understand. And—more important—I could
not show it, even though I *could* plot its orbit. I could compute
roughly that this planet, when at its closest proximity to us and
to Mars, as it is at present, would appear to us terrestrials as
slightly smaller than the moon But—' He flicked on a light,
illuminating a small screen. 'Here's the Solar System; not in
scale of course, but as our ignoramuses tell us and think it to
be.'

I saw the ordinary chart of the sun with its revolving planets,
such as I had seen them (excepting the parvenu Pluto) since
childhood. Then my uncle clicked on another switch, and a

large circle of light started on a moving orbit, beyond the asteroid belt, somewhere between the paths of Mars and Jupiter.

'There,' exclaimed my uncle, 'is Saltus, the invisible planet; and that is approximately its orbit. When I wrote that article for the *Sentinel Courier* I had no actual proof of its existence— at least, no visible proof. Now I have what, to me, is visible proof You have heard of Dr Hans Wertherberg, the great German archaeologist—unquestionably the greatest that ever lived?'

We both nodded, perhaps a trifle vaguely. But somewhere the name rang a bell in connection with mammoths.

'He was captured in Germany and sent to Siberia by the Russians. Being old and feeble they let him tinker about in his own way. There is a heart-rending story of how he discovered in an ice-flow the frozen body of a whole, perfectly preserved mammoth. He couldn't speak Russian so as to tell his guards and the neighbouring peasants of the immense value of their find. To those half-starved, ignorant people it meant meat—fresh meat—and he was obliged to watch them gorge themselves on a carcass which was probably millions of years old. Finally, seeing the hopelessness of his plight, he ate some too, and declared to me it tasted as fresh and palatable as any steak from the butcher's!

'But it served its purpose. After that he became a sort of pet of the Soviets, and they even gave him men and supplies to help him with his excavations. This enabled him to discover something of far more interest archaeologically than the mammoth. He unearthed certain pre-prehistoric drawings, scratched on the walls of buried caves. These drawings, in his opinion and my own, antedate by millions of years anything discovered hitherto. When released, he smuggled photographs of them out, and brought them to me before he died. You shall see for yourselves.'

He switched on another light; and we saw on a small screen what might have been a sketch by a young child.

'There is Man—our earliest ancestor by an incalculable number of years—but without a doubt he is Man. He stands upright, bearing on his shoulder some primitive tool or club. And there is our sun—the same sun we see today: and we recognize it as the sun rather than the moon by the lines emanating from it which express its rays.' The picture was changed.

'And there is Man, this time lying asleep beneath a full moon: and we distinguish the moon from the sun by the fact that it has no emanating rays. You will notice, too, that there is what looks like a small sun in the corner. It is far too large to be either Venus or Mars, our nearest known neighbours. I believe it to be the planet Saltus, depicted at a point in its orbit far from the earth. Look again. The man is lying asleep, and there is the moon, a crescent now; but you see another globe, almost as large as the moon or the sun. That, I believe, is Saltus, the so-called "lost" planet, as it appeared to our ancestors when in closest proximity to the earth. It is exactly as we should see it now, this very evening, if it were not—invisible.'

He turned his attention to the other chart of our solar system. 'Here we have its present position, near Mars, and with Mars at its nearest to the earth. Such a proximity, according to my calculations, occurs once every twenty-eight years and forty-seven weeks.'

He stopped, waiting for a torrent of questions, which I for one was too stunned to put. Finally, Trant's voice came, haltingly, like a schoolboy's.

'But, sir? If it *was* there, and if it is there still, as you say, why can't we see it? Planets don't just disappear—?'

'How do you know they don't, young man? Take the group of stars and planets which we call Andromeda. Although nearly a million light-years away from us, it is constantly changing. Stars larger than our sun explode, disappear and re-appear like fireworks.

'So do their families of planets—each one perhaps larger than our Jupiter. Nothing is impossible, and nothing 100% predictable. The so-called comet of Halley, due in 1986—but I am off the point. Your question was a good one and I can give you only my guess in answer. Saltusians are, scientifically, aeons ahead of us. Some millions of years ago they possibly discovered the secret of invisibility, and, for reasons best known to themselves, they decided to make their world invisible—or, more probably they moved it and themselves into another dimension. Imagine the consternation of our earliest forbears when their second moon suddenly disappeared!

'That they had learnt the secrets of space-navigation is obvious. My own belief is that they colonized the planet we call Mars and abandoned it for some reason, using it merely as a sort of fuelling station. Perhaps they found it lacking in some basic element they needed. Certainly, they have never to our knowledge been much interested in our earth, except as an object of curiosity.'

'But why—? I just don't get that,' I put in.

'Let me try and explain myself better.' My uncle sighed patiently. 'Try to imagine yourself as Christopher Columbus. Europe is a planet moving on a fixed orbit. The Azores Islands are another planet, and America another more distant planet. There are times when your Europe orbit brings you very close to the Azores orbit—a mere ride in a speedboat, but nothing much to see when you get there. And there are inevitably times, though less frequent, when, by merely refuelling at the Azores (Mars) planet, you can take another little jaunt in a speedboat to the America (Earth) planet. Perhaps its potentialities have been exhausted millions of years ago by your ancestors. It is not worth exploitation on a large scale: but there are always Columbuses fired by nothing more than curiosity, or a desire for a short trip—'

'You mean,' said Trant, 'that when this invisible planet, Mars and the earth are in closest conjunction, which arrives roughly every twenty-nine years, we are favoured with a visit?'

'Exactly,' said my uncle. 'Probably nothing more than a Saltusian kid on an Earth spree."

'And we can't see them because they are in a different dimension, but they can see us, and they can nourish themselves by—'

Trant broke off at the sound of the telephone. My uncle picked up the receiver. 'It's for you, Mr—er—'

Trant seized it from him. 'Yes, yes . . . still in Braeside . . . a little boy . . . Bobby Needick . . . trimming a Christmas-tree on the lawn . .'

I felt a cold sweat breaking out all over me. The Needicks were near neighbours, and Bobby was a close pal of Barbara's. No one except those few concerned were aware of the awful danger. Our evening edition had not yet appeared, and no police warning had been given so far as I knew. The children in our garden suburb might well be running about as freely as ever.

'His mother left him for less than two minutes to answer the phone. When she came back—same thing. Even the red balloon.' Trant took up his hat. 'Better get going'

I must hand it to Uncle Edgar that he did not let scientific curiosity entirely outweigh his humane feelings at this third tragedy. He even made vague, clucking noises of sympathy. But as we piled into the car, he could not help saying: 'Perhaps there will be visible tracks if those idiotic policemen . . .'

Personally, I was not thinking of tracks or policemen. I was thinking only of Barbara—for it was not yet her bedtime, and she might well be putting the finishing touches to our modest Christmas-tree on the lawn. I requested to be dropped off at my home.

When we reached our suburb it was light as day, with a full moon, street lights and the rows of illuminated Christmas-trees.

It was only two days before the great festival of love and good-will, but I was gripping the revolver in my pocket and there was murder in my heart—murder for that Saltusian 'kid on an Earth spree', as my uncle had put it.

As I reached the house, my worst fears were realized. Barbara was on the lawn alone, gaily tossing the last strips of tinsel on to the branches of our tree, from which hung balls of red and silver amongst the electric candles.

I jumped out of the car, falling on to the snow that banked the sidewalk. But I did not lose my grip on my revolver.

'Oh, Daddy—you do look funny—' she began, and ran towards me. And as she did so a red, or rather, a pinkish globule seemed to detach itself from the tree and follow her. I flung my left arm around her, pressing her to me, but even as I raised my revolver with my right hand, I felt Barbara being lifted from my grasp by some powerful and invisible force. The sphere, or whatever it was, was a yard or two away from the tree now, and hung just above my daughter's head.

I fired twice, three times over Barbara's shoulder, full into that pinkish globule. Then, gradually, I felt the tension on her relax. The sphere had vanished, but—and this I hardly dare to set down—I distinctly saw my three bullets hanging in the air, motionless, on a level with my head. They were discovered later, near the Christmas-tree, in a small patch of pinkish snow.

But my first interest was to get my poor bewildered Barbara safely into the house; and then to ossify myself with half a tumbler of neat Bourbon.

Not long afterwards my uncle arrived. He had witnessed the shooting from the car, and had spent a happy half hour peering about in the snow.

He seemed satisfied, and not at all upset by the tragedy which had nearly overtaken his great-niece.

'I think,' he said, rubbing his knotty old hands together,

'that we have proved they are vulnerable to even such simple terrestrial implements as a revolver.'

'Thank God for that,' I said fervently.

'And this time I have prints—prints which enable me to add something to the composite picture I have in mind.'

Then he went over to my desk and started what looked like a doodle.

Finally, he handed the result to me. 'Not accurate, of course—and I imagine the size would be roughly equivalent to that of *Homo Sapiens*. We shall never know. I fear. Those filaments are what we would call "arms", and also the—er—tubes by which it nourishes itself. Even if visible, they would be thinner than the thinnest needle.'

I looked in horror at the gruesome and quite indescribable creature he had sketched, and labelled: 'YOUNG (?) SALTUSIAN'.

It had the three-toed feet of an ostrich, and thinnish legs, surmounted by a box-like torso from which emanated numerous fine filaments. In the centre of the box, in a position roughly equivalent to that of the human stomach, was a round circle. The head was shrouded and indistinct except for two wing-like ears. The general aspect was improbable and sinister.

'And the red balloon?' I asked. 'Where does that come into the picture?'

My uncle looked at me with mock severity over his spectacles. 'You haven't read your H. G. Wells, young man; otherwise you'd know that when an invisible creature nourishes itself on a visible substance, that substance remains visible until it is digested by the invisible stomach. There was a pinkish material under your Christmas-tree: I think that will be found to be human blood, partly digested. Remember that our friend had visited the Needicks, before coming to you, and—'

'Stop!' I cried in utter revulsion. 'It's—it's too ghastly!'

My uncle spread out his hands and shrugged. 'But we've got

a lot to be thankful for. So far they've 'come but single spies'—young Columbuses, urged by curiosity to visit a decadent world. In twenty-eight years, forty-seven weeks, they may decide to come in battalions. Perhaps—'

But he did not finish the sentence, because at that moment my wife came in and cheerfully announced supper.

Q PATRICK

'Q Patrick' was a pseudonym used by two British-born writers Richard Webb and Hugh Wheeler for more than 20 mystery novels, a 'theoretical reconstruction' of the infamous 1892 Lizzie Borden murders and many short stories. The two also wrote together as 'Jonathan Stagge' and 'Patrick Quentin', under which pen name Wheeler published eight more books after the collaboration ended.

Rickie Webb was born on 10 June 1901 in Burnham-on-Sea, Somerset, and emigrated to America where he worked for a pharmaceutical company in Philadelphia. Before his collaboration with Wheeler, Webb wrote two novels with Martha Mott Kelley using the pen name 'Q Patrick', derived from combining her nickname 'Patsy' with his own, adding the 'Q' for a touch of mystery. In 1933, Webb's writing partnership with Kelley came to an end when she married and moved to London, and he wrote the third 'Q Patrick' novel on his own. Two more novels followed, co-authored with Mary Louise White, a Quaker journalist who would go on to serve twelve years as Literary Editor of *Harper's Bazaar*.

Hugh Wheeler was born on 19 March 1912 in Hampstead, London, and in later years he would claim that he had started writing fiction when only eight years old. He was nineteen when he first visited the United States and, after graduating from University College, London, he emigrated there in 1934. He would live in America for the rest of his life, becoming naturalised in

1942. Away from crime fiction, Wheeler was an acclaimed librettist. His best-known work is perhaps his revision of the book for the 1974 production of Leonard Bernstein's *Candide* for which he won an Antoinette Perry Award for Excellence in Broadway Theatre, but there are also his Tony-winning books for *A Little Night Music* (1972) and *Sweeney Todd: The Demon Barber of Fleet Street* (1979), both developed in collaboration with Stephen Sondheim. Wheeler also had some success in the theatre, particularly with his first play *Big Fish, Little Fish* (1961), whose original production secured a Tony for its director, Sir John Gielgud. Wheeler also wrote a single novel under his own name, *The Crippled Muse* (1951).

In interviews after Webb's death, Wheeler claimed that the collaboration had initially come about because their families had been close friends in Britain. In 1940, they took over the rent of a place in Tyringham, Massachusetts and they later bought an eighteenth-century farmhouse, reputed to have once been a tavern, on the thickly wooded Chestnut Hill Road in nearby Monterey. But then their friendship began to fracture. Wheeler joined the US Army Medical Corps while Webb was posted overseas with the Red Cross. After the war, Webb's health began to decline and he all but completely stopped writing in 1952. In 1959, he returned to England, where he died in 1966.

Although Wheeler's later career moved into award-winning scriptwriting and musical theatre, he continued to write crime fiction as 'Patrick Quentin', eventually receiving a special Edgar from the Mystery Writers of America for *The Ordeal of Mrs Snow* (1961), a collection of stories mostly written before he and Webb had parted ways. In 1987, Wheeler was hospitalised with pneumonia and he died in Pittsfield, Massachusetts on 26 July 1987, leaving unfinished the book for a stage adaptation of the film *Meet Me in St Louis*.

'The Red Balloon' was first published in the magazine *Weird Tales* in November 1953.

TERROR

Daphne du Maurier

Bridget woke up with a start.

Somewhere something had fallen; perhaps a slate from the roof, or maybe it was only a door banging on the floor above. She did not know this, of course; at six years old it is difficult to reason about strange noises, or about anything that happens in the middle of the night. Half-past nine was the same as midnight to Bridget.

For a few minutes she lay awake wondering what it was that had woken her. She no longer felt tired or sleepy, her mind was alert, and every nerve was on edge Then she opened her eyes and looked around her. At first everything seemed black, pitch black, but as she became accustomed to the darkness the furniture in the bedroom gradually began to take shape.

A queer, ghastly shape.

This was not the same room as the one in which she had undressed. She saw that Nanny had not come up yet, because the bed was empty.

But what is empty? The pillow must have slipped a little, for something bulky lay in the corner by the turned-down sheet. A piece of blanket had become untucked at the side; it was rolled slightly and stretched across the centre of the bed. Yet it was not like an ordinary piece of blanket, this rolled object, it was an arm—a cold, white arm—with no body near it, with no person to whom it belonged.

A loose arm hanging from nowhere . . .

Bridget shrank back in her bed and turned her eyes away, but this time they fell on the wardrobe at the end of the room. It looked huge and sinister, far taller than in the daytime; it seemed to stretch as high as the ceiling.

And there was a dark, inky black corner just by the side of it.

She tried to think of what was kept in that corner, but she could not remember; surely it had never been there before?

Then something creaked.

Sweat broke out on Bridget's forehead, her heart thumped under her little white nightgown; her body burned, but her feet were icy cold!

There . . . another creak . . . Again.

Her eyes were now glued to the wardrobe, whence the sound had come.

Slowly—very slowly—the door opened. The gap grew larger and larger, creaking with every inch; soon it would swing right open.

And what would be inside, waiting, waiting?

She dared not move now, because the slightest sound would tell them that she was there; if she kept quite still with her eyes closed perhaps they would go away and forget all about her.

She lay silent, without a movement, and then, in spite of herself, the dread impulse came over her to look; her head turned. and her eyes were drawn, as if magnetised, towards the wardrobe.

The door was wide open.

And inside—inside where Nanny's clothes hung in the daytime, her coat, her mackintosh, her grey costume—were three shadowy figures, silent and mysterious.

Three mocking priests, with gaunt, dark bodies, and no faces.

Bridget knew they were watching her; they were waiting for her to move, when they would creep from their hiding-place, creep with soft, terrible steps towards her bed, and lift great white hands with thin, hollow fingers.

But the silent priests did not move, and she turned her head.

She waited, waited for some sound to warn her, some sign to tell her that they were coming to her—but nothing happened. This was worse, this sudden absence of any sound, this dead still quiet. She listened—she could hear Silence.

A faint humming sound in her ears, then gradually it buzzed louder, until it became a roar like a mighty wind. She opened her eyes again, and saw that the square, dressing-table had turned into a square, hunchbacked animal, with thin, queer-shaped legs.

It stood beneath the window ready to pounce. The cord of the blind was rattling against the window pane—someone was trying to get into the room.

Yes, at either side of the window, where the curtains generally hung, there were two evil women with long black hair. These were more frightening than the priests; these were witches with claws instead of hands; they had the same faces as a woman in a book she had once seen. She remembered the book, a large old book with a brown cover, and the pictures were horrible.

Supposing all the pictures had become alive, and were going to steal one after the other through the window!

Bridget swallowed—the sound of it seemed to echo through the room, but she could not help herself, she had to swallow again. Her throat was dry—she tasted dust. Everything in the room now took a special shape. The fireplace was a yawning cave; the table a gigantic toad; the chairs were stunted dwarfs.

If only Nanny would come up; if only she could get out of this terrible room into the kind, warm Day Nursery, flooded with electric light.

What if snakes came down the chimney—long, black, wriggling snakes—and glided along the floor and coiled themselves round the bedposts?

The floor became thick with bodies of dead cats —she had seen one in a gutter once—grey, furry cats; and mice, thousands of headless mice . . .

Bridget began to cry, and the sound of her crying frightened her.

The Things had heard; they were all coming near her. The priests bowed, the witches waved, the animals crept quietly, quietly . . .

The air suddenly became thick with stifling blankets; she was going to be suffocated, the ceiling was sinking down upon her. With a strangled scream Bridget climbed out of bed, she stumbled across the floor and flung herself panting against the door. 'Nanny, Nanny, come quickly!'

They were all coming nearer her, long, distorted shapes grinned at her, large crooked hands thrust themselves forward to grasp her.

Above her hung great gaping mouths.

Her feet stood in a pool of blood . . . She was lying on the floor now, screaming into the carpet.

Then the door opened, and someone turned on the light.

It was Nanny. Bridget flung herself upon her, sobbing hysterically.

'Nanny, Nanny, take me away; don't let them get at me; I'm so frightened, don't go away! Oh! save me!'

The nurse shook her crossly. She was irritated at having to come upstairs from her cup of cocoa in the kitchen, but Bridget's screams had alarmed her and she was afraid there might be a fire.

'What do you mean by making all that noise?' she said sharply. 'You ought to be fast asleep hours ago instead of shouting and screaming. I should be ashamed if I were you. I won't have any nonsense, do you hear me?'

Bridget's screams rose higher and higher; she begged and pleaded to be taken downstairs; she clutched on to the nurse with clammy, wet fingers; she grovelled on the floor; she almost licked her hand.

'You stop where you are; do you understand?'

Bridget was picked up and thrust back in her bed.

'Will you be quiet at once?'

Nurse was gone in an instant, and the light was put out.

The door closed behind her, and there was a sound of retreating footsteps.

For a moment the child was too amazed to think. Then came realisation—she was alone.

Long shadows crept across the floor . . .

DAPHNE DU MAURIER

The author, biographer and playwright Daphne du Maurier was born in London on 13 May 1907. She was the granddaughter of George du Maurier, the famous author and *Punch* artist, and her parents were the actress Muriel Beaumont and Gerald du Maurier, a playwright who would later be knighted for his contribution to theatre. However, du Maurier showed no great interest in a career on stage and, while her father hoped she might consider a career in film, she was more interested in becoming a writer. One of her earliest appearances in print was a brief profile of the 'gods and goddesses' of the Wimbledon championships, which was published by the *Weekly Dispatch* in 1928. Over the next three years du Maurier wrote numerous short stories as well as poetry and opinion pieces, many appearing in the *Bystander*, a leading British periodical. She also began writing a novel, *The Loving Spirit* (1931), which chronicles the lives of four generations of the family of a Cornish shipbuilder.

In 1932 du Maurier became engaged to Major Frederick 'Boy' Browning, an officer in the Grenadier Guards. They were married on 20 July at the parish church of Lanteglos-by-Fowey, which features in *The Loving Spirit*. In the next five years, du Maurier produced two of her best books: *Gerald—A Portrait* (1934), a biography of her father; and *Jamaica Inn* (1935), which deals with the wreckers who made the rock-strewn Cornish coast a death-trap for ships in the nineteenth century. Around the time of the novel's publication, Browning was advised that he was to be posted to Alexandria. Du Maurier went with him and began work on a biography of her grandfather and *his* notorious grandmother, Mary Anne Clarke. While in Egypt, she also sketched out the plot of her most famous novel, *Rebecca* (1938), in which a woman finds it harder than she could ever have imagined to be married to a man who has been married before.

Du Maurier's main contribution to the war effort was a series of propagandic 'true stories of war-time Britain', which after publication in various newspapers were collected in *Come Wind, Come Weather* (1940) with all proceeds going to the Soldiers', Sailors' and Airmen's Families' Association. This 'moral re-armament' collection was very popular, leading to a second edition which included a delightful new story, 'Mrs Bromley Beats the Bombers'. The booklet's tremendous success led to du Maurier being asked to make a broadcast to Canada and the United States from a London air raid shelter alongside an actor playing Tom Osborne, a character from one of the stories. It also led to a commission to write forward-looking advertorials for Sunlight Soap.

Du Maurier's next novel was *Frenchman's Creek* (1941) and in 1943 she leased 'Menabilly', a large, semi-derelict house which had provided the basis for 'Manderley', the setting for *Rebecca*. While she worked in Cornwall on *Hungry Hill* (1943) and *The King's General* (1946), the war was beginning to turn. Browning, who now held the rank of General, was made Commander-in-Chief of British airborne troops and played a crucial role in ensuring the invasion of Nazi-occupied Europe was successful, despite involving—in his famous words—'a bridge too far'. His absence inspired du Maurier to work on 'The Return of the Soldier', a contemporary melodrama that was eventually staged under the title *The Years Between* (1944). It revisits the central theme of *Rebecca* in an entirely different way and concerns the difficulties faced by couples separated by the war and their efforts to rebuild their lives. Du Maurier enjoyed playwriting and her final play, *September Tide* (1948), centres on a widow who falls in love with her son-in-law.

By the 1950s, du Maurier had become astonishingly successful. More novels appeared, roughly one every three years, but towards the end of the decade her husband had a nervous breakdown and he died in 1965. Over the next ten years, she wrote numerous short stories and three new novels: one was *Castle Dor* (1961), a story by Sir Arthur Quiller-Couch left unfinished at his death and completed by du Maurier as a tribute to him and its Cornish setting.

When her lease expired in 1969, du Maurier left 'Menabilly' and moved into its dower house, 'Kilmarth', which provided the setting for her penultimate novel, *The House on the Strand* (1969). Her final novel was *Rule Britannia* (1972), an alternate history of the United Kingdom in which the Government, having failed to integrate with continental Europe, decides to enter into union with the United States. The plan is resisted by a handful of Cornish farmers led by 'Mad', an 82-year-old actress whom du Maurier based on her friend Gladys Cooper.

While du Maurier is sometimes disparagingly referred to as a romantic novelist, the description is wholly inadequate. Her richly detailed novels are imbued with insight, suspense and uncertainty. Given these skills and her ability to write vividly yet economically, she was particularly adept at short fiction, with two prime examples being the horrifying 'Don't Look Now', adapted into an outstanding film directed by Nicolas Roeg, and 'The Birds', an eco-horror story that was the basis for a thrilling but flawed film directed by Alfred Hitchcock, who had previously directed rather better films of *Jamaica Inn* in 1939 and *Rebecca* in 1940.

Daphne du Maurier died in her sleep at 'Kilmarth' on 19 April 1989, and her ashes were scattered in the sea off the Cornish coast.

'Terror' was published in the 26 December 1928 issue of the *Bystander*.

THE GREEN DRESS

Anthony Berkeley

Miles Carrington gazed round the comfortable studio with appreciation. 'I say, old man,' he said sincerely, 'this really is most awfully good of you.'

Fletcher smiled complacently. 'Not a bit! Well, as I was saying, the rent here is paid for a year, and I've stowed all my private things away in that cupboard. Everything else is open to you. You can move in tomorrow if you like.'

'It will be a bit of a change from my little attic,' said Carrington appreciatively. 'And you won't be wanting it even when you get back from your honeymoon?'

'No. I've given up painting for good.' Fletcher paused thoughtfully. If he felt in the least ashamed of his forthcoming marriage to that elderly but wealthy widow, Lady Seymour, he certainly showed no sign of it, in spite of the fact that his reasons were so glaringly obvious. 'To tell you the truth,' he continued airily, I shouldn't be coming back here in any case.'

'Oh? Why?'

'Unpleasant associations!' For a moment it seemed to Miles Carrington that a look almost of disgust flashed swiftly across the speaker's face; but if so, it was gone again so quickly that he could not be sure whether his eyes had not deceived him. 'In fact, old man,' Fletcher continued perfectly naturally, 'it's really you who are doing me the favour by living in the place till my tenancy's up.'

'Of course, if you put it like that—!' Carrington laughed.

'I do. Besides, if you'll let me say so, Miles, I've often wondered whether there wasn't some way in which I could give you a bit of a leg up. I mean, I've always admired the way you've stuck to the game, though the shekels can't have been rolling in any too fast. Couldn't have done it myself.'

'No, they certainly haven't,' Carrington smiled.

'But you're a sticker. You'll get there one day. And you can't imagine what a help a decent studio with a decent address is in that way. Very mundane, no doubt; but unpleasantly true. Well, I've got to run off now and get a few things done. You stay here and explore if you want to. See you at the church tomorrow morning, I suppose?'

'Rather!' Carrington agreed, shaking hands warmly.

'So long, then. Oh, by the way, you'll find some props and costumes that may be useful to you in that oak chest over there. Cheerio!'

With a smile of contentment Carrington began to explore his new home.

Fletcher had not been wrong when he called Miles Carrington a sticker. It takes a sticker to subsist for five years in a tiny attic in Battersea and devote his attention to the portrayal of cheerful gentlemen in their underclothes and elderly ladies distressed by violent pains in the back in order to scrape together a bare living, when his soul is yearning after nymphs and dryads and green trees and such more fitting subjects for his brush. As Carrington installed his meagre collection of household goods in Fletcher's studio the day after that gentleman had departed to Italy with his unblushing bride, he knew that this was the opportunity of his lifetime and registered a number of earnest vows to make adequate use of it.

Having arranged his belongings to his satisfaction, he proceeded to make a more thorough examination of the studio's contents.

Almost the first thing to attract his attention was the oak chest to which Fletcher had referred—a massive piece of mediaeval craftsmanship standing nearly three feet high and with a lid so heavy that Miles had to use both hands to lift it. Inside was a motley collection of draperies and costumes, which he tumbled out on the floor beside him as he delved further into the chest's recesses.

Suddenly he paused. The last armful taken out had left uncovered some material of a most delicate shade of green. Miles lifted it out almost tenderly and examined it.

It was a little dress of stiff green silk of early Victorian period, very simple and, in some curious way that Miles could not define, extraordinarily appealing. He gazed at it for some minutes, turning it about in his hands. It seemed to him such a fragile little wisp of a thing, and yet somehow so inexpressibly characteristic. He began to conjure up pictures of its wearer—her charm, her dainty beauty, just the way she would smile. The thing fascinated him.

He exclaimed aloud, 'That's the setting for my first decent picture!'

The lucky sale, a few days later, of a lady with an outsize smile to a firm of toothpaste manufacturers provided Miles with enough spare cash to enable him to employ a model for a couple of sittings, and he set to work at once.

It was some time before he could fix upon a pose that satisfied him, but in the end he decided to paint the girl in the green dress sitting in a chair, her hands resting on her lap, her head turned a little to one side, and just the suspicion of a roguish little smile curving the extreme corners of her mouth.

The model settled into her pose and Miles, with a strange feeling of elation that sent a thrill through his whole being, began to rough in the lines of the figure.

Yet at the end of the two sittings he had succeeded in producing only the makings of an excellent portrait of the green dress—and nothing more. Half a dozen attempts at the face of its wearer had been painted indignantly out. After that he could not afford a model any more.

By this time the question of the girl's face was beginning seriously to worry him. He could see with his mind's eye exactly the one possible face that would be hers; yet without a living model to work from it seemed impossible that he could grasp its essentials with sufficient clearness to pin them down upon his canvas. And the thought of giving her any other face was almost painful to him.

On the day after the model had left he put the green dress upon the lay figure, fixed it in position and began to try, with something akin to desperation, to hit off the outlines of the face and head; a lucky chance, a few fortunate strokes, might put him in the way of getting it down as he saw it. Completely absorbed, he worked fruitlessly all day long until the gathering twilight of the winter afternoon began to obscure his vision. Then, glancing across in the dim light towards where the green dress shimmered mistily upon the model's throne, he saw a girl's head above it and the very face of which he had dreamed.

He caught his breath and stood transfixed. There she sat, just as he had imagined her, the sweet face tilted a little to one side, her small feet Just peeping out from beneath the folds of the dress, her little hands clasped loosely in her lap; but now she wore white lace mittens on them. He could even see the gentle rise and fall of the dress on her bosom. He shut his eyes, then opened them again quickly. No; she was still there.

With a bound he reached the electric light switch and turned it on. There was nothing on the model's throne but the green dress, stiff and unnatural upon the lay figure. He turned off the light again and the girl sprang into view once more.

Miles stumbled back to his easel, seized his brush and began to paint feverishly.

After that it was always the same. There was no explaining

the thing. Each evening, as the light began to fail, the lay figure was transformed into the living, breathing girl herself. That is, as long as Miles remained a sufficient distance away. If he approached nearer to the throne, as he summoned up enough courage to do once or twice as time went on, it was to see nothing but the lay figure once more.

He spoke to her once or twice, timidly, almost as if dreading to hear her answer. But she never did answer; only she seemed to move her head a little and glance more directly at him than before. At these times she smiled, too; but such a pathetic, utterly wretched little ghost of a smile that Miles could hardly bear to see it. For that reason he left off speaking to her.

Yes, that smile of hers. That was the only point upon which Miles had been wrong in his mental picture. She might have smiled roguishly once; but not now. Now there was nothing but a terrible wistfulness, a hopeless sadness in her face that made Miles ache with pity for her even as he strove to transfer it to his canvas. She seemed a symbol of dead hopes and wishes unfulfilled.

Miles accepted it all without question. During the day he worked at his advertisement sketches; at dusk he stepped into another world and sent his soul out in search of another soul, that they might mingle together and be painted into the picture under his hand. That the whole thing was impossible; that he was suffering from a dangerous delusion; that there could be no girl there at all—these things did not worry him. The girl existed. He saw her. She wished him to paint her, and paint her he must. That was all. Miles knew well enough that the whole thing had been foreordained from the beginning. The why and the wherefore apparently did not concern him.

And so the picture was finished.

It was a masterpiece, Miles knew that. Gazing at it as it stood on its easel in the studio, he compared it with his previous work and marvelled that his could have been the hand to paint it. All the ineffable pathos, the utter hopelessness of the poor little dream original was there, even the pose, with its drooping shoulders and inertly clasped hands, had taken on an aspect of almost intolerable melancholy. Just to glance at the picture brought a lump to the throat, one pitied the poor child so.

In due course he sent it to the Academy. It was accepted without hesitation.

That was Miles' first step upon the ladder of fame. 'The Green Dress', as he had called the picture, attracted the inevitable attention that was its right. Every day for months there could be found a knot of people in front of it, spellbound before this incarnation of misery, talking only in hushed whispers as if fearful that the girl in the picture might overhear them. The critics predicted a blazing future for its talented artist.

Work began to crowd in upon Miles. Fashionable women wanted their portraits painted by him; letters from business firms interested in art arrived by every post. He found himself famous. Also there came numerous offers, some of them really magnificent, to buy 'The Green Dress'; but these he put aside. Somehow he could not make up his mind to part with it; the picture seemed to have become almost a part of himself.

And the strange thing of it all was that in his new work Miles found himself able to maintain the high standard which he had already reached in his great picture. In his more matter-of-fact moments he realised that the inspiration which his work must have lacked before had come to him at last. But more often he felt just as if somebody was standing at his elbow, guiding his brush; and at these times he liked to think that the dream girl of the picture was trying to show her gratitude to him in return for his fulfilment of her wishes.

Yet one must not think that Miles was getting morbid. It was a thoroughly sane and healthy feeling of his, in spite of its fantastic absurdity. He believed in the kindly friendship of the girl in the green dress as one believes in the protective powers of the angels.

And then Fletcher returned from Italy.

Bursting with loud congratulations he appeared in the studio late one morning just as Miles was preparing to go out to lunch, and the two men shook hands warmly.

'It's great!' Fletcher exclaimed. 'Of course I knew you'd get there one day. Told you before I went away, didn't I? But this terrific jump, old man! How did it all happen? I'm simply aching to hear.'

'I'm blessed if I know!' Miles confessed with a smile. 'I just painted a girl that I saw somehow in my mind, and—well, the picture happened to catch on with the public. That's all.'

'Nonsense! People don't make such a fuss about a picture unless it really is the goods. By the way, you used that old green dress in—in the oak chest, I gather?' Fletcher's voice retained its genial note, yet somehow it sounded a trifle forced in his last words.

Miles' sensitive ear caught the altered inflection. 'Yes. You don't mind, do you? I understood you to say that—'

'Mind?' Fletcher interrupted, a trifle too boisterously. 'Good Heavens, no! Why on earth should I mind? Of course I made you free of the contents of the chest.'

'I thought you sounded a little—?' Miles paused doubtfully.

'Of course not! What an extraordinary idea! Well, let's have a look at the picture. I've been longing to see the original. Saw a rotten reproduction in one of the illustrated dailies, but it was so blurred I couldn't make out the face at all. Got it here?'

There was no disguising the anxiety in Fletcher's voice this time. And now that Miles looked at him more closely, it seemed as if his whole manner was unnatural. He appeared to be labouring under a terrible excitement—an excitement actuated

(Miles gazed at him incredulously, but the thing was plain enough) by real fear.

'Have you got it here?' he repeated impatiently.

'Look here, Fletcher,' said Miles kindly, 'you're looking a bit rotten this morning. Tired or something, aren't you? Let me mix you a drink.'

'Drink be blowed!' snarled Fletcher. Then he caught the amazed look in the other's face, and made a visible effort to pull himself together. 'I've come to have a look at this picture of yours,' he said, with a twisted smile. 'Why be so modest about it?'

'Oh, all right. It's here.'

Miles shrugged his shoulders and walked across to an easel. The gesture with which he removed the cloth that hug before the picture was almost a caress. He heard a grasp behind him and wheeled quickly about. Fletcher was staring at the picture with wide, horrified eyes; his face was dead white and little drops of moisture were gathering on his brow.

'Good Heavens, Fletcher, what on earth is the matter?' Fletcher took no notice. He was muttering to himself. Miles could see his lips moving and bent forward to catch the low, husky words.

'I knew it would be—I knew it would be! Oh, my God, what does she want with me? What does she *want*?' His gaze was torn from the picture and his starting eyes fell upon Miles. 'What does she *want*, Carrington?' he shrieked.

Miles darted forward just in time to catch the toppling figure before it fell to the ground. Fletcher had fainted.

That night Miles woke up suddenly, with a feeling that something was wrong. He sat up in bed, straining his ears into the darkness. Then he heard stealthy sounds coming from the direction of the studio and knew what had roused hm.

'Burglars, by Jove!' he muttered, getting noiselessly out of bed.

His bedroom opened directly into the studio, and he eased the dividing door ajar with soft caution. A small circle of light was wavering jerkily about the opposite walls; as he watched, it picked up the covered picture on its easel and rested there.

Quick as thought Miles sprang for the man who was holding it, clamped an arm about his neck and bore him heavily to the ground. 'Got you!' he exclaimed triumphantly.

'All right, Carrington,' said a sulky voice beneath him. 'No need to throttle me.'

Miles sprang to his feet in amazement and switched on the light. 'You, Fletcher? Good Lord, what on earth are you playing at?'

Fletcher rose unsteadily. His face was white and his eyes wild. 'I suppose a chap can come to his own studio if he wants to, can't he?' he muttered, avoiding the other's eyes.

'Of course. But why come in the small hours of the morning and pretend to be a burglar? My good chap, it's no good looking like that; that's what I took you for, and so would anybody else under the circumstances. Sorry if I hurt you, but you were rather asking for it, you know.' Miles was feeling not unreasonably somewhat annoyed.

'Well, I — I didn't want to knock you up at such an unearthly time, that's all. I had a spare key and didn't think there was any need to disturb you. Nothing to get peeved about, old man.'

Miles laughed. 'Perhaps I was disappointed for the moment—I should have liked to have captured a real burglar. Well, what is it you've come for, anyhow?'

'Oh—something—something I found I was needing from that cupboard of mine,' said Fletcher awkwardly. 'Nothing worth bothering you for.'

'Well, there's the cupboard; you'd better take what you want and run home to bed.'

'Er—yes, I will.' Fletcher began to feel in his pockets. 'I'm blessed!' he exclaimed with ill-disguised relief. 'Left the key at home! Well, I'll take your advice and go home to bed. I can pop in tomorrow morning for what I wanted, can't I?'

Miles looked at him curiously. Then he took him by the shoulders and pushed him suddenly into a chair. 'You'll have a drink first,' he remarked, as if stating a fact rather than asking a question.

'Yes, I would like one,' said Fletcher eagerly. 'I'm—I'm not feeling very well today, as you know. Don't spare the whiskey part of it.'

Miles mixed the drinks in silence and handed a glass to Fletcher. 'Well, here's luck!'

'Good health!' Fletcher drank thirstily, and Miles noticed that he threw a glance towards the corner in which the covered easel stood before doing so.

For a moment there was silence. Then, 'And now, Fletcher,' said Miles sternly, 'I want to know the *real* reason why you came here this evening!'

Fletcher started violently. 'But I told you! To get—'

'Rot! You invented that excuse on the spur of the moment. I saw you doing so. Now look here, Fletcher, there's some mystery going on here. What's it all about?'

A cunning look came into Fletcher's face. 'Mystery?' he repeated blandly. 'I don't know anything about a mystery. If you're talking about that melodramatic faint of mine this morning, I told you that I was feeling rather cheap after twenty-four hours' travelling; that was all.'

'And what about that girl in the green dress?' asked Miles quietly.

'Wh-what about her?' Fletcher returned shakily and cast another apprehensive glance over his shoulder towards the easel.

'You seemed uncommonly interested in her,' said Miles slowly. 'Perhaps you'd like to see her again? I'll take that cloth off.' And he made as if to rise from his chair.

'No!' exclaimed Fletcher shrilly. 'No! Don't do that!'

'Then tell me why not,' said Miles, sinking back again.

Fletcher took another drink. 'I don't see why I should be put through this cross-examination,' he said doggedly. 'If you really want to know why the picture startled me—and I admit it did for the moment—it was simply because your girl reminded me rather strongly of a little model I had a few months before I was married. The likeness rather took me aback. I say, you might give me another drink, will you? My nerves are always rotten after travelling.'

'You didn't appear any too glad to see her again,' Miles remarked, pouring a generous allowance of whiskey into the others' glass and splashing a little soda on top of it. He knew the line to take now.

Fletcher took a long drink. 'No,' he replied complacently, wiping his mouth. 'To tell you the truth, I wasn't. I had a bit of trouble with her.'

'Oh?'

'Yes; you know what these girls are.' Fletcher was beginning to warm to his theme, as Miles had known he would; he was the sort of man who boasts of his love affairs.

'Why? What happened?'

'Oh, the usual sort of thing. One kisses 'em, you know, and—and that sort of thing.' Fletcher leered reminiscently. 'They expect it. This little girl was foolish enough to take it seriously. Thought I was going to marry her, if you please! I had an awful job with her when she found out I had rather different intentions, I can tell you.'

'Did she take it badly?'

Fletcher looked up sharply, as if he realised that he had said more than he intended. 'Yes, she did.'

'What did she do?' asked Miles carelessly, though his heart was thumping terribly. Things were becoming plain to him at last.

'Oh, I don't know,' Fletcher hedged.

'Tell me!'

Fletcher shrugged his shoulders. 'Threw herself in the river, the little fool!' he said shortly. 'Any more questions?'

Miles rose to his feet. Poor, poor little girl in the green dress! 'No, I don't think so,' he said with weary disgust. A sudden thought struck him. 'And you painted her in the green dress, too?'

Fletcher started. 'How on earth did you know that?'

'I didn't. I—I just guessed.'

'Damned good guess, then! Yes, that was the first time she sat for me. After that we didn't worry about dresses, green or otherwise. Well, I'll be toddling now and look in for those things of mine tomorrow. Good night, old man.'

'Good night, Fletcher.'

Miles turned back to his bedroom again, sick at heart.

Fletcher did not come the next morning. He came in the late evening, boisterously cheerful and smelling strongly of drink. Miles, who had already determined to cut short his occupation of the studio and break with the man, received him with no great show of welcome; but Fletcher affected to notice nothing and insisted on remaining to have a night cap.

Miles slept very deeply that night.

He woke in the morning with a splitting head and a tongue like leather, and racked his aching brain to discover the reason. Only two things could have made him feel like that: drink and drugs. As for drink, he had only had one weak whiskey and soda the evening before, and that only because Fletcher had pressed him so hard. As for—

Miles clutched suddenly at his forehead. 'My God!' he said aloud. 'Could he possibly have—?'

He staggered out of bed, drank a hurried glassful of water and made his way into the studio.

Yes! He was right. Fletcher had been there! The picture was

lying on the ground in front of its easel, face downwards and surrounded by splinters of broken glass. Miles crossed the floor and picked it up. Then he groaned. The face was slashed across and across till it was quite unrecognisable!

What could have possessed the maniac? Yes, that was it. Fletcher must be a maniac! That explained everything. Or did it? Miles gazed gloomily round the studio, striving to piece the puzzle together.

Suddenly he stiffened and his face blanched. A man was kneeling in front of the oak chest, his head inside and his arms hanging inertly by his sides, the heavy lid resting on the back of his neck. Miles stared at him in horror, and it was a full two minutes before he could force himself to cross the room, lift the lid and look at the face.

Yes, it was Fletcher. He had known that instinctively as soon as his eyes fell upon him. And he was quite dead—must, in fact, have been dead for some hours. Miles gently laid the head down and prepared to lift the body from its ironical position.

It was only then that the full horror of the thing dawned upon him. He stepped back, breathing heavily, and stood transfixed, hardly able to believe the evidence of his eyes.

For wound tightly about the dead man's neck in a fantastic embrace were the two arms of the little green dress.

ANTHONY BERKELEY

Anthony Berkeley Cox (1893–1971) is one of the most important writers of the Golden Age. Cox had a playful approach to the business of writing crime and detective fiction. His penchant for twisting tropes and confounding expectations undoubtedly played a major role in the genre's development away from a simple linear narrative—in which characters are introduced, a crime is committed, clues are solved and the criminal is detected—into a more complex form in which almost anything can happen. Cox's 'great detective', Roger Sheringham, is virtually the antithesis of Sherlock Holmes, arrogant rather than showily omniscient and unlikeable rather than unclubbable. Nonetheless, with only a few lapses from greatness, the detective stories that Cox wrote as 'Anthony Berkeley', as well as the smaller number of psychological thrillers published as by 'Francis Iles', should be on the bookshelf of anyone who professes to love crime fiction.

Cox was born on 5 July 1893 in Watford, north of London, and educated at Sherborne, a boarding school in Dorset. After school he went to Oxford and after coming down in 1916 with a Bachelor of Arts degree from University College, Oxford, he enlisted in the British Army, serving in France. After being demobbed, Cox embarked on a career as a humourist, producing countless short stories and comic sketches for a huge range of magazines while, working with J. J. Sterling Hill, he expanded a twenty-minute vignette into a futuristic opera, *The Merchant Prince*. He also started to write crime fiction, exclusively so once he found it paid better than other genres.

His first crime novel, *The Layton Court Mystery* (1925) was published anonymously and in many ways it set the tone for his career as a crime novelist. There was an ingenious problem, a surprising solution and—in the form of Roger Sheringham—a surprisingly fallible detective. In just under ten years, Sheringham appeared in ten novels published as by 'Anthony Berkeley', and these included one of the true masterpieces of the Golden Age of crime and detection, *The Poisoned Chocolates Case* (1929). Cox was never without a sense of humour and in all of his Anthony Berkeley novels his tongue is firmly in his cheek, a tendency deplored by some contemporary reviewers. As well as incorporating humour and taking an iconoclastic approach to the genre's 'rules', Cox found the history of crime a ready source of inspiration, using several infamous crimes as the starting point for a detective story. He also broadcast on the BBC and its predecessor 2LO. Finally, as the self- styled 'first freeman' of the Detection Club, the dining society for crime writers that he and others had created in 1929, Cox played a key role in developing ideas to raise funds, including an anthology of crime writing as well as the Club's novel *The Floating Admiral* (1931) and other multi-authored stories.

When Cox tired of playing with the detective story, he decided to take a new direction, and as Francis Iles wrote two powerful psychological mysteries—*Malice Aforethought* and *Before the Fact*—filmed by Hitchcock as *Suspicion* (1941)—as well as a third less successful novel, before abandoning writing altogether. From the mid-1940s, other than a few propaganda stories featuring Sheringham, some other short fiction, a few radio plays and two collections of limericks, Cox focused not on writing crime fiction but reviewing it, which he did until shortly before his death on 9 March 1971.

'The Green Dress' is an undated typescript with the byline 'A. B. Cox'. This is its first known publication.

THE HAUNTED HOUSE

A. Fielding

'I've made a mistake—a great mistake—in taking the Manor. I realise that now, when it's possibly too late.' Mr Terry rested his head on a trembling hand in such an attitude of hopeless dejection that it amounted to despair. 'As a member of the Psychical Research Society I naturally was interested—but I wish to Heaven that I'd never heard of the place.'

Mr Marshall helped his visitor—and recent client —to a whisky and soda with the benevolent solemnity of a Harley Street specialist handing over an infallible prescription.

'I'm extremely sorry to hear this, but perhaps the feeling will pass. Lord Ivymere was never troubled by the bell-ringing, and—eh—so on. I warned you of the legend, but as you say—ahem . . .'

Mr Terry bubbled something into his glass which the other interpreted as regretful assent.

'Of course, the Manor is in other respects a delightful property,' Mr Marshall continued soothingly, 'and if I may say so, it was let to you at a remarkable bargain.'

'Including the ghost.' Mr Terry gave a weak smile. The house-agent responded a trifle uncertainly. He was not quite sure how far to go in acknowledging the ghost of Spondon Manor.

'Well, the ghost has hitherto been—what shall we say—historic. That's it, historic. Not—'

'Something much more than I ever bargained for.' Mr Terry sank back again into his gloom. 'Do you believe in presentiments, Mr Marshall?'

Mr Marshall having a very strong one at that moment that Spondon Manor would shortly be in his hands again to let once more—at a commission—cheerfully said that he did.

Mr Terry eyed him sombrely.

'Well,' he said, rising heavily—he was a thick-set man of about fifty, with keen, grey eyes and the jaw of a fighter, not at all the sort of man generally troubled with visitors from the other world—'well, I've a presentiment, and a black one. I'd clear out bag and baggage if my son, Beresford, could be moved. Unfortunately, the doctor says that's out of the question.'

He eyed the stick which he took from a chair beside him as though it, too, were a messenger of doom.

'I'm sorry to hear that Mr Beresford Terry is no better,' Marshall said politely.

'Worse.' The other's face darkened still more if that were possible. 'We keep all this from him, of course, and the two nurses, so far, seem to be sensible women; but, well, I wish we were well away from the whole place. It's got on my nerves. You see,' he creased his felt hat thoughtfully, 'it's one thing to take a manor with a bell that rings before a death and a piece of knotted rope found beneath it in the morning when you are all well, and it's another, damnably another, thing when your son's ill with the worst bout of malaria he's had in years. We've cancelled the house-party of course, and what with half the servants gone you can't imagine a drearier hole than the Manor is just. now.

Marshall stiffened. He did not let holes.

'I hope Saunderson has remained?' he asked, by way of tactfully suggesting that where that admirable butler kept the flag flying, life could never be unendurable.

'Oh, rather! I don't know what we should do without him.'

'That's just the expression his lordship used so often,' beamed Mr Marshall, who hoped that the conversation was now definitely salvaged on to lighter ground.

Terry paused in the act of lighting a cigar.

'Well, I've written this morning to town asking any two members of the P.R.S. to come down and investigate. You can't think what it's like to have your only son as ill as Beresford is, and then to've heard that damned bell, twice over now, ringing away up on its rafter, and find that twisted rope lying beneath it, and know the legend, that it means a death coming to someone in the house. If there were any possibility of hocus-pocus—but there isn't. There isn't!' He shook hands in an agitated way, and almost ran to his car.

'Well, well!' Mr Marshall laid aside his expression of sympathetic gloom till it should be wanted at Mr Terry's next call. 'What a lot of people there are in the world who don't know their own minds, Hallett. Here's that chap grumbling about a bell ringing when he expressly took the Manor in order to study—let me see, what did he call it?—spirit manifestations, that was it. Spirit manifestations!'

Hallett, glad of any interruption to lighten the curse of Adam, shook his head.

'Of course it's all nonsense,' Marshall was no longer talking to a client; 'the Spondon Manor ghost was just a bit of family swank, you know. Interesting, perhaps, like Pipe Rolls, but just as much out of date.'

'He certainly seemed to have the wind up all right.'

'Nerves!' Mr Marshall lumped all unusual behaviour under that heading. 'Or else someone in the house is playing some foolish prank. Now then, about this sale of the Mortimer cottages . . .' and Hallett clicked on again.

Over a game of billiards at the Why Not, however, he related the morning's visit to his chum, Daly.

'You should have seen him, Bob, white-faced and trembling, telling old Marshall about the bell that rings at midnight in the hall at the Manor without anyone touching it. You bet if Terry walks about much overhead the bell would ring! He must weigh eighteen stone.'

Robert Daly listened attentively. He had a reason for being interested in anything that concerned Spondon Manor. He met it in person soon afterwards. The reason—a very pretty one—finally held him at arm's length.

'Do be more careful, Bob, someone might see us!'

'Why not?' Bob asked brazenly. 'Do 'em good. Christmas comes but once a year!'

May Broderick adjusted her hat.

'But what's all this nonsense that's going the round of Spondon about the ghost?' he asked, only waiting his opportunity to make her do it all over again. 'Have *you* heard that bell?'

She caught his arm.

'That's why I asked you to meet me here! '

'Oh.' He straightened. 'That was why, was it?'

'It's your chance come at last, darling! Mr Terry's written to the Psychical Research Society this morning—he read the letter aloud to Mr Beresford in front of Nurse Macleod and me, asking them to investigate with him. He offers to put any two of them up for a week. Now then, darling'—Miss Broderick's hat again suffered an eclipse, and was retrieved later from her left ear—'why don't you investigate too? You're ever so much cleverer than that silly society. You're a reporter—well, here's something really worthwhile to report! Oh, Bob, it'll make your name and your fortune at the same time.'

'And we'll be married and live in London town,' Bob finished by way of capping the picture.

He was excited though.

'Sounds a good suggestion,' he agreed. '"Ghost of well-known Derbyshire Manor House interviewed by our Special

Correspondent. Gives its impression of winter conditions as compared with the good old days of Canute." The ghost dates from Canute, doesn't it?'

'Thereabouts. Spondon Manor was built by accident on the place a hermit. cursed when he was hung beside his chapel. The bell tolled as he died, and tolls now whenever a death is coming to anyone in the house.' She shivered a little. It was a cold day in mid-December.

'Look here, you don't believe that stuff, eh, dearest?'

'I don't know. I'm not sure . . . I wonder if I'm right to suggest your looking into it, Bob. I only came down yesterday, and at first it seemed such a silly story, but—'

'But?'

'There *is* something wrong about the house. I'm not a bit nervy, as you know, but there's a feeling—an atmosphere of— well, it sounds ridiculous, but really it's an atmosphere of horror—since that bell rang last night.'

'It did ring? You heard it?'

'Oh, clearly. I was in bed. It rang at midnight, as it always does—if it rings at all.'

'Convenient hour, not too many people around. But how do you know so much about the correct time, and the history of the place?'

'The butler told me. He's fearfully worried about it. I ran into the hall when I heard the sound. I didn't see the bell actually ringing, of course, only the person who is going to die sees that. But anyone can see the bell still vibrating afterwards.'

'Are they pleasant people?'

'Quite nice. Of course, the position's a little awkward. Doctor Nesbit wired for me without asking anyone's leave, it seems, because he doesn't think Nurse Macleod up to her work. And, certainly, her ideas of a temperature chart are weird. On the whole she's been very decent about my being put in charge of Mr Beresford.'

'What's he like?'

'Oh, ordinary. Fearfully nervous about himself. Talks of nothing but his symptoms and how bad he is.'

'And how bad is that really?'

'Pretty bad. Much too much so to want to hear that bell toll overhead.'

Bob thought over what she had told him. It sounded queer.

'And how about a piece of rope left beneath the bell; did you see that interesting relic?'

She opened her little handbag.

'There! I sneaked it off Mr Terry's table.'

Bob examined the knotted cord attentively. The noose was just the size of a man's throat, and it was knotted tight.

'I saw Mr Terry in church yesterday. He passed the plate around. Looked a clever chap. What does he say?'

'Nothing to me, of course, but he nearly had a collapse in the hall last night.'

Again Bob stood looking down at that noose, and thinking hard.

'Darling, I want you to give up the case. Leave as soon as you can pack up. I'll explain to the doctor. I don't like your being mixed up with tolling bells and rope-ends.'

'But I couldn't think of leaving my patient!' Nurse Broderick quite obscured his little fiancée.

'Yes, but you see, darling, I don't believe in ghosts, and if this isn't a ghost . . . then there's something funny up.'

'But what? In books, of course, there's always someone who wants the house for some reason or other, but that's not true here. And it isn't done for a joke, for there's no young people.'

'No, I didn't think it was done for a joke. How does Beresford take the bells?'

'He doesn't know of them. His room is right away from the main part. I slipped in last night before I ran into the hall. He was fast asleep.'

'It's a funny story,' Bob maintained. 'Before Lord Ivymere left for South Africa that bell hadn't rung once in a lifetime, so Hallett told me, and since this man has taken the house it's rung three times. Three times in not quite a month! I'll interview Mr Terry today, and see if he'll let me prowl around a bit—but in any case I wish, darling, that you'd be a sensible girl—'

The awful figure of Nurse Broderick loomed so imminent that he contented himself with a very satisfactory hug of May.

'Tum-tiddly-hi-ti, tum-tum-tum!' hummed Robert, a little on the sharp side, as he walked back from his interview later in the day with Mr Terry. Things were going well or the humming would have been flat.

The tenant of the Manor House was delighted at his offer of help. There was no mistaking his genuineness.

'An independent trained observer! The very thing we want!' He himself made no secret of his conviction that the recent happenings were due to supernatural agency, but he thankfully gave Daly *carte blanche* to write what he liked and go where he liked, and insisted on putting him up. Daly got a provisional promise from a London editor to 'look at his stuff' and went to bed with high hopes.

From the landing outside his bedroom he could look down into the big hall and up at the bell high above. The central hall at the Manor had no ceiling but went up to the uncovered rafters of the roof, and from the highest and smallest rafter hung a little bronze bell—the bell. A field-glass and a flashlight photograph of his own convinced Bob that there was no wire or thread running from the bell, and that the rafter was absolutely inaccessible.

Yet only a few hours later at midnight Bob was wakened by the sound of the bell ringing furiously, not tolling as hitherto. He leapt out of his room. From the next one bolted Terry in his pyjamas, his face ghastly, his eyes horrified.

Below them in the hall lay the butler, apparently staring up at the bell over his head which was silent but still quivering. The light was very dim, only one bulb being on. Terry darted past.

'Switch on the lights,' he shouted, evidently quite beside himself, 'the man's dead! Help!'

Robert's head drummed. As for Terry, he was sobbing and swearing. A perfect picture of panic. One glance at the dead man's face made Daly feel the neck. Deeply embedded in the flesh was a tightly twisted noose. He and Terry had hard work to cut it loose. They tried to get some air back into his lungs, but the doctor stayed their well-meant, useless efforts. The man was quite dead, strangled by the mate to the noose that reposed in Robert Daly's bag.

Into Manchester Bob went on his bicycle and sent off a despatch that left him with exactly 9¾d to continue life on, but which the London editor amplified instead of cutting.

Bob hardly knew where he was during the next day. The Derbyshire constables kept the crowd at bay, the deputy chief constable was closeted with Terry and his son, who could no longer be kept in ignorance of what was going on. A private detective interviewed all and sundry, and obviously looked on Robert as the most probable solution of the mystery. And in the thick of the morning down came two leading members of the P.R.S., or, to be accurate, one leading member from London and one from a similar Australian organisation.

Solemn-faced, spectacled men both, with an air of portentous gravity. They were turned over to Daly, for he seemed to have stepped into the post of confidential secretary.

'The bell,' observed Mr Grey, the Englishman, 'is quite impossible to get at in any way.'

'Quite impossible,' intoned Mr Herbert Townley. Bob had opened his eyes at the name, for Mr Townley was interested in other things besides ghosts, and his name was known in other realms besides those frequented by spirits.

'You saw the bell ring?' Both men had their notebooks out. Bob gave a very accurate account of what he had seen.

'You saw no one in the hall besides the butler?'

'No one. I would swear that no one could have been there. You see, it's very barely furnished. No place to hide that I can find.'

'Was he—warm when you touched him?'

Bob nodded. He did not like to remember that moment.

'I understand from the police superintendent that he was a most respectable man, known to the neighbourhood from his boyhood. This certainly is a most interesting affair,' and Mr Grey tapped his note-book reflectively.

'It certainly is!' agreed Daly.

As for Mr Townley he only nodded and spent the rest of the day crawling on his stomach, like the serpent after his little joke went wrong in the Garden of Eden. By dinner-time he and Mr Grey had a very fair idea of the drains and water-pipes and were nearly at one about the position of the principal cellars. Evidently the Society took its work seriously. Mr Terry was no use to anyone. He reiterated that as soon as the doctor would let Beresford travel, both would be off, never to darken a haunted house again. Mr Grey considered him a backslider and was hardly mollified by the offer to stay on as long as he liked and investigate to his heart's content. The night after poor Saunderson's terrible death the household was not disturbed, but the night after that came again the clanging of the bell, came again the little loop of tightly knotted rope lying on the floor below. According to tradition the bell never rang two nights in succession, and the third night also was a blank, but on Christmas Eve Mr Townley, who had a bed made up for himself regularly on a couch in the hall, was disturbed by a hand laid very gently on his arm. It was just eleven o'clock. Mr Townley was not asleep. It was Bob who bent over him, and there was a rather strange look on the young man's face.

'I think I've discovered the clue to the ringing of the bell. There's an odd bit of mechanism in the cellar that I'd like to show you. Mr Grey's there already. This way—' and noiselessly they tiptoed along a corridor. Robert flashed his torch for a second down a flight of stairs.

'Here we are!' he murmured, leading the way.

At the bottom he switched on the light of a cellar room.

'It's in there—in the next room! Mr Grey's—' Townley stepped past him, wheeled, and an automatic swept out.

'Up with your hands and—' The voice was low, but no longer either Australian or solemn. There was snap enough and to spare in it and in the eyes fixed on Bob's. But he did not finish his sentence. A cloth was flung over his head from behind, and springing forward Daly dashed the pistol aside and knocked him out very neatly.

Then, with a grunt of satisfaction, he trussed him and gagged him, with the help of Miss Broderick, whose silent feet and deft throw had just reversed the tables.

An hour passed. Midnight struck. The bell! The clanging, crashing bell! Out on to the landing jumped Mr Grey.

Down below swayed Townley's grey head. He was struggling with three men. Beside him a girl rang a hand-bell and screamed, 'Help him! They'll kill him. Police! Police!'

In a second leap Mr Grey was in the hall below.

Even as he sprang three of the men tried to jump apart—out of sight—but the lights were full on now, and his automatic controlled the situation. As for the bell-ringer, she was on her knees beside a figure on the floor, and sawing at a cord around his neck, while she sobbed wildly.

'He told me it was perfectly safe! Don't put that pistol down! He told me it was perfectly safe!'

Grey was certain that he was having a nightmare. Not his usual one of seeing a train depart with all his luggage and money on board, nor yet the dear old second-best, in which, attired only in a top hat, he found himself mounting the stairs of Buckingham Palace to be knighted by a startled sovereign, but a totally new one.

He was holding up, like the villain of a melodrama, his host, Mr Terry, and two strangers. On the floor lay a Townley who was not quite Townley.

At that moment, out from a door that seemed to lead downstairs stepped a man with a cut on his jaw whom he had never seen before, and yet who was vaguely familiar, while at the head of the stairs, surveying the scene with interest, stood Herbert Townley. Undoubtedly the ghost-hunter and millionaire, and yet vaguely unfamiliar. He, too, held an automatic.

The man on the floor gurgled something.

'You told me it wasn't dangerous!' sobbed the girl, materialising a jug of water from somewhere, and holding it to the swollen lips.

'Nor was it, or if it was it was worth it!' croaked Daly, getting up and steadying himself by her shoulder. 'That's the police. Just on time.'

The stranger who had come in by the door stepped forward.

'Ah, superintendent, I see you've brought some constables with you. Perhaps you'd like to see my card first.'

The police officer took it with goggling eyes that only fell on it by an effort. The name made him give the man another look.

'Someone arranged with us over the telephone to be on hand and come on in by a window left open when a bell should ring. And someone else—'

'You have your warrants to arrest Horniman, Mitchell, and Bolton? The man whom Daly had gagged spoke with the voice of authority. Good. These are the three men. I give them in charge, as I told you over the 'phone, for the murder of Saunderson and the attempted murder of Mr Townley.'

'At the inquest yesterday, which was adjourned, sir, no evidence was brought forward'—the superintendent spoke deferentially, but he clearly intended to know where he was stepping.

'I should hope not! There's plenty. A part of it looks to me as though it could do with a whisky and soda!'

'Not in this house!' Daly said hoarsely. 'And who in blazes are you?' But the man with the cut on his jaw was solely concerned with the police officer.

Arthur spoke only to him. 'First as to Horniman. I see you've heard his name before. That's him! That little chap there.' He pointed out a sullen figure whom the dead Saunderson had called Nurse Macleod.

'As for the other two, they're new to you as yet. I'll fill in the details when they're out of the room.'

There followed the usual caution; handcuffs were clicked on, and the constables collected the three silent men like so many dropped cards.

'Don't take 'em outside,' Daly squeaked, 'not outside—reporters camped around the house—my stuff this!'

'I should say so!' Braddon, ex-inspector of New Scotland Yard, and head of a private inquiry office, agreed heartily, 'distinctly yours! Like the cut on my jaw. Take 'em off into that room there. Saunderson suspected the men from the first, though he thought that they were after the Ivymere silver and pictures. He little guessed the crime intended. But he watched them, and the evening before they murdered him he wrote to me that things were getting a bit beyond him. I'd been called in once in a house where he worked. After posting that letter he evidently gave himself away somehow, poor chap. For his death wasn't intended from the first. But once it became a necessity they decided to use that too as bait. I got his note together with the morning paper telling of his death. The paper incidentally mentioned that Mr Townley, "the Australian mine-magnate, well known for his interest in spiritualism", was going to look into the extraordinary affair. Had intended to go down to Spondon even before this last development. That let in daylight! That explained why the Haunted House mystery had figured so prominently before the town for the last fortnight. Of course it was haunted! That was the only bait that would lure Mr Townley down here. I caught Mr Townley with one foot in the car, and he was able to explain a letter Saunderson had picked up and enclosed. He gave a reason for all this stage-work, a reason that would have been buried with him if all had gone according to plan. Mr Townley and Bolton—alias Beresford—'

'But he *was* ill!' broke in Nurse Broderick; 'he bad a temperature of 104 degrees this evening!'

'Wonderful what a plug of tobacco will do if held in the armpit! Old soldier's trick! Well, Mr Townley and Bolton owned a ruby mine in Burma. Mine fizzled out. Mr T. wanted to publish the truth. Bolton said he had discovered another—the real thing on the same property. Mr T. agreed to wait till New Year, but not a day later, for the proofs to be planked down. Bolton agreed but decided that it might be simpler to plank down Mr Townley instead. He searched high and low for a haunted house to suit. A damsel wringing her hands along the picture gallery or a gent with his head under one arm wouldn't be of any use to him. Spondon Manor was *It*. Bolton took the house furnished for six months and moved in with Mitchell and Horniman. Mitchell, a one-time gentleman, was from Buenos Aires—on the run! And Horniman's a capital woman impersonator, and very broad-minded. The three started the show and nearly got you, sir.'

Mr Townley raised his eyebrows.

'Impossible with two guardian angels actually struggling together for my safety! Why, I've been watched over like an heir apparent. Mr Braddon only let me come on condition that he should pass for me, and I be disguised as the valet. But don't forget to tell about the bell.'

'Nice little idea that. Crawling over the roof, I found one chimney too many. It was just over the bell. Inside it—it was a dummy—was another bell with an electric wire running to a clock in Bolton's room, which was generally stopped—on account of the poor patient, eh, Nurse?'

'So Nurse Macl—that man, told me.' Nurse Broderick was still a long way behind the facts.

'Bolton had a Chinese weather-vane from Wembley added to the house, with Lord Ivymere's permission, and incidentally had this chimney fitted on too. He himself's an expert electrician. By setting the clock in his room going and putting the alarm to whatever hour he liked, the bell on the roof rang. A hole was cut immediately over the visible bell, and the sound came down perfectly. Also a small black rubber ball that hit the edge of the bell and set it vibrating. Ball to be picked up later on. It was finding that clock going that made me sure there'd be trouble tonight. That's all for a first instalment, I think.' Braddon rose.

'The superintendent and I have to run into Manchester now to speak to the chief constable. I'll send your wad off for you, Daly, if you like. Hear your story later.'

'You're a sport!' Daly said warmly, handing over the pad on which he had been scribbling for dear life.

May was dropped with friends, and the three men went on to Daly's lodgings.

'Well, I suppose you know where you are?' Grey said, patiently. 'But my name really *is* Grey. I'm sorry to be so dull, but honestly the P.R.S. asked me to come down here with Mr Townley—this Mr Townley or the one we've just left—or perhaps it was Mr Daly, and the young man I took for Daly was really a Mr Townley.'

Townley laughed.

'Clear us up, Daly. How did you come to take a hand?'

'Those knots left on the floor were all tied by a left-handed man. I'd seen Mitchell in church; he was left-handed. When he jumped out of his room the night poor Saunderson's body had just been laid beneath the bell, his face had big drops of sweat on it. Considering he wasn't supposed to know that the man was dead, I couldn't see why.'

'But what made you get throttled in my stead?' pressed Townley.

'I'm a reporter,' Bob said simply, 'and I wanted the whole story.'

'You nearly got an epitaph instead.'

'As soon as I heard your name,' Bob went on, 'I decided, like Mr Braddon, that the plot was against you. You see, I guessed Macleod was a man fairly early. Wrist and forearm always do give that game away; so May and I thought that we'd make sure of your safety anyway. One Saunderson was enough! We tied Braddon up in a cellar room.'

'I know. I found him there a few minutes later.'

'How?'

'He had left a trail of birds-eye from his couch. We decided to wait and watch events. They were worth watching. But go on with your yarn.'

'I got a grey wig and made up as much like you as I could; then I lay in Braddon's place and waited. Those men moved like cats. I never heard them when they pounced. But May heard! She rang that bell of hers like the town crier who's lost the king, and that was all.'

Townley took out his cigar and looked at Bob.

'You've nerve, young man. I like nerve. You've brains. I like brains, too. Look here. You're wasted in England, where the underwood's too thick for a youngster. Come out with me to Queensland. I'll give you a salary you'd take twenty years to work up to here. What say?'

'Done,' Bob said promptly, 'if I can come as a married man.'

'All the better. Room out there for twenty wives.'

'Not if May is one of them!' Bob said with a grin.

'I'm sleepy or I should have put it differently. Here's luck to us all and a Merry Christmas. And now I'm off to bed.'

A. FIELDING

'A. Fielding' was the author of 25 novel-length detective stories published between 1924 and 1944. All but two feature Inspector Pointer of Scotland Yard, and they are similar to the police mysteries of Freeman Wills Crofts and John Rhode. Like the detectives created by these better-known writers, Pointer is a plodder and he methodically investigates cases such as *The Tall House Mystery* (1933) in which a guest is murdered during a party while dressed as a ghost, and the Christiean *Mystery in the Rectory* (1936). Arguably, the best of the Pointer mysteries is *The Footsteps that Stopped* (1926), which the publisher Collins boldly, if rashly, promoted as the new *Roger Ackroyd*.

Who then was 'A. Fielding'?

At least one contemporary magazine identified 'A. Fielding' as 'Archibald Fielding', while in the United States the novels were attributed to 'A. E. Fielding'. *However*, contemporary notes against titles by 'A. Fielding' in the British Library catalogue identify the author as Dorothy Feilding.

So *who* was Dorothy Feilding?

She *might* be a woman of that name listed in 1930s electoral rolls as living in Sheffield Terrace, the same street as Agatha Christie, together with a man called Alfred Edmund Anthony. *However*, while Mr Anthony's initials might *perhaps* be significant, little more is known about her.

She *might* be Lady Dorothy Mary Evelyn Feilding who was born at Newnham Paddox, Warwickshire, on 4 October 1889, the second daughter of the Earl and Countess of Denbigh and distantly related to the novelist Henry Fielding. Lady Dorothy's parents were wealthy land-owners and she was educated at home and later at a convent in Paris. While two of her sisters became nuns, she took an active part of the social and sporting life of Warwickshire but still found time to do good deeds. In August 1914, after a short spell working in a cottage hospital, she travelled to France where she served with Hector Monro's 'Flying Ambulance', a Red Cross unit attached to the Belgian Field Army. For her work in the trenches—as described in *The Sketch* as 'the gayest of nurses in the grimmest of wars'— Lady Dorothy was awarded the Order of Leopold by King Albert of Belgium in 1915, and in 1916 King George V presented her and five nurses with the Military Medal for bravery in the field. In July 1917, she married Captain Charles Moore of the Irish Guards, with whom she had four daughters and one son. After the war, she went to live at her husband's home in Ireland where she ran the estate and lived a quiet life, ideal conditions *perhaps* in which to write. *However*, Feilding died of heart failure in south Tipperary on 24 October 1935, nearly ten years before the last 'A Fielding' title was published. On top of that rather problematic fact, Lady Dorothy's grandson has stated that the family are not aware of any evidence to suggest that she wrote a word of fiction, let alone 25 novels and a handful of short stories.

So 'A Fielding' *might* be someone else entirely . . .

'The Haunted House' was first published in *The Sphere* on 24 November 1924 where the author was credited twice: once as 'A. Fielding' and once as 'Archibald Fielding'.

PERSONAL CALL

Agatha Christie

(*Confused noises of a cocktail party in progress*)

VOICES: (*Jumbled*) 'Hullo Pam, you're looking wonderful. Marriage seems to agree with you.'

'Come on in, old man. So glad you could make it.'

'Pam's about somewhere.'

'Darling, have you heard about Mona?'

(*Telephone rings. Unheeded for a moment or two*)

MRS LAMB: 'Ullo, 'ullo . . . Yes, Kensington 34598. Wot? Just a moment, please. I can't 'ear you.

(*A door shuts. Cocktail noise reduced to faint background*)

'Ullo, yes?

OPERATOR: Can Mr James Brent take a personal call, please, from Newton Abbot?

MRS LAMB: I'll try and get 'old of 'im but there's a party going on.

(*Door opens. Increased noise and scraps of conversation*)

VOICES. 'Mary, it's lovely to see you. It's been simply ages.'

'Hullo, Johnnie, you must meet my wife. She's somewhere about.'

'Cocktail, or would you rather have sherry?'

MRS LAMB: Please, sir—please—

JAMES: —We certainly are—but how we're ever going to manage on this travelling allowance I don't—eh, what?

MRS LAMB: You're wanted on the 'phone, sir.

JAMES: What—now? Who is it?

MRS LAMB: It's a personal call, sir, from something Abbas.

JAMES: People will ring up at the most inconvenient moments. John, get Mona another drink. Hullo, Lois, lovely to see you. Pam's about somewhere—

(*Cocktail noises fade as the door shuts*)

Hullo?

OPERATOR: Is that Mr James Brent speaking personally?

JAMES: James Brent speaking.

OPERATOR: Just a moment, please.

(*Pause. Voice sounds faintly*)

Go ahead please. Mr Brent is waiting.

FAY: (*Her voice sounds remote and rather unearthly*) Hullo James?

JAMES: Who's speaking?

FAY: Don't you know? (*Slightly mocking laugh*) It's Fay . . .

JAMES: (*Not yet reacting*) Who did you say? Sorry, the line's bad and there's a lot of noise going on here.

FAY: (sounding nearer) It's Fay . . .

JAMES: (*Startled*) What did you say?

FAY: It's Fay, James? Don't you remember?

JAMES: (*Upset*) Who are you? Where are you speaking from?

FAY: I'm at Newton Abbot station . . . Where you left me . . .

JAMES: What's that? (*Angry*) Who is this?

FAY: I told you. I'm Fay . . . You remember Fay? I'm waiting for you to come and meet me.

JAMES: Meet you? What do you mean?

FAY: I'm waiting at the station. At Newton Abbot.

JAMES: Look here, one of us is mad. What are you talking about? And who are you?

FAY: How often have I got to tell you that I'm Fay . . .

JAMES: If this is a practical joke, let me tell you that it's a very heartless and silly one.

FAY: It isn't a joke, James. I'm here—waiting. You'll have to come.

JAMES: I've never heard of anything so preposterous . . . how dare you pretend—

(*Door opens. Noise of party is heard*)

PAM: So that's where you are, darling. Telephoning! For goodness' sake come back. People are pouring in. We want some more cocktails mixed. (*Her voice changes*) Why—darling—what is it?

(*Slamming receiver down*)

JAMES: (*Speaks angrily*) A cruel, silly, practical joke! You'd think people had something better to do—

(*Shuts door, sudden hush*)

PAM: Darling—what is it? Who was it ringing up?

JAMES: (*Furious*) How should I know? But I'm going to try and find out.

(*Dials*)

Can you possibly carry on for a few minutes without me, Pam? I'll be along as soon as I can, my sweet.

PAM: Yes, of course . . . (*Pause*) You're really upset, aren't you, darling? What did whoever it was say?

JAMES: Hullo—hullo. This is Mr James Brent. Kensington 34598. You put through a personal call to me just now. Can you tell me where it came from? Yes . . . Yes . . . You'll ring me back? . . . As soon as you can . . .

(*Replaces receiver*)

Sorry Pam, but it really made me see red.

PAM: But who *was* it?

JAMES: I'll tell you all about it later. Do go now, darling. The party will be getting out of hand.

PAM: It's being a great success. That's really the trouble. All right, darling. I'll cope. But do come soon.

(*Door opens. Noise. Shuts*)

(*Softly*) Fay . . . I wasn't dreaming it . . . She said *Fay* . . . And

it was her voice, too . . . Who the devil can have been playing
a trick on me . . . ?

(*Telephone rings. Receiver off*)

OPERATOR: Mr James Brent? I have made enquiries. No
personal call has been put through to you today.

JAMES: What? But I—

OPERATOR: No personal call has been put through to you.

(*Replacing receiver*)

JAMES: (Softly, shaken) But I don't understand. I don't understand . . . I heard her . . .

(*Door opens. Party noise*)

PAM: (*crossly*) Really, James, if you've finished telephoning you
might come along. You just stand there looking as though
someone had socked you on the head!

JAMES: I really am sorry, Pam. I'm with you.

PAM: Who was it who rang you up?

JAMES: Oh—just somebody trying to be funny.

PAM: What did he say? (*With a slight change of tone*) Or was
it a she?

JAMES: I don't know . . . I mean, it was a she . . . It was nothing
particular.

PAM: (*A little forced*) Darling, you're not leading a double life,
I hope? I shouldn't like that at all.

JAMES: (*Also forced*) You're the only woman in my life, Pam.
I can assure you of that.

PAM: You'd have to say so, anyway! But something seems to
have shattered your morale.

JAMES: (*With feeling*) I just don't like silly jokes.

PAM: Well, come on, back to the scrimmage. By the way, I
asked Evan and Mary in for bridge tomorrow. I haven't seen
Mary for ages—and one can't talk at a show like this. Is that
all right?

JAMES: Quite all right.

(*Party noises louder as James and Pam re-join the party*)

Hullo Evan, not seen you for ages . . . I hear you're coming
in to bridge tomorrow? Good show . . .

(*Party fades out*)

(*Tune in noises of a railway station. Train rushes through
with scream of engine*)

PORTER: Mind them cases, Joe. Yes ma'am, what is it?

FAY: Please can you tell me where I can find—

(*Voice drowned by shunting*)

PORTER: Sorry, ma'am, couldn't hear you. What did you say?

FAY: The telephones?

PORTER: Out by the booking office. Over the bridge.

FAY: It's a trunk call I want.

PORTER: The first box.

FAY: Thank you . . .

2ND PORTER: Hullo, Bert? Seen a ghost?

PORTER: 'Tis funny, you saying that. That woman who was
asking me the way to the telephone boxes—reckon as I've
seen her before somewheres . . . and seems to me as when
I saw her, 'twas something to do with a death . . . I can't just
call to mind—

(*Train comes in slowly*)

Newton Abbot. Newton Abbot.

(*Train noises, then suddenly silence*)

FAY: Hullo. I want a personal call, please . . . To Mr James Brent.
The number is Kensington 34598 . . . This number is—Newton
Abbot [?] . . . Yes . . . Yes . . . How much did you say the
charge will be? Yes, I've got the money ready . . .

(*Fade*)

(*Tune in to bridge four*)

EVAN: —And I've got the best heart *and* a trump.

PAM: That makes us two down. Sorry, James. Your deal, Mary.

MARY: Cut, please.

JAMES: Jumping to four spades was a bit rash, Pam.

PAM: I've had an awful head today—after the party yesterday,
   I suppose.

EVAN: Jolly good party, Pam.

MARY: Yes, indeed. Evan and I drank far too much.

PAM: Oh, one must do something to cheer oneself up nowadays.

MARY: One heart.

JAMES: Three diamonds.

EVAN: Pass.

PAM: Four clubs.

   (*Telephone rings*)

   Oh bother!

JAMES: Mrs Lamb will answer it. What did you say, four clubs?

MARY: Double four clubs.

JAMES: Four diamonds.

EVAN: Double four diamonds.

PAM: Yes, Mrs Lamb, what is it?

MRS LAMB: It's a personal call, sir, for you.

JAMES: (*Upset*) For me? All right— (*Slowly*) I'll come.

PAM: Darling—you don't think—

JAMES: It's quite all right. Probably Smith, about that transfer.
   (*Door closes*)

EVAN: Wonder whether it's still raining.

   (*Pulls curtains, opens window*)

PAM: (*Confidentially*) He got a personal call yesterday from
   somewhere or other, and it upset him dreadfully. He told me
   it was someone playing a silly joke on him, but he wouldn't
   tell me what the joke was . . . You know, Mary, it really quite
   worried me . . .

MARY: (*Confidentially*) Have you got an extension?

PAM: (*Confidentially*) Yes, in my bedroom. Do you think—

MARY: (*Urgently*) I would . . .

PAM: (*Artificially and loud*) I must just run upstairs and powder
   my nose.

EVAN: You women . . .

(*Fade*)

JAMES: Hullo—yes?

VOICE: Just a moment, please.

(*Click*)

Go ahead—you're through.

FAY: James? It's me again . . .

JAMES: Fay!

FAY: Yes, Fay . . .

JAMES: Now look here, what's the meaning of all this? What kind of a game is it?

FAY: It's not a game, James.

JAMES: If you think you're going to get me rattled—

FAY: You needn't be so upset. I just want you to come and meet me.

JAMES: Meet you? Where?

FAY: At Newton Abbot, of course . . . That's where I am now.

JAMES: A likely story! I checked up last night, it may interest you to know, and no call from Newton Abbot had ever been put through.

FAY: But I *am* at Newton Abbot . . . Wait—I'll push the door a little bit open. Then you can hear—

(*Faint sounds of trains and station noises*)

PORTER: (*Very faint*) Newton Abbot . . . Newton Abbot . . . Torquay and Kingswear train. Change for Plymouth and Cornwall . . .

FAY: You hear?

JAMES: (*Shaken*) I don't believe it.

(*Train noises shut off*)

FAY: Haven't you even noticed what time it is?

JAMES: What do you mean?

FAY: The time . . . *It's a quarter past seven* . . . Don't you

JAMES: (*Hoarsely*) Shut up.

FAY: How rough you are, James darling . . . But you do see what I mean, don't you?

JAMES: (*Hoarsely*) I don't know what you're talking about. What the Hell do you want, anyway?

FAY: I want you to come and meet me here.

JAMES: Where?

FAY: Oh dear, have I got to open that door again? I told you before, I'm where you left me. And I can't leave there until you come.

JAMES: This has got to stop, I tell you! It's got to stop.

(*Faint melancholy scream of an engine*)

Hullo—hullo—hullo—Are you there? Damn!

(*Slams down receiver*)

(*Door bangs. Another opens on to—*)

EVAN: —and I still feel, Mary, that kids don't really appreciate— Hullo, James, put through a successful deal?

JAMES: What deal?

EVAN: (*Facetiously*) Or was it a bit more personal than that, old man?

JAMES: (*Shortly*) Nothing important. Where's Pam?

MARY: Powdering her nose—oh! Here you are, Pam.

EVAN: Now where had we got to? Four diamonds doubled. Your shout, James.

JAMES: Oh—er—pass.

PAM: (*With acid sweetness*) Are you finding it difficult to keep your mind on the game, dear?

JAMES: No, of course not. What do you mean?

EVAN: What's the matter, Pam? Not feeling faint or anything, are you? You look very queer.

PAM: It's just my head. I told you I had a bad head.

MARY: (*With decision*) Look here, I think we'd better stop. It's nearly half past seven, and we've only Just started this rubber, Pam's not feeling well, I can see. Come along, Evan. *Evan!*

EVAN: All right—don't kick me. So long, you people. See you again after you come back from abroad. When are you off?

JAMES: Day after tomorrow. I am looking forward to it, I can tell you. Nowhere like *la belle France* for a holiday.

EVAN: (*Facetiously*) Ah, but you shouldn't take the wife! (*Laughs heartily*)

JAMES: Don't you believe it! It's going to be our second honeymoon!

MARY: (*Urgently*) Come *on*, Evan.

JAMES: I'll see you out.

(*Voices recede*)

EVAN: So long, old man . . .

JAMES: 'Bye, Mary . . .

PAM: (*To herself, loud and scornfully*) Second honeymoon!

MARY: (*Very faint*) 'Byeee . . . enjoy yourselves . . .

(*Front door bangs*)

JAMES: (*Returns, whistling*) Sorry about the head, Pam. Too much gin yesterday evening?

PAM: (*Acidly*) Too much gin covers everything, doesn't it?

JAMES: Hullo, is something the matter? Pam, darling, what have I done to make you look at me like that?

PAM: Nothing.

JAMES: Nonsense, I can see there's something. Have I said something tactless? I'll mix you a small brandy and soda. (*Clink of glasses*)

PAM: (*Dramatically, after a slight pause*) James, *who is Fay*? (*Glass drops with a crash*)

JAMES: Damn! What do you mean—Fay? What do you know about Fay?

PAM: I know that she's a woman who rings you up on a personal call, and that she wants you to come and meet her somewhere and that she seems to know you—rather well:

JAMES: So—you were listening in just now?

PAM: Yes.

JAMES: My dear girl—you've got the whole thing wrong. You simply don't understand.

PAM: (*Bitterly*) You're only too right, I don't!

JAMES: It isn't the least what you think.

PAM: Isn't it?

JAMES: No, of course it isn't . . . (*Hesitates*) As a matter of fact—well, Fay's the name of my first wife.

PAM: You told me her name was Florence.

JAMES: So it was. But I always called her Fay.

PAM: (*With irony*) So your former wife, who has been dead for over a year, rings you up on the telephone! Most remarkable.

JAMES: Don't you see, it's some wicked, stupid, practical joke? Ringing me up and pretending to be a dead woman.

PAM: And it happened yesterday, too? And that's why you were so upset?

JAMES: Naturally. It's a particularly cruel and heartless thing to do.

PAM: But how extraordinary! Why should anyone do such a thing?

JAMES: Plenty of batty people in the world, I suppose.

PAM: But, James . . . her voice . . . did you recognise her voice? You did, didn't you? *That's* why you were scared—as well as angry . . . *It was Fay's voice* . . .

JAMES: It sounded like it . . . but, of course . . .

PAM: Where was it she wanted you to meet her? Some railway station or other?

JAMES: Newton Abbot.

PAM: But why Newton Abbot? And what has the time—a quarter past seven—got to do with it?

JAMES: Because— (*Pause. Goes on sulkily*) I've never cared to talk about it much. Too painful. She was killed in an accident there, you see.

PAM: (*Awed*) At a quarter past seven?

JAMES: (*Reluctantly*) Well—er—yes. Oh, you might as well hear all about it. She'd been getting faint—had dizzy spells. We were going back to London after a holiday we'd had on Dartmoor. We were standing on the platform waiting for the train. I went to get a paper from the bookstall. She must have felt faint and—and pitched forward on to the line just as the express came in.

PAM: Oh, darling, how tragic for you.

JAMES: Yes, you can see why I—never cared to talk about it.

PAM: (*Vaguely*) Yes . . . yes . . . of course . . . James, yesterday—you were ringing up to find out where that personal call came from. What did they say?

JAMES: They said no personal call had been put through to me . . .

PAM: (*Draws in breath with a startled noise*) (*Awed*) Suppose . . . it's *true* . . .

JAMES: (*Sharply*) What?

PAM: (*Quick and breathlessly*) I've Just been reading a book on psychical research. Really . . . the most extraordinary things happen . . . Suppose it really *is* Fay? Suppose her spirit is there—at that railway station—waiting for you . . .

JAMES: (*Angrily*) Do you think I believe that sort of nonsense?

PAM: Nobody would play that sort of joke—*nobody* would. And you recognised her voice . . . ? Queer things do happen. People who die violent deaths are earthbound, they say

JAMES: (*Sharply*) Who said she died a violent death?

PAM: (*Surprised*) But she fell under the train, didn't she?

JAMES: Yes . . . yes . . . of course . . . For Heaven's sake, don't go on talking about it. To forget—that's all I want—to forget! Let's talk about ourselves. Let's think how lovely it will be to get to the south of France. The mimosa will be in bloom, and the Mediterranean will be—oh, so blue! Why, when we get out of the train—

PAM: Why don't we go by air? Much more fun.

JAMES: (*Sharply*) No, I hate air travel.

PAM: Trains are so stuffy and take so much longer.

JAMES: (*Decidedly*) No, we're going by train. I've got the tickets and everything. That's all settled, dear.

PAM: (*Rebelliously*) Trains! James, let's go down to this place—what is it—Newton Abbot?—tomorrow. Before we go away. Let's be there, in the station, at a quarter past seven.

JAMES: (*Violently*) Of all the idiotic suggestions! We'll do nothing of the sort. A lot of silly superstitious rubbish! It's nothing but a hoax, I tell you: And anyway, we've got other things to do tomorrow—all sorts of things. We've got an appointment with the lawyers—our two wills to sign.

PAM: (*Diverted*) I leave you everything I've got. And you leave me everything you've got! (*Gaily*) But I get the best of the bargain! You're really quite a rich man, aren't you, darling?

JAMES: Yes, it's annoying that my capital is tied up the way it is. But the money's there all right. (*Laughs boisterously*) You may be a rich widow one of these days!

PAM: Oh, darling—don't . . .

JAMES: Dearest, I was only joking . . . But you're right. One shouldn't joke about the things that really matter. You and I are going to have long years of happiness together.

PAM: (*Dreamily*) Long years of happiness . . . I'll try and make up to you for—for all that you must have suffered.

JAMES: That's my sweet girl

PAM: Did you care very much for her? For Fay, I mean?

JAMES: Not as I care for you! You've got something—I can't explain it—but you're absolutely different from any other woman in the world.

PAM: Darling. (*A kiss. She sighs*) Poor Fay . . .

JAMES: Oh, do forget about Fay!

PAM: I can't . . . Do you think—she'll ring up again tomorrow at the same time?

JAMES: For goodness sake! You speak as though she exists!

PAM: Well, do you think that whoever it is who is hoaxing you will ring up tomorrow at the same time?

JAMES: (*Angrily*) I don't know and I don't care! I shall make a particular point of not being in at that time. And the day after that we shall have left England, and this fine practical joker can ring up until she's blue in the face. If I had the least idea who it could possibly be—

PAM: Don't get all het up, darling. Why . . . you're shaking all over.

JAMES: (*Hoarsely*) it's all so completely pointless . . .

PAM: Unless it really *is* her . . . in some extraordinary way that we don't understand—

JAMES: (*Quite unnerved*) Stop it, Pam! stop it!

PAM: (*Her voice fading*) So you do believe that spirits can come back to earth . . .

(*Pause.*)

(*Fade in*)

PAM: Milk, letters, papers bread, laundry—I think that's everything, Mrs Lamb.

MRS LAMB: Don't you worry, ma'am. I'll look after things for you while you're away.

PAM: Thank you, Mrs Lamb, I'm sure you will. Well, it's after seven. You'd better be getting home.

MRS LAMB: Wouldn't you like me to stay until Mr Brent comes back?

PAM: No, I shall be all right. I don't expect he'll be long. You get off home.

MRS LAMB: I'll be here first thing in the morning. And I'll bring along that packet of luggage labels you asked me to.

(*Telephone rings*)

Shall I answer it, ma'am?

PAM: No, I will. Good night, Mrs Lamb.

MRS LAMB: (*Faintly*) Good night, ma'am.

(*Front door shuts. Receiver lifted*)

PAM: (*Answering 'phone*) Hullo? (*Nervously*) Who—who is that?

MR ENDERBY: (*Very precise voice*) This is Mr Enderby of Enderby, Blenkinsop and Lucas. Can I speak to Mrs James Brent please?

PAM: Mrs Brent speaking.

MR ENDERBY: Ah, good evening, Mrs Brent. You are feeling better, I trust?

PAM: (*Blankly*) Better? I'm quite all right.

MR ENDERBY: Capital. Capital. I rang up to acknowledge the receipt of your will, duly signed and witnessed. Your husband brought it in this afternoon. It is quite in order. I am not quite clear, however, what you wish done with it? Shall it remain in our keeping? Or would you like it sent to your Bank? I understand that you and your husband are going abroad tomorrow.

PAM: Yes, we are. Perhaps you had better send it to the Bank. They have all my share certificates and things like that. The singers Bank, the Notting Hill Gate branch.

MR ENDERBY: Yes, yes, I have the address from your husband. Then that is all quite in order. Allow me to wish you a very pleasant trip and no more of these dizzy fits.

PAM: Dizzy fits? What do you mean?

MR ENDERBY: Your husband seemed quite worried about you. But I trust that they are not serious. Much wiser to rest quietly at home today, and not come to my office.

PAM: But James said that it was *you*— (*Stops abruptly*)

MR ENDERBY: Hullo? Hullo?

PAM: Nothing.

MR ENDERBY: Ah, I feared we had been cut off. As I was saying—now what was I saying?

PAM: You were saying that James was worried about my health. That's all nonsense. I'm perfectly well.

MR ENDERBY: (*Archly*) Ah, these devoted husbands! Over-anxious—always over-anxious. But it's a fault on the right side.

PAM: Perhaps. Well, thank you, Mr Enderby, for ringing me up.

MR ENDERBY: Not at all. Not at all. Bon voyage.

(*Pam replaces a receiver*)

PAM: (*In bewildered voice*) Dizzy fits? *Dizzy fits?* I've never had anything of the kind . . .

(*Telephone rings*)

It's just on a quarter past seven . . . I wonder . . . (*Pause before she takes up receiver and speaks*) Hullo? Yes?

OPERATOR: Can Mr James Brent take a personal call from Newton Abbot?

PAM: (*Draws in breath sharply*) Oh! I—He's out . . .

OPERATOR: Can you say when he would be available?

PAM: I—I don't quite know. This this is *Mrs* James Brent speaking, perhaps I would do instead . . . ?

OPERATOR: Just a moment, please.

(*Dead silence and quite a considerable pause. Then very faint train noises*)

FAY: (*Much weaker than before*) . . . So far away . . . it's very difficult . . . can you hear me?

PAM: This is Pamela Brent. Who are you?

(*Far off melancholy scream of an engine*)

FAY: I'm Fay Mortimer . . . I know who you are . . .

(*Engine approaches*)

Don't travel with him by train . . .

(*Banshee wail of engine increases then fades*)

PAM: What? I couldn't quite hear you?

FAY: (*Distinctly*) Don't—travel—by—train—with *him* . . .

(*Train enters station. there is a woman's piercing scream, the shouts of other people. Then the whole thing shuts off like a tap being turned off*)

PAM: Hullo . . . hullo . . . hullo

(*Jerks receiver up and down*)

Hullo . . .

(*Sound of front door opening*)

JAMES: (*Whistles a tune. From hall*) Pam, where are you?

PAM: I'm here.

JAMES: Hullo, what's the matter? You look as white as a sheet.

PAM: James, what was your first wife's name?

JAMES: (*Puzzled*) I told you—Fay—

PAM: No, I mean her maiden name.

JAMES: Garland—why?

PAM: It wasn't *Mortimer*?

JAMES: (*In a panic of rage*) Where did you get hold of that name? Who's been telling you things? Come on now—tell me at once.

PAM: Ouch! You're hurting me.

JAMES: (*Shouting*) Tell me where you got hold of that name?

PAM: (*With meaning*) She said it through the telephone . . .

JAMES: (*Shaken and frightened*) You mean . . . it's happened again?

PAM: Yes. She said her name was Fay Mortimer.

JAMES: Oh, my God! (*Pause. Then he speaks in a subdued frightened voice*) I must have a drink . . .
(*Chink of glasses*)
Ah, that's better . . . You'd better have one, too, Pam.

PAM: (*Hostile*) I don't need one.

JAMES: (*Nervously*) I'm sorry I lost my temper—but this sort of thing—it gets a man down. Thank goodness we're going away tomorrow—right out of England.

PAM: I'm not going.

JAMES: What's that?

PAM: I'm not going.

JAMES: But why not? What's happened?

PAM: I'm not going abroad. (*Pause*) I'm going down to Newton Abbot.

JAMES: You'll do nothing of the kind!

PAM: You can't stop me. If you won't come too, I shall go alone. We've got to find out what all this means . . .

JAMES: It's a stupid, cruel, practical—

PAM: Don't say that again! It isn't true. Whatever it is, it isn't a joke. *I* think—I think—it's *her* . . .

JAMES: Her?

PAM: Fay . . . come back . . . or never gone away . . . Just waiting there—where she died . . . Waiting for you to come.

JAMES: Stop it, Pam! Do you want to drive me mad?

PAM: *You* think so, too . . . Oh yes, you do . . . We've got to go there and find out . . . If you won't come with me . . .

(*Fade out as James speaks*)

JAMES: (*Sulkily*) Of course I shall go if you're going . . . But I don't like it—

(*Gradual tuning in of train and station noises*)

PORTER: Stopping train to Plymouth on the other side. Up the stairs.

WOMAN: Paddington?

PORTER: This platform. Seven fifteen du in a fu minutes.

WOMAN: Is there a Restaurant Car?

PORTER: Yes, up forwards.

MAN: Torquay?

PORTER: Seven fifty-five. No. Two. Over the bridge.

STATION ANNOUNCER: (*Booms out hoarsely*) The next train on No. two platform is for Exeter and Paddington only. Exeter and Paddington only.

JAMES: Well, Pam, I hope you're satisfied. This is Newton Abbot station, and a pretty pair of fools we look.

PAM: Don't be cross about it. I just felt that we *had* to come.

JAMES: See any ghosts about?

PAM: Don't take up that sceptical attitude! We've got to be helpful—to be receptive.

JAMES: Helpful? To whom?

PAM: To Fay, of course.

JAMES: How you can believe this—this farrago of superstitious nonsense?

PAM: I don't believe exactly. I've just got an open mind. And don't you see? If nothing happens, we'll be free of it. *You'll* be free of it. Because it's been getting you down. You've kept saying it's all a hoax, but actually you've been like a cat on hot bricks. Because, in your heart of hearts, you do believe.

JAMES: I haven't the least—

STATION ANNOUNCER: (*Drowning James' speech*) The train standing on platform three is the stopping train for Plymouth. All stations to Plymouth.

PAM: It's nearly time now. Whereabouts was she standing when it—happened?

JAMES: (*Hoarsely*) Up at the end of the platform. Well forward.

PAM: Let's go there.

(*A goods train clanks through slowly*)

Just about here?

JAMES: (*On edge*) yes. I—this is pretty ghastly, Pam. It brings it all back so.

PAM: I'm sorry, darling. I can see how awful you feel. But I'm sure we are doing the right thing. Now you were both standing just here?

JAMES: (*Quickly*) I wasn't. I'd gone to the bookstall. To get a paper.

PAM: Yes, I know. But you left Fay here?

JAMES: Yes. She was quite all right when I left her. But she'd been having these dizzy spells—

PAM: (*Suddenly remembered*) James, why did you tell Mr Enderby that *I'd* been having dizzy spells?

JAMES: (*Startled*) I never—what on earth do you mean?

PAM: Why didn't we both go to his office as we arranged?

JAMES: Because I thought you had quite enough to do. Why shouldn't he send a clerk along with the papers?

PAM: But the excuse you gave him was that I had fits of giddiness?

JAMES: Nonsense. Of course not. I can't imagine where he got hold of that idea.

PAM: According to him—he got it from you.

JAMES: What do you mean—according to him? You never saw the old boy.

PAM: He rang me up—last night. That's how he happened to talk about—dizzy spells. (*Softly to himself*) Damnation.

PAM: What did you say?

JAMES: Nothing.

PAM: (*Thoughtfully*) It would be easy to fall over on the line here—if one did—feel dizzy . . . Or if someone *pushed* you . . . (*Sound of approaching train. engine whistles*)

PORTER: (*Rather far away shouts*) Exeter and Paddington train.

FAY: *So you did come, James . . .*

JAMES: (*In utter panic, half screaming*) Fay . . .

FAY: Yes, it's Fay . . . I've been waiting here for you . . . ever since you pushed me under the train that day . . .

JAMES: I didn't . . . I didn't . . . keep her away from me . . . Don't . . . don't . . . I never did . . . I never meant to . . . it was an accident . . . just an accident . . . I didn't mean to push you . . . keep away from me . . . keep away . . .

PORTER: (*Shouting*) Look out, sir!

(*Train comes in*)

Blimey! He's gone over . . . (*Shouts*)

JAMES: (*Screams*)

PAM: (*Screams*)

(*Swallowed up by noise of engine*)

(*A moment's silence, then murmurs against a very distant background of station*)

INSPECTOR NARRACOTT: She's all right . . . coming round now . . . Take it easy . . . There . . . like that . . .

PAM: Where . . . where . . .

INSPECTOR NARRACOTT: You're in the stationmaster's office, Mrs Brent. I'm Inspector Narracott. Just you drink this little drop of brandy. There—that's right.

PAM: James? Is he—was he—?

INSPECTOR NARRACOTT: He was killed instantly. This has been a great shock to you, I know, Mrs Brent. But in a way, you've been lucky. You were going away with him on a journey abroad so I've heard—and maybe you wouldn't have come back.

PAM: Not come back?

INSPECTOR NARRACOTT: There have been three accidents that we know of. One in Northumberland and one in Wales and one here last year. Attention was drawn to the strange similarity of those accidents. In each case, the husband had mentioned previously to someone that his wife was subject to fainting or dizzy spells. And in each case, when the accident happened, the husband claimed he had gone to the bookstall to buy a paper. In Northumberland it was a Mr and Mrs Carter, and in Wales it was Mr and Mrs Emery—and down here he called himself Mortimer. But *it was the same man*. But there was no actual evidence. And so—this lady here volunteered to help us . . .

PAM: (*With a gasp*) *You* . . . It was you who spoke to him—on the platform . . . But you can't be Fay—you're cleverly made up, but you're not young enough.

FAY: Fay was my daughter. Our voices were always exactly alike and we looked sufficiently like each other for me to pass as her in the dim light this evening. James Mortimer had never met me.

PAM: You trapped him.

FAY: He murdered her. I always knew it, but I had to break him down. The first time I rang him up I was in London, but I pretended it was a personal call from Newton Abbot. The second time I really did speak from Newton Abbot. The third time I rang up, he was out—

PAM: And you spoke to me instead.

FAY: (*Surprised*) Spoke to you? No, I never spoke to you.

PAM: But you did! You warned me.

FAY: You're wrong. I just rang off.

PAM: But *someone* spoke to me. Someone told me not to go on a journey with him . . . Someone with a voice just like yours . . . (*With rising hysteria*) Someone . . . Who . . . ? Who . . . ?

(*A last faint banshee wail from an engine dying into silence*)

AGATHA CHRISTIE

Agatha Christie (1890–1976) is the world's most popular writer of mystery and detective stories. As well as dozens of novels and short stories featuring her principal detectives, Hercule Poirot and Jane Marple, she wrote the world's longest-running play, *The Mousetrap*, and is the author of *And Then There Were None*, the closed circle mass murder mystery that is the archetype for countless other books and films in the crime and horror genres.

Christie was born in Torquay, Devon, where each year the International Agatha Christie Festival celebrates her life and legacy. Largely self-educated, one of her main joys as a child was in writing dramatic sketches and performing them with her siblings to entertain her parents. She also wrote poetry, the form in which she was first published, and more than 150 short stories. In the mid-1910s, in response to a challenge from her sister, she wrote a novel, *The Mysterious Affair at Styles*, which first appeared as a newspaper serial in 1920. Nothing would ever be the same again.

That first book introduced the character of Hercule Poirot, a retired Belgian police officer who comes to Britain as a refugee and goes on to enjoy a second career as a private detective. Initially, Poirot was very much in the style of Sherlock Holmes, especially in the early short stories, but he quickly became very much her own creation. As the biographer Christoph Irmscher neatly put it in a recent piece in the *Wall Street Journal* reviewing Mark

Aldridge's essential companion, *Agatha Christie's Poirot: The Greatest Detective in the World*, Christie's unfailingly immodest sleuth is 'the perfect embodiment of the impossible, inextinguishable hope, shared by readers everywhere, that all problems can be solved'.

In creating Poirot, Christie was inspired by the Belgian refugees who had fled to Torquay after the outset of war in Europe: they included the Count and Countess de la Roche, who recounted appalling atrocities, which in turn might have inspired Christie's supernatural short story 'The Hound of Death'. Retired naval commander Michael Clapp has suggested that Christie might specifically have been inspired by Jacques Hamoir, a former Belgian police officer who lived in the area and whose son, tragically, was drowned off the Cornish coast in 1916.

As well as Poirot, Agatha Christie created Miss Jane Marple, an elderly woman living in a small village in Kent who, despite what one might assume to be a mundane and unremarkable existence, has what one of her friends describes as 'a natural flair for justice [and] a natural genius . . . for investigation'. For Miss Marple, Christie captured elements of the personality of her own grandmother, Margaret Miller, as well as some of the traits of her grandmother's friends, which she had already drawn on to create a character in her most infamous—and, for some, best—Poirot novel, *The Murder of Roger Ackroyd*, published in 1926.

Although Christie created many other series characters—the irrepressible Tommy and Tuppence Beresford, Christopher Parker Pyne, Superintendent Battle and Colonel Race, as well as the not-entirely-natural Harley Quin—it is Hercule Poirot and Miss Marple for which she is most famous. Quite simply, Poirot and Marple stand head and shoulders above their contemporaries, loved as individuals in books and on screen, and look set to endure—if not forever, certainly for many years to come.

A longer biographical note about Agatha Christie can be found in the first volume of *Bodies from the Library*, together with her first published short story, 'The Wife of the Kenite'.

Personal Call was written especially for the BBC's Light Programme and produced by Ayton Whitaker. The play was broadcast live on 31 May 1954 and featured the return of Inspector Narracott from *The Sittaford Mystery* (1931).

THE WOMAN WHO CRIED

H. C. Bailey

It is still a good room. They have mixed the old, austere furniture with some plump splendour. They have covered the walls with oily pictures of themselves and other animals. Still, its fine Georgian shape gives it calm and dignity. At the south end, a triple window looks out over the silver and lavender hazes, and the crowded mystery of London streets.

The Burbidge family has lived there on the hill at Highgate for a hundred years of orderly, restrained affluence. Since the tallow-chandler of 1810 emerged from Saint Mary Axe they have never been in danger of relapsing or getting any further. There is not one failure on their record, or anything else of interest. The present Mrs Burbidge is a good example of the family taste.

The blinds were half drawn, lest the sunlight should come into the room vigorously. Mrs Burbidge sat erect on a chair where she might have been comfortable, and her fingers were flaccid on a piece of embroidery. Her violet dress suggested tightness wherever it could. Her sallow face was insignificantly pleasant, and when she moved it shook, like a mask swaying in front of nothing. Above it rose a rampart of frozen curls.

Her daughter, Mary, who was fidgeting at flowers on the piano, went quickly to the south window, stared out a moment, and came quickly back again. As though she were eager to hear something, she stood tremulous, and so looked oddly small and fragile. Beneath the mass of her black hair her face had the clear delicacy of porcelain, but it was thin and sharp. Again she went to the window, turned, hesitated, and went back. 'So nervous,' Mrs Burbidge breathed in a thick voice. 'Dear me, just like your poor aunt.'

There was a moment's silence. Then Mary cried out: 'What did you say?'

'Oh my dear!' Mrs Burbidge started heavily. 'So very abrupt. I don't know what's come over you lately. Not at all nice to be so restless and nervous. Answering so sharply, too. Quite disturbing. Really just the manners of your poor Aunt Amy. One might actually think you had something on your mind. And I'm sure you've everything that a girl ought to want. Dear me, how your father used to argue with her—'

'Do you think Mr Hall can have gone?'

Mrs Burbidge sat still more erect in the pain of wounded dignity and propriety. 'Really, my dear! You're positively rude. I don't know anything about Mr Hall, and I hope you don't. Quite an inferior young man. I must say I thought it rather impertinent his calling on your father. And if there's one thing more than another your father can't endure, it's impertinence.'

Mary hurried out into the garden.

'Really!' Mrs Burbidge protested. Then sadly to her embroidery: 'I always told poor Amy it was digestion.'

At this moment away in the library the large, portly form of Mr Burbidge was swelling. The long face of Mr Burbidge was becoming rosier. He stared at Tom Hall, a short, square man, with surprise and indignation. Tom Hall had just made clear his desire to marry Mary Burbidge, and the income of Tom Hall, as Mr Burbidge approximately knew, was £250 a year, with a prospect of attaining £300 before his employers dismissed him with a small pension. Mr Burbidge's fatherly affection was outraged. Let us be fair. He would have suffered if Tom Hall's income had been thrice as much, for he found his daughter a useful and pretty piece of furniture, and to part with her would be uncomfortable. Fortunately, she was a good, dutiful girl, who felt the claims of her parents. This preposterous proposal, this penniless impertinent, irritated him even to sarcasm: 'Of course, your income enables you to provide for a wife's comfort.'

'Mary says she's not afraid of two hundred and fifty a year, Sir,' said Tom Hall, without shame.

Mr Burbidge stammered: 'If you think it's honourable to speak to my daughter without her father's consent, Sir, I can only say, Sir, it will do you no good.'

'I beg your pardon,' said Tom Hall.

Mr Burbidge made several times the sound which is written 'Pshaw!'

'I don't agree that it was dishonourable. I didn't conceal anything. She's not a child. She's twenty-six.'

'Her age is no business of yours, Sir,' Mr Burbidge cried. 'As for your notions of what's honourable, Sir, they're of no importance. I've only one thing to say to you, and that is that you'll cease from annoying my daughter.'

'I haven't begun,' said Tom Hall.

Mr Burbidge fumed. 'You're impudent, Sir. I'll not discuss the matter further. I shall know how to protect Miss Burbidge.' He rang the bell.

'She won't need protection.'

Mr Burbidge stared and relented a little. 'Then I shall have a better opinion of you, Mr Hall. There must be no communications—'

'I beg your pardon. She's not your property.'

'My property?' Mr Burbidge gasped.

'She belongs to herself. I'll see that she doesn't forget that.'

'Upon my word!' Mr Burbidge began.

'Good afternoon,' said Tom Hall.

After the door was shut Mr Burbidge discovered several things which he ought to have said, and, strutting, said them to the empty room and began to feel that he had annihilated Tom Hall. So he went to tell his womenfolk how he had done it. You have, perhaps, seen a cock, after some encounter with a disrespectful dog, return, ruffled but grandly, to his hens. Mr Burbidge's gait was of that kind.

He came into the drawing-room and sat down elaborately. Mrs Burbidge would have thought it improper to ask him what was the matter. Also, she knew that he would explain more than sufficiently. She stared stolid, dutiful attention. 'My dear,' said Mr Burbidge, 'a most unpleasant thing—'

'Here is Mary,' said Mrs Burbidge, and Mary came through the window in a hurry.

'It is just as well that Mary should be here,' said Mr Burbidge, and coughed.

'Has Tom gone?' Mary cried.

Her father and mother stared at her as though she had said something indecent. Then her mother gasped, 'Good gracious!'

'Oh don't! I'm not a baby,' cried Mary.

'I don't understand you,' said Mr Burbidge with dignity. 'I may say you surprise me. This—er—this manner is most unusual and unsuitable.' He cleared his throat. 'Now, Mary, you force me to ask you whether you knew what was Mr Hall's business with me today.'

'I knew, yes,' said Mary, with an odd, tremulous defiance. 'I asked him to come to you.'

'You asked—oh, my dear child!' Mr Burbidge was overcome. 'Really, this is distressing.' His wife echoed the word. 'The man must have misled you shamefully, my dear. It's impossible, quite impossible.'

'Why, please?' said Mary.

'Really, Mary,' Mrs Burbidge protested. 'You mustn't argue with your father.'

'My dear,' said Mr Burbidge, 'this is one of the matters in which you must allow me to know best. I have to consider your future. I assure you, this is impossible—preposterous. The man cannot afford to support a wife.'

'I don't want to go on living like this—too much of everything and nothing to do.'

'My dear,' said Mr Burbidge, 'you don't know what you're saying. You have been brought up in a certain degree of comfort, and if you were deprived of it we should have to fear for your health. You have never been strong—'

'Oh, I hate to hear all that. You've always tried to keep me shut in as if I couldn't live out of a hothouse. I'm sick of hearing about my health. I'm just like other girls. Only you always want to keep me shut in and wrapped up and lying down.'

'Mary! What are you saying?' Mother and father stared their bewilderment.

'Oh, it is dreadful, isn't it?' Mary's laugh was hysterical. 'Do you think I like being tied up in cotton-wool? Didn't you want to live, Mother?'

'You are talking very rudely,' said Mr Burbidge, with dignity. 'Very ungratefully, I must say. A very unpleasant spirit. I see that some most unpleasant ideas have been put into your head. Now, Mary, I saw at once that Mr Hall was a young man of no principle, but I must say I'm surprised to find that he has been able to set you against your father and mother.'

'Please tell me what you told him,' said Mary fiercely.

'I told him that he was to hold no further communication with you. I expect you—'

'I'm not your property,' Mary cried.

Mr Burbidge was for a while speechless. To have that awful heresy flung at him a second time, and by his daughter, hurt him. 'I expect you not to meet him again,' he said feebly.

'Is that all?' Mary cried, and waited a moment. Mr Burbidge could not condescend to answer such a tone. 'I think you were horrible to him,' said Mary, and hurried out. She did not want them to see her cry.

Your pity is requested for two melancholy parents. They would as soon have expected their tables and chairs to show fight as Mary to rebel. She had always been so sweetly dutiful and submissive. And they conceived themselves to have treated her with the tenderest care. They were always anxious that she should not risk her health is too much of anything—exercise, amusement, travel, work. They had kept her, as it were, with the blinds down and the windows shut on life. And hitherto she had always been gently grateful. They had counted upon her living with them, sweet, docile, attentive, till they had no more use for her. It would be only a daughter's simple, easy duty to loving parents—a slight return for all they had done for her. They would be much surprised, even now, if you suggested that there was something of the vampire about them.

So far, this story, dealing, as you justly complain, with dull and common facts, has been put together from the evidence of all the characters. For what follows, I depend upon Mr Burbidge alone, who will not be suspected of imagination. He does not believe it now as much as he did. He begins to be shy of it, to make odd and pathetic efforts to laugh at himself, which is not his natural role. But this is how he told it while it was still invincibly real.

After appropriate lamentations, he decreed to Mrs Burbidge that they should not mention the matter to Mary again for some time. She was naturally excited, he said, but would calm down if she was left alone. They would treat her just as usual, merely showing a little quiet regret at the way she had behaved.

They had, as you may imagine, an awkward, glum dinner. Mary said nothing more than she was compelled. Her manner was jerky and pugnacious. She looked, Mr Burbidge relates, like somebody at the dentist's. He kept up a heavy conversation with his wife, chiefly about building land. He fancies that she was not so attentive as usual and recalls that once or twice he broke off a sentence because he could not remember how he had begun it. Also, they felt cold during dinner and had the windows shut. It was July. But all this seems very easily explicable.

After dinner, Mary went at once to her room. Mr Burbidge sat with his wife in the drawing-room which I have described, and according to their established habit, he read the evening paper, while she played patience. They are fond of artificial light, and the display of electricity in the room is tiresomely brilliant. In a little while Mr Burbidge began to feel trouble in his eyes. He grumbled and looked at the lamps but could not be sure that they were duller than usual. Yet when he tried to read again the light seemed dim. His wife, who had been watching him uneasily, agreed that there must be something wrong. Mr Burbidge condemned municipal supplies of electricity and struggled on with his paper. After a time his wife said nervously: 'Robert, don't you think there's something queer about the room?'

Mr Burbidge testifies that he cannot imagine why he should have started. It appears, however, that he did not start excessively. Then he said, 'All nonsense, Louise; the light's bad;' and he changed his seat grumbling and still read his paper. Mrs Burbidge sat still, with her hands on her cards. She seems in some strange way to have been frightened.

Then Mr Burbidge heard a woman crying. He started round and looked at his wife, but it was not she. 'Did you hear that?' he cried, but before he spoke he knew that she did. 'Must be Mary. You'd better go to her.' Mrs Burbidge shivered as she rose. Mr Burbidge always says that she checked and stood still on her way to the door.

He was disturbed. He dislikes any display of emotion, and particularly grief. After Mrs Burbidge went out, the sound of crying ceased, but still he felt uneasy. If Mary was going to make a tragedy, the house would be very uncomfortable. He thought that she was behaving inconsiderately. And while he blamed her, there came to him a queer consciousness of someone in the room. It was plainly absurd, but he could not get rid of it. He sprang out of his chair and began to look behind curtains and screens. There was, of course, no one to be seen. He was very annoyed with himself as he took up his paper again. It is curious that he still remembers some phrases from the report of an insignificant trial. While he read, something in the depths of his mind was hammering at him the announcement that he was not alone. He read on resolutely.

Mrs Burbidge came back. 'She says she hasn't been crying. I'm sure she hasn't. And she was very rude about it,' she said plaintively.

'One of the servants, then,' Mr Burbidge growled. 'I always told you that new housemaid looks flighty.' He went on reading.

Mrs Burbidge sat still, with her hands on the cards. Then she began to look about her nervously. 'Robert, Robert,' she whispered, 'I'm sure there's someone in the room.'

Mr Burbidge bounced out of his chair. 'Perfect nonsense,' he cried. 'You know you're making a fool of yourself, Louise. And the light's bad. I must say, the light's bad.' He rang the bell and fumed and fidgeted till Wallis, their shaggy Butler, came. 'Oh yes. Wallis, has there been any disturbance among the servants tonight? I mean—I thought I heard one of the maids making a noise—crying, you know. Hysterical, perhaps.'

'No, sir, not at all.' Wallis was surprised and reproving. 'Certainly not, sir. We have none of that kind here.'

'Oh, very well, very well. I suppose you don't know what's wrong with the light?'

'With the light, sir?' Wallis was plainly amazed. He stared at it, and blinked, and stared back at Mr Burbidge.

'Don't be a fool!' Mr Burbidge snapped. 'You see it's bad, don't you?'

'I can't exactly say that I do, sir.'

Mr Burbidge told him that he was going blind, and when he retreated turned upon Mrs Burbidge. 'You're upset, that's what it is, Louise. Your nerves are the trouble. You'd better get to bed.' Mrs Burbidge, without protest, began to put her cards together. She was very limp, and dallied, and when at last she rose went to fidget with vases and trinkets in different parts of the room. This annoyed Mr Burbidge, who called out: 'For Heaven's sake, don't fuss like that. Why don't you go?'

Then Mrs Burbidge began to cry. It appeared that she did not want to go upstairs alone.

There is nothing else definite to be described in that night. They slept badly.

That they begin the next day with a feeling of weariness and depression is not surprising. Mr Burbidge does not remember much about his daughter at this stage; but fancies that she wore an air of distant hostility. He did not enquire into her feelings. That, of course, is what you would expect of him. I mention it as evidence that it was not anxiety about her that created his trouble.

The curious thing, he considers, is that while he was uncomfortable all day, his uneasiness was vastly increased when he came into the drawing-room in the evening. The light did not trouble him, but he complains that he did 'could not concentrate'. He read and did not know what he was reading. He is not lucid in describing a state of mind, but he seems to have felt as if some memory, or fancy, or emotion, which would not become definite, was trying to attract his attention. Something kept jerking and knocking at his mind. And it produced a queer, impotent melancholy. He was wretched and could not tell why. He observed that his wife appeared in the same condition. In fact, she looked so miserable that he was angry with her.

Now, on this second evening, Mary stayed in the drawing-room with them. She only spoke when she was spoken to, and they only spoke to her upon trivialities, for her attitude, though civil, was cold and aloof. Mr Burbidge makes the odd comment that she seems to be defying them to do their worst. This touch of melodrama seems out of place.

It was clear, at any rate, that she did not feel the wretchedness which enveloped them. She was sewing something briskly, almost fiercely, and whenever he glanced at her energy Mr Burbidge felt weak. The room seems to have been singularly silent. At least, I suppose that is what Mr Burbidge means when he refers to a very odd sensation—as if things were happening all round him which he could not hear. After the silence had weighed on them through ages—or about an hour—he heard faintly, just as on the night before, a woman crying. Almost before he had time to glance at his wife she screamed.

'Whatever is the matter, Mother?' cried Mary.

Mrs Burbidge, who was shivering, stared at her. 'Didn't you hear it?' she muttered.

'Hear what? I only heard Father jump.'

'Jump? What do you mean? I don't jump,' said Mr Burbidge angrily.

'Oh, very well.' Mary's tone was calmly indifferent.

Mr Burbidge and his wife looked miserably at each other. They did not again hear the woman crying, but the queer burden of depression was not lifted. When they were alone together upstairs, Mrs Burbidge broke down and became like an hysterical child. Mr Burbidge has not seen her so in thirty years' experience.

Mrs Burbidge said in the morning that the room must be haunted. This was incredible. Nothing had ever happened there. It is hardly possible to imagine that anything could happen in a room so calmly ordinary. The house has been in the Burbidge family for all its one century of existence, and their edifying records include nothing of violence, or passion, or mystery. No one has ever died or suffered there, except in a quite ordinary and respectable way. Mr Burbidge explained that to her at length, and she said it would be the death of her. She seems to have been eloquent about it, which is not within her normal keep capacity. At least, she affected Mr Burbidge profoundly, who recalls that he began to be afraid they were out of their minds.

Two people more severely sane I have not met. But his alarm is comprehensible. Their distress, depression, fear—what name you please—would not leave them. They woke day after day weary and wretched. Outside the house Mr Burbidge felt himself more at ease, though never free. As soon as he was inside again he was once more enveloped in the queer, gloomy anxiety. It was always heaviest in the drawing-room, but he felt it all over the house. On some days they would hear more than once that sound of a woman crying. Sometimes two or three days passed without it. Once, he recalls, everything in the room seemed to be quivering, like a cinematograph scene. Very often he had that strange feeling of someone unseen in the room with them, and almost always his mind was straining to realise something, some thought, or memory, or emotion, quivering in the deep levels of consciousness. All this was shared by his wife, and by no one else.

Mary, it was plain, felt nothing of it. Through these weeks she was bustling and energetic, taking, as usual, the greater share of the household affairs, and facing her parents with a faintly hostile reserve, completely captain of her soul. They agreed that nothing but her pride had been touched by the prohibition of Mr Hall. Mr Burbidge congratulated himself on his wisdom. He had much need to feel proud of something.

The worst night of all came very near the end. They had a dinner-party of their ordinary kind, and so there were some dozen stolid, dull people in the drawing-room. Mary was singing and Mr Burbidge had a notion that he had never heard her sing so well. Then something stabbed at his mind. He felt someone watching him. With twelve people in the room that seems easily possible. But this, as he records it, was like being watched by someone whom he could not see. By that triple window, there stands an uncomfortable Louis XVI chair. Mr Burbidge jumped around to stare at it. It was empty, and yet his distressed mind told him that someone was there watching him. He went across the room, he tried to get out of sight of it, and still felt some unseen creature staring at him . . . He talks about torture, a violence of language unusual in him. Apparently, he felt sure he was going mad . . . Which is all very absurd, but hardly so absurd as the thought of Mr Burbidge harassed by anything merely mental or spiritual.

I suspect that when his guests were gone he collapsed. There is something which he slurs over. At all events, that night Mrs Burbidge and he agreed that they must get away for a long holiday. But on the next day, their cousin, Mrs Hay, of Manchester, was coming on a visit. Mrs Hay is a vivid little woman of many uncommon interests, who was not much in favour with the Burbidge family till she married, rather late, a warehouseman of some wealth.

In their depressed condition they found her overwhelming. She saw that they looked worn and told them it was because they took life too easily. She found cause to congratulate Mary, whom she had never seen looking so brilliant. Mrs Burbidge herself remarked an unusual vivacity in Mary, who nevertheless went early to bed on the plea of a headache. So they were left alone in the drawing-room with Mrs Hay. In a very little while Mrs Hay's vigorous conversation began to flag. 'Isn't there some-thing odd about this room?' she said sharply.

Then Mrs Burbidge gasped and swayed in her chair. 'Do you notice anything?' said Mr Burbidge and remembers that his voice surprised him. Then he heard a woman crying.

'Ah! What's that?' said Mrs Hey. The silence which seemed something heavier than silence came over the room . . .

'Did you hear it? said Mr Burbidge.

'Good heavens! Of course I heard it. It came from that chair.'

She pointed to the Louis XVI chair by the window. 'It was Amy crying.'

You have not forgotten Mary's poor Aunt Amy, whose nervous ways Mrs Burbidge lamented in Mary. But of late Mary has not suggested her poor aunt, and otherwise Aunt Amy seems to have been too insignificant to be remembered.

'Amy?' Mr Burbidge said. 'Amy? Oh, but preposterous of course . . . Besides, Amy never was crying. Nervous, of course, and restless, but always agreeable. Very naturally. Such a peaceful, happy life. Quite beautiful.'

Mrs Hay laughed. 'That's what you call it. I remember Amy in that chair crying . . . crying . . .' After a moment she turned with some ferocity on Mr Burbidge. 'Do you mean to say you never knew? You knew George Lake.'

'Of course, I knew that my father forbade her marriage with George Lake. And, considering the vulgar woman Lake afterwards married, I'm sure it was a very good thing for Amy.'

'A good thing! Oh, you Burbidges! I think that was the most thoroughly selfish thing that your father ever did. Amy made him comfortable. He liked Amy's pretty face about the house. He just fed on her vitality. So she mustn't marry. Oh dear no! Her duty was to him. And the man was poor. And she wasn't strong. So she had to fret and fuss away her life shut up here. And George Lake went to the dogs. Ugh! It makes me sick when I think of it . . . How she cried! . . . Have you heard her before?'

Mr Burbidge fidgeted and coughed. 'I must say—that sound—there has been something curious of the kind.'

Mrs Hay looked at him hard. 'I wonder why . . . She was just the age of your Mary.'

Mr Burbidge became aware that his wife was crying. 'Really, really, this is too fanciful. I'm afraid we have frightened Louise. Come, come—' He shepherded her to bed. He remembers that Mrs Hay cried too. He found this real visible weeping round him quite comfortable.

You may guess what counsel the night brought Mr and Mrs Burbidge. After all, the worst of their faults is an absence of imagination. They make up for that in some degree by not being wholly reasonable. I do not suppose that, even with the strange fear still haunting them, they believed all Mrs Hay's proclamation of the woes of poor Aunt Amy. What they did believe Mr Burbidge has always been shy of telling me. The poor souls were in no case to quarrel with any explanation of their trouble which offered them a way out. The notion of Aunt Amy from the world of the dead interfering with their respectability to prevent Mary from being sacrificed to the Burbidge family comfort, from being wasted as her own life had been—doubtless that seemed fantastic. But so many horribly fantastic things had happened. And to believe this would at least put some reason into them, and provide a way of escape. For, if they let Mary marry, their troubles ought to cease.

Do you wonder that they arose in the morning resolved to speak to Mary, and feeling very noble about it? But it had been very late before they could sleep, and it was late when they came down. Mary had made her breakfast and had gone out. But Mr Burbidge went to his office more nearly happy than on any day since his interview with Tom Hall. It was incredible (or, at least, preposterous), but the depression, the fears, the strange knocking at his mind were gone.

He came home early, and found his wife in the drawing-room. She smiled at him. He had hardly been in the room a moment before he knew that it was all pleasant and normal again. He kissed Mrs Burbidge, and sat down heavily, with a great longing for sleep . . . In a little while a letter was brought him. He stared in amazement at Mary's writing. He wrote that she had been married to Tom Hall that morning and hoped that he would let her see her mother sometimes.

'I think,' said Mr Burbidge, 'she might have treated us with more consideration.'

Such is the narrative of Mr Burbidge. As I have said, he begins to show a desire to laugh at it and explain it away. He seems to think it's improper to believe that a dead woman tried to tell him something. I do not find that he sees anything pathetic in the affair.

H. C. BAILEY

Henry Christopher Bailey was born in London on 1 February 1878, the only son of Henry and Jane Dillon Bailey.

In his day, H. C. Bailey was regarded to be one of the top writers of crime and detective fiction, adored by readers and respected by critics. Such respect was, however, at times, a little grudging. Bailey had two main characters—Dr Reginald Fortune and Mr Joshua Clunk—and despite their popularity, reviewers frequently warned that they were at times 'irritating', urging readers not to be deterred by their more grating characteristics: in Fortune's case, these were cherubic good humour and an affected manner of speech; and in Clunk's a tendency to quote from the hymnal. Mannerisms and habits aside, the work of H. C. Bailey is unusually atmospheric and his crime and detective fiction is underpinned with notions of morality and decency. There is nothing quite like it.

Of the two principals, Fortune is the stronger. In an essay written for the BBC and first broadcast in 1934, Bailey described how he had conceived Fortune in the 'darkest days' of the First World War when the challenge of creating a detective had provided a welcome distraction from his work as a war correspondent. Bailey explained that Fortune had been born a little under 50 years earlier, i.e. in the late 1880s, and said he had attended Charterhouse and Oxford. By contrast, Bailey was a little older and had attended the City of London School and Oxford. Bailey had been popular, winning a scholarship and elected by his peers to be School Captain, whereas Fortune's time at school and university had been without 'any particular distinction'. Fortune had been destined to become a doctor, unlike Bailey who seems destined to have been a writer from the crib, with his lengthy first novel appearing in 1900 as a serial in *Longman's Magazine*.

Nonetheless, the creator and his main character do have some things in common—'an old-fashioned mind', to quote Bailey, and a strong sense that what matters most is what is right, whether or not that coincides with what the law allows. These qualities were certainly well-suited to a journalist working for the *Daily Telegraph*, the right-wing British newspaper that Bailey joined in 1911. In a career in journalism lasting a little under 50 years, Bailey reported on the two world wars and several notorious crimes, including the trial of the French serial killer Henri Landru. He also contributed dozens of pieces, sometimes anonymously, on subjects as diverse as séances, thieves' slang, good living and the delights and dangers of a Victorian childhood. And when he wasn't writing at work, he was writing at home: a dozen historical romances, 20 novel-length mysteries and over 100 short stories, more than 80 featuring Fortune, who also appeared in Bailey's only radio play, a mystery that was included in *Bodies from the Library 4* (2021).

Towards the end of the Second World War, Bailey decided to wind down his long career as a journalist and novelist. He retired from the *Daily Telegraph* in 1946 and together with Lydia—his wife of over 35 years—he moved permanently to North Wales where they had holidayed for many years. He died at home on 24 March 1961.

'The Woman Who Cried' was published in the *Daily Telegraph* on 5 August 1912.

THE WITCH

Christianna Brand

What do you do when you know that your husband is plotting to murder you?

It was at my father's funeral that first I saw Gereth—coming across the room to me, so tall, so darkly handsome in his fierce Welsh way, weaving his way through the occasional tables with their loading of brass ornaments and china bric-a-brac, the vases of dusty pampas grass, the big central table groaning with funeral baked meats, presided over by 'Aunt Blodwen' in her blowzy mourning bombazine—who was no aunt to me but by courtesy, having for so many years reigned as my father's house-keeper . . .

'She'll never marry now,' Aunt Blodwen was saying, chattering among the women, hardly troubling to lower her voice. 'Twenty-four and—well, never been a pretty girl, not to my mind, and I can't say that that London of hers seems to have done her much good . . .' She had forgotten, I suppose, that despite my English education I would still understand some at least of my native Welsh. 'But she won't want, mind. He's left her a nice little competence.'

And so I saw him coming across the room to me: Gereth Morgan, my one, my only—whatever the future might bring, my for ever and ever love—coming across that stuffy, crowded room and so into my life . . .

He confronted me. 'Forgive my intruding, but you look so pale. Are you faint? Let me take you out to the fresh air.' And he put a hand to my elbow and half propelled me, my stiff, braided black stuff skirts brushing through the foolish little tables, across the room and out through the bobbled velvet curtains, into the cool garden. 'Sit here on this balustrade and just rest quietly a little while. You won't be missed.'

I took off my bonnet with its heavy trimming of black crêpe and leaned my forehead against the cold stone of an ornamental urn. 'That at least is true,' I said.

He thought, perhaps, that I should regret it—coming out with it so bitterly and in front of a stranger; he began to talk a little hurriedly, a little volubly, covering over my outburst. He was here representing his college in London where my father had had some connection. And he introduced himself: 'Gereth Morgan—poor music teacher; who will never now, alas, be a great concert pianist as once he hoped, astonishing all the world . . .'

I bowed back to him. 'And Laura James, poor spinster; who will never now, alas, as once her Aunt Blodwen hoped, be the gracious married woman, astonishing society. But who has her nice little competence to make up for it.'

He was taken aback. I had not doubted that he would recognise the quotation, had come to my rescue only because he observed that I overheard the gossip about me. Meeting him in that atmosphere, it did not occur to me that he might not speak Welsh. But he continued to stand there quietly, spoke kindly, making excuses for my ill-mannerly roughness. 'Your spirits are depressed at present, you are in mourning—'

'Outwardly,' I said.

Once more he checked: made me a second small bow, half ironical, half a sort of genuine respect. 'Miss James, it seems, is a young lady who dispenses with conventional dishonesties.'

'My father was a cold man,' I said. 'Cold and unloving—

though I was his only child, without other relatives—motherless and friendless; but for him, alone in the world.' And now there was no longer even my father. 'As I am still,' I said.

Why did I tell him? Why did I say it? What was he to me then but a cool stranger, civilly kind? But my heart seemed as though it would burst with its bitterness, my never great self-esteem had been shattered by my aunt's confidential asides—by the knowledge that her opinions were shared by the rest. And why should they not? Where the fashion was all for clear pink and white skin, for little rosebud mouths, for curly golden 'bangs' on marble foreheads, my own face was too square, my skin too brown, my nose not little and tip-tilted; my mouth was too wide, my hair—my hair hazel coloured, unruly, for ever escaping in foolish tendrils from my neat braids and buns. And—twenty-four years old! 'She'll never marry now . . . Never been a pretty girl, not to my mind . . .' Fatherless now and very friendless; alone in the world. 'As I am still,' I said.

He looked down at me. He smiled: that smile, half tender, half teasing, that I was to come to know so well. 'But there is always the nice little competence,' he said.

And six weeks later, I was a married woman—not astonishing society, certainly, but established blissfully in a home of my own—furnished lodgings in Pimlico until we could find somewhere more permanent; and begging him for the hundredth time, as I sat with him over his breakfast tray, to regard the money as his own, to give up the wretched school to which he should even now be rushing off to begin the day's work, and start to build a career of his own. 'My dearest dear, I have told you a thousand times—I won't touch a farthing of it.' He was sorting through the morning's post, thrusting into his pocket one envelope—I caught sight of a faintly familiar handwriting, huge, beautiful and bold—consigning the rest to the fire. 'What would you live upon—while I set off on long, expensive journeys for one ill-paid appearance after another. There is not enough for both.' There was truth in this; it would be a slow business and the famous competence was not a very large one, after all

But I insisted. 'You who are so brilliantly talented—'

'So brilliantly mediocre,' he corrected, laughing. 'It is Lynn who has the genius.' His young cousin, Elline, was studying the harp at the college of music where he was a tutor. He laughed. 'Or so you would think, to hear my Aunt Hannah talk.'

'You must take me to visit your Aunt Hannah, Gereth. I ought to be meeting your family, or they'll think it odd.'

'It's been so nice, just the two of us,' he said. Just you and me. And it will be freezing in that gloomy old house in the wastes of a Carmarthenshire winter. Let us wait for the spring.' He put up a hand lazily, that strong, brown flexible pianist's hand of his, and caught at my own hand and held it a moment against his cheek and kissed it and gave it back to me: a small hand but as brown and square as his own, not as I should have loved it to be, soft and white with tapering fingers, a hand for the bride of such a man as he. 'I must go, my love. I shall be back early; I have to go to this function tonight.' He stood brushing the London dust from the in-curling brim of his hat. 'What shall you do with yourself today?'

'Spend it sorting out the wedding presents,' I said.

Not an arduous task: there were not very many, our marriage had taken place so quietly, we were both orphaned and much alone in the world. I started to tidy away the breakfast things to be cleared by the landlady, straightened cushions and flounces, drew back the curtains on the dark London morning, extinguished the gas lights. One crumpled envelope had escaped the fire. I stooped to pick it up and as I tossed it into the flames, observed a Carmarthenshire postmark, unwontedly clear, and the date. Had Gereth then heard from Aunt Hannah today? How odd that he shouldn't have mentioned it—especially when the question of a visit to her had arisen. Was it her letter that he had tucked away into his pocket with an air of . . . ? I thrust from my mind the thought that it had been an air of—of apprehension, of furtiveness. Had his aunt, perhaps, actually proposed the visit which he was anxious to postpone? But then again—had that been an old woman's writing, so bold and clear . . . ?

I went into the small room where our little store of gifts had been laid away; and knew at once whose handwriting it had been. For here was the amulet—Gereth's wedding present from Dorion Rhos.

Dorion Rhos, whom they called in Carmarthenshire Dorion y Gwrach, which is Dorion the Witch.

I had forgotten it. There had been a small wrench to my heartstrings when it arrived, so strange an offering, so strange a message, from the girl he had loved in the past—had for a little while deeply loved, as he had confessed to me, in his long ago, boyhood past. Now the pang came again as I took up the small package, almost with reluctance pulled away the paper wrappings. Within the little square box a ring, curiously wrought in three colours of gold: pale gold, dull gold, red gold; and a folded note. 'Gereth,' Dorion had written in her big, beautiful, flowing hand, 'I send you no marriage gift. But here is something for your wife. It is an amulet against the Evil Eye. It has been in my family for all time, but after all, of what use is it to *me*? Tell your Laura to wear it—she will need it if ever she comes down to Wales.' It was signed with a flourish: Dorion the Witch.

Gereth was not home early after all, but in fact rather late; later than he should have been, for he had an evening appointment at some all-male function where wives were excluded. I had long ago drawn the curtains, lit the gas, made all cosy and bright for him to come back to; and in the bedroom had laid out his evening dress clothes, the tail coat, black silk waistcoat, white shirt, pleated and tucked. 'So you'll just have time for a glass of sherry, dearest,' I said, greeting him in the hall, taking his overcoat. Sit down and rest, I'll bring it to you.'

'Thank you,' he said briefly and went past me into the sitting room, peeling off his tight working jacket, tossing it on to the arm of one chair while he subsided into another. He looked very pale, I thought, tired and strained. 'They kept you late, my love?'

'I had to see Lynneth,' he said.

He could see his cousin any day of the week. I said, anxiously: 'Is something wrong?'

'No, no nothing; it was nothing especial.'

It seemed odd that, having already an appointment, he should make himself so late seeing Lynn about 'nothing especial'. But I was full of my discovery of the amulet. 'Look what I came across today among the presents—from your one-time lady friend in Carmarthenshire.'

'From Dorion?' he said sharply.

The ring was on the little finger of my right hand. I took it off and dropped it into his palm. 'Do you know anything of it? What does it mean?'

'She's told you what it means,' he said, rather irritably. He had never spoken so to me before, never spoken to me before with un-love. 'It's a magic against the Evil Eye.' He turned the ring over in his fingers. 'This must be Welsh gold. The mines, you know, are quite near to Hendre Drom.'

Hendre Drom was Aunt Hannah's house. 'Are there gold mines in Wales?'

'And you a good Welsh girl!' he said. 'Of course there are. There are two, and ours is still working. It dates back to Roman times. Heaven knows how old this ring may be.

'A family possession—why should she send it to *me*?'

He shrugged. 'After all, as she says—of what use is it to her? It's she that has the Evil Eye.'

A chill wind blew for a moment through the snug little room—the dear little room with its lace curtains, looped back within curtains of dark velvet, with its bright fire burning, the clock ticking away beneath its glass dome on the draped mantelshelf, a wind as chill as any from across the snow-capped mountains of Carmarthenshire. 'But Gereth—you don't really believe it? That she's a witch?'

He lay back in the chair, his long legs, slender in their close-fitting plaid trousers, thrust out before him, feet braced against the brass fender. Small fears thrilled through my heart. I thought: How remote he seems! He said: 'Of course she's a witch. Everyone in the valley knows that Dorion's a witch.'

'But—is that not just their ignorance?'

'It depends upon what you mean by ignorance,' he said.

He turned the strange ring over, a rough cabalistic sign, sharp edged, in its three colours, pale gold, dull gold, red gold. 'Who knows?'

'Her father no doubt boiled up herbs and made cures—'

'And his father and his father before him and his father's father.'

'Yes, but—what were they but quack doctors, after all—curing country folk? And Dorion—well, she doesn't even cure people, does she?'

'No, indeed,' said Gereth. He gave a short, bitter laugh. 'She makes them worse.' He quoted: '"Oh, what can ail thee, knight at arms, Alone and palely loitering?"'

The little clock ticked on. I knew that he should be dressing for his dinner, but somehow the conversation had gone so strangely wrong, I could not bear to let him leave me a whole evening under this vague threat of his hostility. I had meant to bring in Dorion's name lightly, so that he might as casually reveal to me that he had that morning received a letter from her—might confide, even, that it had shaken him more than he had expected. I would have said at once, safe and confident in his love, 'I know, I understand, I honour you for not too easily forgetting; have no secrets from me.' But now . . .

But now he sat, darkly brooding, and I wished I had never brought up the subject at all. I protested, trying to speak casually: 'Dearest, isn't this all just nonsense? Because her father was a "wizard", because she lives alone and remote in the mountains, because she's wild and—and free and—'

'And beautiful,' he said.

'Very well, and beautiful—'

'And her singing tears out the very heart of you; even only to remember it—'

'Because she's a pretty girl, Gereth, and can sing,' I said, and could not keep the impatience from my voice, 'and the country boys fall under her—her—'

'Spell,' said Gereth.

'We speak easily of coming under the spell of a woman's charms. What else is this but that the local young men are attracted to a good-looking girl—and the credulous farming people, jealous perhaps for their own daughters, ascribe it to witchcraft.'

'You have it wrong,' he said. 'These are my people, I know them. They know well enough what they mean when they say that Dorion's a witch.' He sat with his handsome dark face sombre in the flickering light, staring into the fire, his thoughts two hundred miles away. 'The very beasts of the fields are under her spell,' he said. 'Even the sheepdogs, so close that they know the very minds of their masters—even they will leave their Shepherds at the call of Dorion Rhos; and the men themselves go with them, like as not. Every man in the valley's half in love at least with her.' And he quoted again: '"La Belle Dame sans Merci, hath them in thrall."'

My hands shook, my mouth was stiff. I said: 'Including Gereth Morgan of Hendre Drom?'

And the clock on the mantelshelf chimed seven.

He leapt to his feet. 'Look at the time! I should have left the house by now.' He hurried of to the bedroom and within fifteen minutes was back, standing in the doorway of the sitting-room, snapping his fingers in an effort of concentration. 'What was it I came in here for?'

'To have your tie knotted properly, I should think,' I said, jerking myself from my uneasy thoughts, forcing a laugh. He stood impatiently shifting while I re-tied it, broke away from me, dashed out into the hallway, and hitched down his dark evening coat. At the door, he paused. 'By the way, I forgot to tell you what it was I went to see Lynn about. She's not well. I've rearranged my work at the college; we're taking her down to Hendre Drom tomorrow. You and I.'

I stood at the window and watched him hurry off down the street to Victoria station where he might pick up a hansom cab. It was dark by now but the gas lamps were lit in the street and I watched his light, tall figure pass beneath each, move like a shadow out of the shadows into the golden glow, grow bright for a moment, pass out, a shadow into shadows again. A shadow, moving into shadow: my love, my bright, clear love, so suddenly, so cruelly grown remote from me and obscure. Thanks to Dorion Rhos.

He had concealed from me that morning that he had received a letter from Dorion. He had said that we would not go to Wales until the spring, but now without consultation, almost, it seemed, deliberately keeping the news until there was no time for discussion of it, had peremptorily arranged to go. He gave as a reason that Lynneth was ill; but he had said he had seen her about 'nothing especial'. It came to me for the first time—how little I knew of him really, of his background, his character. Perhaps, I thought, he is moody and difficult—musicians, all artists, so often are. Perhaps he isn't sure enough yet to trust me, to say outright: 'I find I am not even yet quite free of the spell of Dorion the Witch.'

He had rounded the corner. I turned away from the window and so caught sight of the jacket he had flung across the arm of the chair.

So that was what he had come for, from the bedroom! I had interrupted him and now he had gone off without changing his things from the pockets of his jacket to those of his evening coat; had gone without his note case, without loose money or keys . . .

I snatched up the jacket and began feverishly to hunt through the pockets, meaning to run out after him, hope to catch up with him before he found a hansom, so that he might at least have the money for his cab fares . . . And in my hurry, picked up the coat half upside-down. His note case slid out from its pocket and lay, gaping wide, on the patterned carpet, and from it tumbled the letter from Dorion.

That huge, bold handwriting, you could not help but see. The letter was written in Welsh, and the first word was *Cariad*, which in Welsh means 'dearest'. Dearest or darling—an endearment anyway.

It is an old letter, I thought: a letter she wrote to him long ago and which he has sentimentally kept. But that was nonsense. The letter was dated 'Wednesday' and there had been the crumpled envelope this morning—which Gereth had so carefully not mentioned bearing Wednesday's date. Besides, I had seen him coming back from collecting the post, slipping this very letter into his pocket.

What of it? I thought. He was in love with Dorion once, he has made no secret of that; and now Dorion won't let him go. Can Gereth help it if Dorion writes to him and calls him 'Dearest'? And yet . . . If only he had not—with that faintly furtive air—hidden the letter from me! I knelt down and with shaking hands gathered up the thick-bunched sheets, shuffled them into their original creases, folded the whole to replace it in the notecase . . .

Who shall say that I was innocent of glancing again at that first page, the page that began with an endearment—Cariad? Who could swear it was all as much genuine accident as the rest had been? If indeed I was guilty, I was soon enough punished. Listeners learn no good of themselves; nor the readers of other people's letters. The words leapt out at me from the page: one word, a phrase, a whole sentence in the big, clear, beautiful handwriting. *The time has come for your wife to die.*

As though a snake had struck at me I thrust letter and note-case out of sight, backed away from it, shuddering and sick. But a glimpse in the mirror of the overmantel of my own white face, brought me back to my senses. It was all a mistake, some idiotic mistake. My Welsh, language of my childhood, had grown rusty; of course I had read the words wrongly. I went over to the shelf, took down my old dictionary and, going back to the window, with one eye anxiously on the street lest Gereth discover that he had no money with him, and come hurrying back for it, looked up the word 'wife'.

But there was no mistake. The word in Welsh can mean just 'a woman' but there was no other woman in Gereth's life. *The time has come for your wife to die.*

A man turned the corner into the street and I started guiltily. But it was not Gereth. And why should I mind? I thought. Why should I be afraid? The moment he returned, I would ask him about the letter, I would ask him to explain . . .

Only—why had he not already explained?

Why, because of this very threat, said my heart; and I tried to find ridicule in a mental rehearsal of such a scene. 'Oh, Laura, by the bye, I have had a letter from Dorion Rhos—the witch, you know—and she says you are ripe to be killed. So come along, let us hurry down at once to Hendre Drom . . .'

Cold in my vitals, the memory of those words of his at the door, ten minutes ago. He had said this morning we should not go to Wales till the spring. And now we were to go to Wales at once.

I steadied myself. What am I thinking, am I mad? Am I imagining that Gereth, my husband, my love, is in correspondence with another woman, with a woman who wants me to die? I thought of the happiness, the tenderness, the ecstasy of these six weeks of our having known each other—and my heart said, Don't be a fool, you fool!—He loves you as you love him . . .

And my head repeated: I have known him for just six weeks.

On the little finger of my right hand gleamed the gold of the amulet. Let me come down to Carmarthenshire, Dorion had written with the gift—and I would have need of it!

With the fingers of my left, I touched the rough, cool gold. Very well. If this is a charm against evil, I thought, let it help me now: if only against the evil of my own imaginings. For though at the time I felt no pang of fear for my own safety, yet I knew that something far more precious was at stake. Without trust in Gereth, what was life itself to me?

As though I were answered, all in a moment I knew what I must do. I took the letter from the note case again and read it through.

I might mistranslate a word, bungle a phrase, get a sentence back to front, my head might be hot with panic, my heart cold with fear—but there was no mistaking the meaning of the letter. A letter, not of passion or longing, but of cool deliberation—one of many such letters, quite evidently, written and answered—*and answered*—over the very recent past. Its implication was clear beyond doubt: that they two, Gereth and Dorion, planned between them to go away together, to be together. '*We will roam the earth,*' wrote Dorion, '*and all the world of music will be ablaze with our names.*' ('A poor teacher of music,' he had said, introducing himself to me, 'who will never now, alas, be a great concert pianist, astonishing the world . . .' And, of Dorion: 'her singing tears the very heart out of you—even only to remember it.' And to me . . . To me he had said with that little half-teasing, half-tender smile: 'But who has her nice little competence . . .'

My nice little competence. Six weeks later, I had been married to Gereth who knew of me nothing but that I was alone and friendless in the world, but with my nice little competence . . . The little competence that would not be enough for both of us were he to take it and set up on his own as a concert pianist: not for *both* of us.

We must have money, wrote Dorion. *And SHE has money; and so the time has come for her to die. You mustn't be afraid. I have the tablets I told you of. Nothing to fear in them; this was my father's secret, I have seen him use the stuff often on sick creatures that must be disposed of. It could be passed off easily as an antidote to fever or pain. And don't let it distress you—it is an easy death, just slipping away into sleep. People may be surprised, may even suspect; but of all people, you least of all could be suspected. And I—? But anyway, we should be far away. On the other hand, better still than the pills would be an 'accident'; then no suspicion at all could attach. A 'fall', a slip on those polished stairs at Hendre Drom . . . Make an excuse, come down here as soon as you can.* Here was a P.S.: *If we can't meet, remember the old, childhood 'post office' between the beech hedge and the wall.*

The note ended simply, *Love, Dorion.* She cares nothing for him, I thought: all she wants is to get money through him, to get away, to exploit this golden voice of hers . . . The voice whose very memory could tear out the heart of Gereth Morgan: of my dear love.

Hooves clip-clopped outside and with trembling hands I stuffed the letter back into the case and the case into the pocket of his jacket, and threw the jacket down again upon the chair. But it was a false alarm and somehow, it was clear, Gereth must have come to some arrangement about his cab fare and be on his way. I stood looking, down into the empty street and, in the darkened window pane, caught a reflection of my own white face—my own plain face, that I had thought could ever have captured the heart of such a man as he. It had been a wonder and a glory to me that one who was himself so handsome and brilliant, should have chosen me. Now I faced the thought, turned back, beaten back into my own old self-disparagement and pain, that it had all been for this—to secure my little fortune for himself and Dorion. The lightning courtship, the impatient marriage—I, God knew, no less eager than he, infatuated, unquestioning . . . And all for this.

What did one do when one had incontrovertible proof that one's husband was trying to murder one?

One sought counsel. But where? To whom could I turn? To Aunt Blodwen, far away in Wales? And anyway, what could she do? Some priest, some lawyer? I thought of the half deaf, quavering old vicar in the parish I had just left; of the solicitor who had handled my father's affairs, down in Wales also, and an old man, dry as dust. The police? I thought of my love and of all it had meant to my starved and lonely heart; thought of Gereth's eyes as they dragged him off to some place unknown . . . And I pressed my palm against the rough gold of the amulet ring and cried out in my heart once again: If you really have magic to help me, help me now! And immediately, as though it had indeed some power, my mind grew calm.

Of course it isn't magic, I thought, any more than Dorion is a witch. But for me it shall be magic and for me she shall be a witch. She is a witch and Gereth is not the Gereth I know and love but a man in the power of her sorcery, under the spell of the Evil Eye. Let me cling fast to this knowledge, I thought, and my way is clear. My mind shall believe this terrible threat to be true, I shall take every step to keep myself safe from it. My heart shall keep faith with Gereth and trust in his love

We caught an early morning train for the long journey to

Wales: a bitter cold December morning with the steam from the engine brilliantly white against a sky heavy with the leaden grey that promises snow. I remember to this hour the smell of the horses, of leather harness, of stables manure, from where the carts and wagons awaited the incoming trains to be loaded up with the mail, with 'luggage in advance'; where the carriages awaited wealthy masters, the grooms with their cockaded top hats, standing at the horses' heads, soothing their nervy unrest. Lynn and I stood close together for warmth, wrapped in our heavy winter mantles: I remember too as though it were yesterday how she held her skirts high, away from the station's dirty floor, above her pretty little button boots. She was very young, only seventeen, if as much as that, a frail creature, very sweet and clinging. I thought that she would not be difficult to influence; and with the very thought, Gereth turned to her and said, 'You still look very unwell. You haven't told Laura yet how you passed the night.'

She started to say that she had slept well: felt in excellent health. But you could see the change come about in the frank young face, you could see her reflect that yesterday Gereth had told her how well she looked and so she must surely be ill? She stammered out that she felt—well, much better, but of course would be glad to be at home. The aunt with whom she now lodged was very kind; but home was home . . .

The carriage was crowded and though bitterly cold, soon unendurably airless from the need to keep the window tight closed against the sparks and smut from the engine. I sat crushed between Gereth and Lynn, my hands buried in my fur muff. Even to bring them out and 'manage' the picnic basket we had bought at the station, to hand round cold chicken and sandwiches, was almost to invite frostbite. I was thankful for piping hot tea handed round by small boys at several of the stations where we stopped; I see the bright copper urns now and hear the chirping cries of 'Cuppa tea a penny, a penny for tea!' We spoke very little; between Gereth's late return last night from his dinner, and the hasty arrangements for this morning's departure there had been no time for discussion; I was grateful for it. The long hours passed. I prayed for them to end, and yet as the end drew near, wished they might be as long again. Here at least I was safe, or might hope to be safe.

Aunt Hannah had sent her carriage to meet us and there was still the long drive to the house. We sat in close silence still, huddled in rugs against the bitter chill of the late winter evening, with stone water hot jars at our feet, rocking with the motion of the coach, lulled by the jingle of harness and the rhythmical clip-clop of the horses' hooves. It was pitch dark when Lynn roused herself to say: 'There are the lights of Hendre Drom.'

Though it marked the end of so many weary hours, I could not seem to be glad. I asked, to make some show of interest: '"Drom" means in Welsh "doom". Why do you call it the House of Doom?'

'It's always been so called,' said Lynn. 'I don't know why. Perhaps, in fact, it does have a rather gloomy air?'

'Not to me,' said Gereth. 'Many of my boyhood holidays were spent here; for me it has meant happiness.'

Happiness, I thought, with Dorion Rhos.

Mrs Morgan came to the big front door to meet us: dressed in the black of her long widowhood, with the tiny, hardly perceptible rattle of jet beads that accompanied her every movement. An ugly woman: a squat, ugly woman, as ugly as a toad, was my first thought: my second a wonder that anyone so ill-favoured could radiate so immense a charm. She took one look at Lynn's pinched white face. 'Well, you don't look well, child, that's certain; go straight up to your room now and let Bronwen get you unpacked and tucked up in your bed and you shall have some supper there.' To me, stumping up the broad, shallow wooden stairs at my side (*A fall . . . A slip on those polished stairs at Hendre Drom . . .*), she said: 'Well, I'm glad you're here at last. Glad I am, to have Gereth safely married; and to a good Welsh girl at that. I like it when like marries like. Why didn't you come before?'

I said, feebly: 'It was all such a rush.'

'What was the hurry?' said Mrs Morgan flatly.

Ah—what indeed? 'Well—we were both alone. There seemed no reason for waiting. I don't know.'

'I do,' said Mrs Morgan. She pushed open a door and ushered me into a vast room where already my luggage had been brought up. 'He was afraid of that girl.'

'Afraid?' I said, trembling.

'She has her spell on them all,' said the old woman. 'And she doesn't like losing a lover. You know that he was in love with her?'

'Yes,' I said. 'He told me.'

'She's no good,' said Mrs Morgan. 'No good to any man.' And she quoted: 'I saw pale kings and princes too, Pale warriors, death pale were they all; They cried, La Belle Dame sans Merci, Hath thee in thrall.'

'Gereth calls her that too,' I said.

'And he's quite right. There are no kings or princes here. And yet . . . All our lads, all our fine young farming men—where are they now? Where's Widow Jones's boy? Drowned himself in a mountain pool, because of Dorion Rhos. Where's the Williams' lads? A pack of wolves, snarling among themselves, over Dorion Rhos. Where are Will James and Dai Rees and Dan Edwards' sons? All gone, cleared off out of the valley for love of Dorion, for fear of Dorion the Witch. Men, women and children, the very beasts of the fields and the mountains—she has her spell on them all.' And she came up to me close, and put her two hands on my shoulders and smiled up into my face. 'And where's Gereth Morgan? Married to a good young wife— and safe, please God!'

I tried to smile back at her. 'Mrs Morgan—will it—will it be necessary for him to see her while we're here?'

'See her? Of course not,' she said sharply. 'I'll take good care of that.'

For the next morning, at any rate, she made sure of it. Lynn, well or ill, was kept in her bed; Gereth led off to a conference on family business. Left to myself, I whistled up the tawny sheepdog, Bracken, and went for a walk along the river's edge.

It seemed to me now a mad thing to have done this; but fast in my mind was the idea that the plot was between Dorion and Gereth—that Gereth must take at least a part in my destruction. That Dorion herself alone might attempt it, did not enter my head. All was Gereth to me—Dorion but some evil, directing hand. I gave her no more thought.

It was a lovely day. Between its eroded sandy banks, the river was in flood from the melting snow, swirling down the valley to the tranquil fields below. Up the mountainside the scrub oak was the very colour of the bracken that burned beneath, so that the whole hillside seemed ablaze.

I came to a rustic bridge that lay across the river, a single larch tree, felled to lie spanning the low banks, its thin branches trailing in the pewter swirl of the water. A second tree formed a precarious handrail three feet above. 'No thank you,' I said, a hand on the sheepdog's head. 'It's very tempting in that lovely meadow beyond; but we'll stay over here.'

Across the river, something stirred in the bracken: the dog pricked his ears and a moment later had shot from beneath my hand and bounded on to the bridge.

A thin, splintering crash as the slender trunk gave; a sharp yelp, a splash, and I cried out helplessly, 'Bracken! Brack!' as the sleek wet head struggled up above the icy rush of the water, caught in the tangled branches of the fallen tree . . .

And out of the blaze of bracken and oak, creamy mane and tail flying—a pony bounded forth, leapt the crumbling, sandy bank and plunged into the stream. Its rider stooped and caught the struggling dog by the collar, hauled him up to the saddle and with a heave and a scramble set the pony at the opposite bank and made the shore. She released the dog in a shower or droplets—and sat on the pony, looking, triumphantly laughing, down at me. So for the first time I saw Dorion—Dorion the Witch.

What I had expected, I don't quite know—some flashing, dark creature, strong and bold, dressed gypsy-fashion. What I saw was a young girl, very thin—too thin—with hair the colour of autumn leaves, carelessly parted, falling, rather straggling, to her shoulders, not plaited up, nor in any way dressed: a girl in a full, rather tattered skirt, flowing out from a tiny waist; with woollen stuff sleeves showing beneath the traditional Welsh flannel shawl. She came closer, slid down from the back of the lovely creamy-maned pony, stood leaning negligently against its arched, golden neck—and I looked into the flower face at the pale, petal mouth, the smouldering grey eyes—and saw there a beauty that was almost terrible. I had had cause indeed to be afraid of Dorion Rhos.

'Well, Mrs Gereth Morgan,' said Dorion. 'So the amulet saved you after all!'

I looked at the splintered trunk of the tree—a tree giving way beneath the weight of a dog! '*You* did this,' I said. 'You arranged it so that *I* should fall.'

'Keep out of my mountains, then,' said Dorion, coolly.

I looked at the dripping dog. 'I might have—I might have been caught and held by the branches. That's what happened to him. I should have been drowned.'

'Nonsense!' said Dorion. 'The river here is not four foot deep. You'd have a ducking as I intended; but no more.'

'Then why need you plunge in to rescue the dog?'

'I did it to show off,' said Dorion, laughing. She turned to the lovely pony and said: 'Broomstick—take a bow!'

The pony thrust out a stiff foreleg, circus fashion, and bent his proud head. 'I shall tell Mrs Morgan,' I said to her, steadily, 'and she will inform the police.'

'Oh, dear—what a terrible threat!' said Dorion. She leaned back, laughing, against the pony's neck, looking lazily across at me with a sideways glance of those smoky grey eyes. '"Away with her! Drown her on the ducking stool! Burn her at the stake!"' She considered it, eyeing me all the time with her mocking glance. 'When they drag me to court, I shall have to take Broomstick.'

'Take the pony—?'

'Sir Ivor—the magistrate—he breeds such ponies, you see; and it was Sir Ivor's son who gave me Broomstick.' She gave a little skip and began to sing in a high, clear fluting, thin little haunting voice: '*Tom, Tom, the magistrate's son, Stole a horse and away did run* . . . Though he didn't run really,' she added. 'Sir Ivor packed him off abroad to be out of harm's way.'

'I see,' I said.

'Besides, what harm have I done to *you*? The tree gave, that's all.' She glanced back at it casually. 'You should blame Dan Edwards for not keeping his bridges in repair.'

I remembered Aunt Hannah's mentioning that name. 'Farmer Edwards has no sons now, it seems, to help him keep them in repair.'

'True: so he has not,' said Dorion. 'I shall have to put a spell upon his trees for him, so that they don't rot away.'

'You might take your spell off his sons,' I said, 'so that *they* do not rot away.'

'Ah, that!' said Dorion. 'It is easier to use magic than to control it. This you must know yourself.'

'I?' I said. 'I have no magic.'

'I think that you have,' said Dorion. 'And I think you could control it no more than I could control mine. I have the magic of making people love me. You have the magic of making people

like you.' She smiled and despite myself I felt the strange fascination of that smile. 'I rather like you myself.'

And I rather like *you*, I longed to say. I can't help liking you,
I know now what they mean when they say that you hold people
in thrall—men, women and children, you hold them in thrall.
How could one believe her capable of murderous intent, this
lounging, thin young creature with her pale mouth and laughing
eyes . . . ? And anyway—surely that was all over now? As I had
thought of Dorion, so doubtless Dorion had thought of me—a
vague, menacing woman who had stolen her love and deserved
to die for it. But now . . . I threw out my hand to her in an
almost involuntary gesture of friendliness and trust. 'I like you
too, Dorion. Could we not be friends?'

She gave a sharp cry. 'The ring!' The rough gold of the amulet,
sharp edged, had rasped her finger; she stood paler they ever,
staring down at it. 'No blood!' she muttered. 'No blood!' Then
she rubbed her other hand over the rough place and lifted her
head. 'You knew! You did it on purpose!'

'I did nothing to harm you. I merely put out my hand—'

'You knew,' she insisted wildly. She thrust out her narrow,
sunburned hand and caught me by the wrist. 'Say it, admit
it—you know!'

If she knows what I know, I thought, frantically calculating,
then surely she must be warned off, surely I shall be safe? I tore
myself from her grasp. 'Very well, then: yes—I know. I saw the
letter.'

But she was looking down at her hand again, muttering again.
'They say that if you shed the blood of a witch, she dies. You
knew that, you did it on purpose.' And suddenly, swiftly, she
lifted her head. 'What do you mean—the letter?'

Too late to retreat. 'I mean that I saw your letter.'

She asked softly: 'A letter of mine? What letter?'

'The letter you wrote last week,' I said. I looked back steadily
into her eyes. 'Your murder plot.'

She took one step forward, then another, till she stood directly before me, looking deep into my eyes. I stared back at her steadily but my own eyes seemed to glaze and waver before the glare of grey. She said: 'Tell me who else you have told about this.'

I was silent, forcing myself not to reply; yet strangely my tongue longed to answer, to say: 'I have told no one.'

Dorion asked: 'What have you said of it? Have you spoken of it to Gereth?'

Keep silent, warned my mind; my lips said: 'No.'

'And anyone else? Have you told anyone else? Answer me, Laura!'

Be warned, said my mind; be warned. But my lips said: 'No.'

Dorion said, very thoughtfully: 'I see.'

The long eyes glanced sideways at the icy grey torrent of the river, hurtling by. 'You would not care now to walk across the bridge, dear Laura, would you? It is not so very badly broken after all.'

'No,' I said.

'Then we shall have to persuade you.' She spoke a brief word to the pony and he lifted his head, reared up suddenly with a flash of steel hooves and brought them down thundering upon the meadow grass. 'A horrid accident,' said Dorion, 'if he had been more close to you. You will be safer on the other side of the river.'

'I shall not go,' I said. And suddenly: 'There are people coming from the house.'

And there, sure enough, starting across the fields towards me, was Aunt Hannah's stout figure, cloaked all in black, with Lynn and Gereth, one each side of her. They called out sharply, seeing perhaps the murderous flashing of the pony's hooves. Dorion swung about, gave them one frustrated, furious glance and then, with a single movement, fluid as quicksilver, was astride the pony and galloping wildly away.

And cry and call as we might—Bracken the dog went with her.

Aunt Hannah was very much upset about the dog. She was afraid that Bracken, uncontrolled, might join a rogue dog which was known to be in the neighbourhood, killing sheep. The penalty for a dog caught worrying sheep is death. She stood in the huge, old-fashioned drawing-room with its heavy carved oak furniture, dispensing tea.

'If we could be sure she would keep Brack with her and not just turn him loose!'

'I'll go up to the cottage, Aunt Hannah,' said Gereth, and get him back.'

I looked wildly at Mrs Morgan. I had had no time to think what next to do; if Gereth now had an opportunity to confer with Dorion, all might be lost. But Aunt Hannah did not fail me.

'Nonsense, boy, you will do no such thing! You would not get the dog back—and likely as not, we should not get *you* back.' She gave a rather forced smile. 'Besides, we have not finished yet in the library . . .'

They went back to their discussion, this time taking Lynn with them. I was left in the drawing-room, alone with my unquiet thoughts.

The room lay at the side of the house, its French windows looking out on to wide lawns, rhododendron-dotted and bordered by a high brick wall beyond which lay the narrow road. I got to my feet and moved restlessly over to the window. Along the road went the clip-clop of a horse's hooves; some farmer, I thought: Dorion's was hardly the only pony in the neighbourhood. I wandered back to my chair, sat down, buried my head in my hands in an effort at concentration. What now to do? To confront Gereth with the truth? To confide in Aunt Hannah . . . ? To tell only part or all to the local police? Along the road, I heard again the sound of hooves. Outside the garden wall, they stopped.

I went back to the window and, in the shadow of the heavy curtains, stood watching. The sun was going down, the light leaving the sky. Halfway, as I peered forward, I could see where the wall abruptly stopped, giving way to a high beech hedge. I remembered suddenly the note at the end of Dorion's letter to Gereth. If they could not meet, he was to remember the 'post office' of their childhood games, between the beech hedge and the wall. Now, where these two met, I seemed to see something move. A moment later and with a scatter of hooves, whatever horse and rider had been there, were gone.

I slipped out of the French window. Sure enough, tucked into a crevice between wall and hedge, not hard to find if you knew where to look—a folded paper. I read it through, peering at it in the evening light, frowning over the difficult Welsh . . .

Why haven't you come? Dorion had written. *I took Brack, I thought that would give you an excuse to follow. Laura has found out—she has read my letter to you. We must act at once, we must get her out of the way before she tells anyone. She has not yet; I forced her to admit it. Now, do exactly as I say—there is no time to argue. I have been down to the gold mines. In the second cave—you remember? We used to play there as children, terrified of the dark—there is the old shaft. It is very deep, there is water at the bottom of it now. I have weakened the barrier around it and spread oil at the lip. In the darkness of the cave, you would not see the pit if you did not know it was there and the cave floor slopes down to it. A boy will bring a message that Brack has been seen running loose in the mines. Bring Laura down there to help hunt for him, bring her to the cave, alone if you can; it will be easy, there are many caves for the others to search while you make this arrangement, you two to take the one with the pit. I shall hide on the far side of the pit. I will flutter something white, she will think it is Bracken and will run straight across the cave to him. Once she slips in the oil, that will be the end.* She had added: *It is not nice, you will not like this way of doing it; but now there is no time for choosing, we are actually in great danger while she lives. You must do it for me, even if you will not for yourself.*

I stood with the letter in my hand and it seemed to me that this moment of terror could never end. But it ended. Voices called my name faintly from the house. I shrank back into the shelter of a dark bush, frantically fumbling with the paper, trying with hands numb with cold, clumsy in their terrified haste, to refold it as before. Footsteps crunched on the gravel path round the side of the house. Gereth's voice cried on a note of uncertainty: 'Laura?' I could not have answered if I would have. He waited there a moment and then turned back.

How long I crouched there, I never knew: sick with the horror, the uncertainty, chilled with the bitter evening cold, yet powerless to move, to force myself back into the necessity to speak, to act—to decide. For surely now silence was madness, surely now I must speak? Heart and head again in the old battle raged, mind cold and clear, heart insisting, *I love him, he loves me, this can't, this CAN'T be true.*

Up at the house, someone was moving about. I saw the French window open, a figure came through, footsteps crunched again on the path, were muffled crossing the long grass, coming directly towards me. I thrust the folded paper back into its hiding place and, moving like a ghost, with thudding heart, crept back into the shadow, the black shadow now in the rapidly fading light, of the rhododendron leaves. A moment later and Gereth stood a few feet from me.

He had not forgotten the hiding place. He took the note, unfolded it, stood straining his eyes over it. Then he folded it again, put it into his pocket and hurried back into the house.

Very well, I thought. Now he has it. Now I shall know. A sort of peace descended upon me, for this meant decision at last. If he acted upon the plan—if he asked me to come down to the caves—then my heart could no longer cling to even a fragment of doubt. Then my mind was made up, I must tell all I knew. If he asked me to come down to the caves . . .

But he will not. He will never agree to this, never, never . . .

I crept back to the house. There was no one about. But as I slipped up the stairs to my room, the door opened and Gereth came out suddenly into the hall. 'Laura! Where have you been? We have been calling for you.' He ran up, he caught me by the hand. 'Come, get your cloak and come quickly. The dog has been seen down by the gold mines. They have gone ahead: I waited, trying to imagine where you could have got to.' He hurried me down to the hall, caught up my thick travelling cloak, wrapped it about me, caught at my hand and insisted: 'Come!'

And so I went with him.

The mine was a quarried-out clearing with several cave entrances visible in the cliff sides. I could hear muffled voices calling, 'Brack! Bracken, good dog, come Bracken, come Brack!' A manservant appeared at the mouth of one of the caves. 'No sign of him yet, sir. Madame's over there with Dai and Mr James. I have Miss Lynn here, she'll be safe with me . . .'

'Very well, we'll take the second cave,' said Gereth, calling back. He hurried me over towards a yawning gap in the quarry side. 'I must keep up appearances before them; but I loathe caves, they sicken and terrify me . . .' (*You remember? We used to play there, terrified of the dark . . .*) 'Will you come with me?' He shuddered. 'I could not do it alone.'

My mind said bitterly: 'Don't trouble yourself. You will not have to do it alone. Dorion is there.' But I said nothing aloud: just went with him, speechlessly.

The cave was very large, dim and dank and cold; and as Dorion had written, from where we stood outlined against the entrance, the floor sloped away and if there were indeed a railed-off pit in the centre, I could see nothing of it. Gereth shuddered again. He called out: 'Brack! Brack!' Do you shudder from loathing of the cave? I thought—or from knowledge of what is planned to happen here?

Silence. Stillness. He took my hand in his and held it. But his own hand violently trembled. I thought: Each test so far he has failed. I shall go all the way—but if the last test fails, if he really lets me go forward to this terrible death . . . But my heart said: He will not. Trust him, be true to your love for him—when the moment comes, he will not. He will betray *her*. Not me.

And I thought of how she had written that he must do it for her sake even if he would not for his own: for they were in danger, now that I knew. (Knew of the first letter—neither of them could be aware that I had seen also the second.) He had obeyed: had been told to bring me here and had brought me here . . .

Across the cave—something moved. I knew my cue. I said: 'What is that, over there?'

'It must be Bracken.' He began to call, but half-heartedly: 'Brack! Brack!'

'He may be injured or frightened,' I said, deliberately. 'Why not go across and see?'

'I?' he said. 'I couldn't. I couldn't go one step further into this horrible place.' And he turned away. 'I'll call the others, I'll get help.'

At least he would not stand there and see it done; but as he moved from the entrance of the cave, I knew that my last hope was lost. I said: 'Very well. Shall *I* go across the cave to him?'

He paused in the entrance. 'Yes, go,' he said. 'I can't. I'll get help.'

Yes, go. Hope faded: all lost. *Yes, go.*

Something stirred again in the darkness beyond and now, as my eyes grew more accustomed, I could sense, rather than see, the deeper blackness of the great, gaping hole, the dim, irregular outline of the broken rail of wooden posts and wire. From outside came the sound of voices calling but I hardly heard them, all my mind was concentrated in a last passion of longing for the sound of one voice alone, one voice calling to me not to go on. Still no word came; and now the blackness was pitch black to my eyes no longer but a dimness which the pit yawned before me, clearly visible—as it would not have been visible had I run forward impulsively according to Dorion's expectation. And before the pit—the evil gleam of the blacker patch of oil where the slope of the cave floor grew still more steeply pitched towards the mouth of the pit. My voice sounded very strange in the silence, echoing hollowly back from the dome of the cave's high roof. 'Gereth,' I said. 'Shall I go on?'

Before me—blackness and death. Behind me—a silence as dear as words, willing me to die. And suddenly I was seized with an impulse to die indeed, to end it all, the hideous disillusion, the bitterness, the pain. How could I live on with this knowledge in my heart, the cruelty, the treachery? I will die, I thought. He is here in the darkness, hiding here, waiting; or outside the cave mouth, closing his ears to it, blinding himself, murderer and coward as well. And if this were true—what was there to live for? I had rather die. I pressed my hands to my face and, self-blinded, took one faltering step forward, away from the sheltering wall of the cave towards the pit.

Hard and cold against my face, the gold of the amulet ring—and brought suddenly to my senses by the tiny, rough shock of it, I stepped back, swung about, made a swift movement to the opening and cried out: 'Gereth! Save me! Don't tell me to go forward, don't let me die—!'

And as I stood a moment outlined against the lightness of the evening outside—the comparative lightness against the blackness of the cave—something darted at me, caught me, whirled me around and all in one blinding moment had released me and with one violent shove sent me teetering backwards, slithering and sliding down the inclined slope towards the pit mouth, powerless to stop . . . slithering, sliding, falling: sucked down to the very edge of the pit, dragged by my own weight down the greasy incline. I felt my legs slide over into nothingness; I knew that the end was near: slowly, inch by inch, dropping down into nothingness: into the pit.

And suddenly a violent jerk on wrist and arm. My clawing hand had caught on a strand of wire from the broken barrier.

I gave one violent upward thrust that somehow enabled me to twist the end of wire about my wrist: slid back, hung there, sick, exhausted, paralysed with horror and fear, face down upon the oil-smeared rock of the floor, my legs actually dangling over the edge of the open shaft. Miraculously, the wire held.

One sound I cried out: one small, feeble cry, chopped off almost before it was uttered. For now she came—Dorion.

I forgot the overstrained wire, the rotting posts of the loosened barricade; I gave one panic-stricken jerk, wrenched myself violently upwards and with my free hand caught at a wooden post. It gave, but my knee had found a small patch of rock, free of the oil; I flung my weight forward, clutched wildly at a second post. The post held. A moment later, bruised, scraped, oil-smeared, dreadfully gasping and sobbing, I knelt safe on the dry rock at Dorion's feet, grasping the wooden post in both my arms as though it were the very symbol of salvation.

Dorion stood looking down with cool concern. 'Poor thing,' she said, as though I were some fly, half drowned at the edge of a saucer. 'But it's no good—you've got to die now.' She went down unhurriedly on one knee beside the post and with her own hands forced my hands apart and, hooking her arm about the post, got her heel to my shoulder and, with a single violent thrust, flung me back towards the pit.

The jerk on my arm was appalling but it meant that the wire was still twisted around my wrist; and the wire held. Above me, Dorion crouched, one arm hooked round the post, the other outstretched as it had been outstretched to push me away and down. *Catch at her hand, drag her down with you, if you are to die, let her die with you, put an end to this evil, this sorcery for ever!*

With my free hand, I caught at the wire above my head, wrenched myself up a few inches, clutched at the still outflung arm. Dorion, taken unawares, tottered dangerously forward and to save herself threw all her weight backwards, dragging me with her. My knee felt dry rock again, I grasped at the uncut wires stretched between post and post, hauled myself painfully up and, before Dorion had recovered her balance, had scrambled to the safety of the barrier and stumbled to my feet.

Dorion staggered up, half weeping with rage and frustration. 'Won't you ever die? You've *got* to die!' she cried and launched herself at me once more. I swung round, lashed out with some blind instinct of self-preservation; heard a brief cry of pain as my right hand caught Dorion's pale face, and then was upon my enemy at last. Dorion's back was to the pit, her heel a few inches from the oil which she herself had spread. I caught her by the wrist.

She hung there: her lovely face, pale as a flower glimmering back at me through the dank gloom of the cave, the grey eyes, brilliant, wide with pleading. 'Laura, don't let me die! Laura, help me, forgive me—save me!' And she screamed out in despair: 'You can't let me die like this—not like this!'

No. Not like that. It was the death that she had intended for me—but I was not Dorion. I caught at a strong post and, with my left arm hooked about it, slowly drew her, dragged her, inch by inch, back from the pit to the safety of dry rock . . . And in that moment the light from the entrance was blocked out, there were voices and footsteps and a blackness about me that was not the blackness of the pit but a velvet blackness, the infinite mercy of unconsciousness.

When I came to I was outside the cave, under the moonlight;

and Mrs Morgan was in command. 'We must get her home.' She bent over me. 'Are you better, child? If the men helped you, could you walk that far?' And as I struggled to my feet, she cried, her heavy face blanched with anxiety and horror: 'what happened? Dorion says . . . Dear God, you might have gone down into the pit . . . I don't understand it, what was Dorion doing there . . . ?' But she did not wait for answers, helping me up, folding a rug about my shaking shoulders. 'Gereth, help her home. And you, Dai, go on the other side of Mrs Gereth and hold her. Dorion—?'

'I'm here, Mrs Morgan.' At the sound of her voice, the cream and golden pony came trotting out from his place of conceal-ment where, I suppose, she had ordered him to stay, and set up a joyful whinnying. 'I heard that Brack was among the caves, Mrs Morgan. He ran away from my cottage and I thought I ought to come down and look for him.' Stumbling between Gereth and the manservant Dai, across the uneven rock, I lifted heavy eyes and saw the angel face turned towards Aunt Hannah, innocently beautiful. 'I shouldn't have taken him. I did it to—to tease Laura, Mrs Morgan, and show her my power. I just—willed him to come with me.'

'Well, we've got him safe now,' said Aunt Hannah; Brack, a short length of broken lead trailing, bounded at Dorion's side.

'But what happened?' cried Lynn, she herself seemed half fainting also with the shock and horror of it all. At a nod from Aunt Hannah, James, the big footman, picked her up in his arm and was carrying her like a child.

'It was my fault,' said Gereth, at my side. 'I shouldn't have left Laura alone there. Well—in fact I didn't know that I *had*; I thought she had followed me out of the cave. We thought we saw Brack there; but he wouldn't come when we called and I said I'd get one of the men to help. I couldn't . . . The cave . . . Aunt Hannah,' he said, shame-faced, 'you know how I am about such things.'

'Yes, yes,' she said. 'Some people are like that. It's nothing to be ashamed of, boy.'

'The pit should be railed off,' said Dai, across me to Dorion. 'It's always been railed off. It's dangerous there.'

'The rail has given way,' said Dorion. 'It's a long time since anyone went there, I suppose. And there's grease or something at the edge . . .'

In one moment, I thought, she will tell them she was trying to save me; that I slipped and she was trying to save me. But Dorion was cleverer than that.

We had come to the roadway now, the narrow road leading back to Hendre Drom, I supported by Gereth and Dai, James carrying Lynn, Mrs Morgan following with Dorion, the lovely pony ambling sweetly along by her side. 'She saved me—Laura saved me! She thought she saw Brack in the cave, she came across the cave: I saw her coming towards the pit, I ran forward to warn her and slipped in the oil.' She came forward, caught Gereth by the arm, looking up at him, sweetly pleading, grey eyes limpid as a child's. 'I'm sorry I was—was horrid to her, Gereth. She saved my life.'

Gereth said nothing. When we came to the house I saw that he was white as death but he said no more than: 'Come in here to the drawing-room, both of you: there's a good fire, sit quietly a moment till they come.' Aunt Hannah had hung back a little with James, slowed up by his burden, carrying Lynn. He made no attempt at any private communication with Dorion. 'I will tell them in the kitchen to prepare tea for you; tea with sugar—I'm sure that's what Aunt Hannah will want you to have.' He went away.

Dorion slid to her knees at the foot of my chair. 'Forgive me, Laura! And thank you.'

Impossible to believe that an evil thought had ever lurked behind those lovely, pleading eyes. 'You are utterly—utterly—wicked,' I said.

'I suppose I am,' said Dorion. She sat back on her heels turned her exquisite profile to stare into the fire. 'Only . . . When people speak of badness, of wickedness—I don't know what they mean,' she said. 'I want—what I want. To get it, I do what I must. It doesn't seem "wicked" to *me*.'

I leaned back in the big chair, too spent and exhausted to answer, even to care. Dorion glanced back at me. She said, almost timidly: 'Are you going to—tell?'

'Yes,' I said.

'No one will believe you,' said Dorion. She could not help a giggle, putting her fingers up over her mouth to hide her impish delight in her own cleverness. 'Did you hear how I explained it all, down at the mine?'

'There is also the letter,' I said grimly.

'Well, but—is there? I mean—where is the letter, Laura? *You* haven't got it—have you? So who will believe in that either? Besides,' she added, eyeing me carefully, 'the letter doesn't concern you—only me. If you accuse me, you accuse us both.'

He had taken me to the cave: had acquiesced—even in that. Or had he? The old struggle—heart against head . . . Gereth had gone out of the cave, said he had gone out of the cave, had believed I followed him . . .

He had taken me to the cave: had read her letter, had taken me down to the gold mine. After that letter—could Gereth be innocent?

She was watching my face; listening to my silence. She knew all my weakness. She said: 'Laura! If I go away—if I promise to go away—alone, I mean—if I promise to leave this place for ever, never to see any of you, *any* of you ever again, never to trouble Gereth or any of you any more . . .' She broke off, her young, thin, beautiful hands placed together as though in prayer; and in her face I saw again that look of almost terrible beauty. 'I could not be in prison, Laura. You couldn't wish that for me! I've never been pent up, never, not even in my own home.

Alone, or with my father—always there were doors left open, let the cold be ever so: no creature, animal or human, could ever be closed in there. To be caught and caged—I had rather die . . .'

Aunt Hannah bustled in, stout and efficient in her rusty black, established Lynn in a third chair, plied us all with tea and sips of brandy. Gereth came across and sat on the arm of my chair. I shuddered away from his touch. 'Please don't. My hands—' I held them out, bruised and abrased

'I'll attend to them as soon as you have drunk your tea,' said Aunt Hannah. 'And Lynn, take your brandy. You too, Dorion.'

Dorion sat on the hearth, her bare legs curled up under the ragged stuff skirt; head bent, very humble and quiet. Bracken ran in and settled himself, tail wagging, at her side. The torn lead still trailed from his collar and she unfastened it. *He must have broken free and run off down to the mines . . .* I thought to myself that doubtless that was true—but he had gone in search of Dorion who already was there.

Gereth stood up. 'Aunt Han, do you not think that Laura should go to her bed? She has had a bad shock, she's exhausted.'

'Very well, help her upstairs then. Lynn had better go too, both you girls would be best lying resting; it's all been a great shock. On the way, Lynn, tell them to bring me my medicine box.' To Dorion she said: 'You had better stay here tonight.'

In comparison with myself, Dorion had suffered hardly at all from the skirmish at the pit head—there was a thin scratch down her cheek where the ring had caught her face in the first struggle, her shabby shoes were more scuffed than ever and now smeared with oil; but that was all. 'I think I'll go home, Mrs Morgan, thank you,' she said.

'You had better stay here,' Aunt Hannah insisted.

'No, I think I'll go home,' she repeated coolly. Aunt Hannah made a move to stop her, but in one swift movement she was across the room. She said in a tone of apology: 'You know me,

Mrs Morgan—I don't like to be cooped up, I like to be free.' She said it to Aunt Hannah but she glanced at me and the glance seemed a silent plea. She slipped out of the French window and a moment later we heard a scutter of hooves on the gravelled drive.

Brack lifted his head. 'Lynn, catch at his collar, quick!' said Mrs Morgan. As Lynn sat holding him, she commanded: 'Now, Gereth—get Laura upstairs.'

Panic rose in me. How can I trust myself alone with him, now that he knows that I know? Dorion had told him in her note that I had seen the letter, that while I lived I was a threat to them both. He must know that I at least suspected them both of having designed my murder down in the cave. I muttered: 'I'll go alone.'

'Let Gereth at least help you up the stairs, child.'

One slip on the polished stairs . . . 'I can manage. Please!'

They let me go alone at last, since—I suppose—I seemed so nervously set upon independence. The big, square bedroom was eerie in the gentle light of its single oil lamp. I pulled off my stained, torn dress, my oil-stained stockings and shoes, and flung myself down on the bed. When Aunt Hannah comes, I thought, I must tell her. I can't go on like this.

But as I relaxed, exhaustion closed in on me: claimed me, imprisoned me, robbed me of thought and speech. I was conscious of a hand, hard and cool, on my forehead and started up, crying out. Aunt Han's voice said: 'Hush, hush, child: it's only me,' and cool cloths were put to my temples, cool water bathed my burning hands, brief stinging pain shocked the cuts and scratches, something followed that soothed. 'I'll leave you now. Just rest and sleep . . .'

Now was the time to tell; but Aunt Hannah's words were hypnotic: rest and sleep, rest and sleep . . . I opened my heavy eyelids. 'I want to tell you . . . I must tell you . . . Gereth . . . Dorion . . .' Then the night came, deep and dark, folding me in.

The door clicked, gently closing. As though at the sound of a pistol shot, I started up, wide awake. 'They are trying to murder me,' I called out, loud and clear: saying it at last, telling it at last—to an empty room.

A board creaked. A tiny draught blew icily round the bed. My eyes, wide, staring into the darkness lit only by the oil lamp in the far corner, caught a glimpse of a star against a brilliant dry winter's night outside. Then darkness fell again and the star was gone. Again the almost imperceptible creak of a floorboard, the faintest brushing of cloth against cloth. Someone had parted the curtains and come into the room.

I lay paralysed into immobility, into silence. And saw Dorion.

She stood beside the bed. She still held the broken dog leash in her hands. She thrust a hand over my mouth. 'Don't make one sound.' Even now her beautiful face held no hatred, no cruelty, only an impatience to get the thing settled, a faintly regretful concern. 'Poor Laura! You didn't really think I'd trust you not to tell? That I'd go away and leave you to it?'

With her free hand, she yanked me forward from the pillow, threw the leather thong of the dog leash around my throat. 'It's all right, I'm not going to strangle you. But one twist of this—and I will, if you refuse to do what I say.' She lifted her hand from my mouth. 'Not one sound! If you scream, I shall tighten the strap—like this.' She twisted it for a brief moment. I saw in her eyes the same deprecatory pity with which she had said she must push me back into the pit

I whispered: 'Dorion—if I swear not to tell—'

'Of course you'll tell,' said Dorion. 'Don't be foolish. You've tried already.'

'If you kill me—they'll know.'

'Only one person will know,' said Dorion. 'Why should the rest suspect? What reason have *I* got to kill you?'

'But if . . . If they find me dead—'

Dorion still held the dog leash in one hand. With the other

she fished from her pocket a little twist of paper and began to unfold it. 'I think it will have to be suicide: don't you agree?'

'*Suicide?*'

'You see—may you not have been afraid that I should one day tell them—as I shall when you are dead—that it was not really true that this evening you tried to save my life? On the contrary, mad with jealousy because you thought Gereth still loved me, you tried to bring about my death. When they all rushed into the cave, of course you had to pretend to be saving me. And I was sorry for you, poor thing, and would not give you away.' She smiled in the soft lamplight, at her own magnanimity. 'But then, of course, you'd know that I knew and in fear, perhaps, or remorse . . .' She had the paper unfolded now and two small white tablets lay in her palm. 'All I want is that you should swallow these,' she said in her sweet, casual way. 'You need not be afraid. It is an easy death.'

She had said the same in her letter to Gereth. An easy death. I have only to accept, I thought, and what, after all, have I got left to hope for—but an easy death? Why struggle on? Without Gereth, without my love for him—what is life to me? To live with the knowledge of Gereth punished, imprisoned, locked away so that I may be safe from him—what is life to me?

'Give them to me,' I said to Dorion and held out my hand for the pills.

She drew back swiftly. 'Be careful! You know what happened last time with that thing!'

On my finger—the gleam of the amulet ring, the ring that Dorion herself had sent to me, defying its powers. But for me, it had power: though it might have no magic in itself, I had sworn, it should have magic for me. And now, as ever, with consciousness of the ring, strength and purpose came back once more. I said sharply: 'Dorion—have you looked in the mirror?'

'The mirror? said Dorion blankly. 'What for?' But she was uneasy, taken aback; I could see some sick premonition dawn in her face. She left me for one brief moment unattended, darted over to the dressing-table and snatched up the hand mirror there and darted back. The lamp glowed softly from its shadowy corner. She sat on the bed, holding the looking glass, its face turned away from her. I put up my hand and cautiously eased the thong from about my throat; but she made no move to stop me, seemed not to see me, to have forgotten me—sitting perched there, staring into nothingness, shrinking away from the shadow of an unimaginable dread. Then, very slowly, with a sort of terrible sadness, she turned so that the light of the lamp fell on her—and looked into the glass.

A face of imperishable beauty—marred only by a thin, red line of dried blood, across a cheek as pale as approaching death.

If you shed the blood of a witch—she dies.

The sound of Dorion's screaming filled all the house.

The long night drew on and I sat alone with Gereth in the big drawing-room where a huge fire blazed: and waited for—I knew not what. Aunt Hannah had got the fainting Dorion on to my bed and administered sedatives. 'Take Laura down by the fire, Gereth, she's chilled to the bone with shock. I'll watch over Dorion. Lynn, you stay here with me.'

To their questions, I had answered flatly—since the marks of the leather thong were still plain about my throat—that Dorion had come in through the balcony window, and attacked me. Later, I would tell Aunt Hannah the whole story; she must tell me what to do. Meanwhile, if I were to be sent off alone with Gereth while they attended to Dorion, it would be wisest to pretend that I innocently supposed Dorion simply jealous because her one-time lover had been stolen from her; to deny any knowledge of the letter if he challenged me, to suggest that Dorion must have misunderstood . . . I had agreed to go downstairs and wait with him.

Lynn stood with her mother at the bedside, looking down

at the lovely face. 'What shall you do, Mama, when she recovers?'

'I suppose,' said Mrs Morgan heavily, 'we should send for the police.'

'The police?' said Gereth sharply, pausing by the door.

'Something must be done, my dear.'

'If we weren't here,' suggested Lynn, hesitantly, 'she could just—just slip out of the window, couldn't she—and ride off?'

'She would be caught and brought back again,' said Mrs Morgan.

'The mountains are wide,' said Gereth.

'A hunted creature? You wouldn't wish that for her?'

'No.' He paused. 'I suppose the police must be told.'

'Take Laura downstairs, Gereth; and Brack—take Brack with you.' But Bracken refused to stir from Dorion's side.

So we sat silent, divided, one on either side of the fire— waiting. Gereth said at last: 'Do you think it's strange of me, Laura, that I should wish not to give up Dorion to the police?'

'Strange? No indeed,' I said with bitter irony.

He glanced across at me, as though surprised at the tone of my voice. 'You don't for one moment suppose . . . ? He broke off. He got up and went over to the French window, parting the curtains to look out on the darkness, anthracite bright, of a starlit winter's night. 'I couldn't help to catch Dorion and cage her in,' he said. 'She's like a wild thing, a bird or—'

There was a padding of paws on the polished stairs and Bracken, the dog, came trotting in. He crossed the room and settled himself by my side. I said coldly: 'Well, *I* have not asked you to betray Dorion.'

He seized upon it eagerly. 'A betrayal! Yes—that is what it would be: a betrayal.' He looked at me almost pleadingly, it seemed to me, across the room. 'I was in love with her once, she was my first love—my only other love. You wouldn't ask me to betray her—would you?' I made no response, sitting in frigid silence; the time when I could pretend, could act a part, was past. He asked at last: 'What are you thinking, Laura?'

'I am thinking,' I said, 'that La Belle Dame sans Merci hath thee in thrall.'

Outside in the hall, the grandfather clock struck ten. The door opened and Aunt Hannah Morgan stood there, solid and square in her black dress. She held Lynn's hand as though she were an unhappy child, in one of her own; and indeed, you could see that Lynn had been weeping. She put out her other hand to Gereth. She said: 'You must find it in your hearts to be thankful. Dorion is dead.'

The minutes ticked by. They spoke in low voices, grouped together, the old woman, Gereth, white faced, and the girl—the girl who had not been so white faced when she was supposed to have been so ill that I must assist in bringing her down here: bringing her down here for no real reason but that my death was planned. I sat huddled in my chair, unremembered, not watching them, not hearing them, given over to a sort of blankness of spirit. Dorion was gone and with the black cloud of evil and danger that had lain over all our lives. But with her going, Gereth also was gone. For how could I live again with Gereth—knowing what now I knew?

Forget it, said my heart. Pretend it never happened. Start again, he need never know that you even suspected him. Without Dorion, Gereth has no reason to leave you, no reason to desire your death. That he should ever have done so was but her sorcery; he was sick with her spell upon him. Forget it all—without him, what is life to you?

You could never forget it, said my mind. You would doubt him for ever: knowing what now you know. And doubting him, you would doubt your own love.

And indeed—what was my love for Gereth: if I could believe this of him? Even from death, Dorion reached out her narrow, beautiful hands and worked her will with our lives. And of what avail was the amulet ring to me now?

But even as I turned it listlessly on my finger, the little group at the other end of the fireplace ended the discussion. 'I'll do it,' said Gereth; but Lynn caught him back by the arm. 'No, Gereth, not you. I'll go,' she said, and went out into the hall. I heard her call to the footman, James; and her voice said quietly: 'James—go at once please, take a pony, go down to the village and fetch Owen Jones.'

We were silent. she said, coming back, closing the door quietly after her: 'James has taken a pony and gone down to fetch the constable.'

The constable . . . I leapt to my feet. 'The police? You can't bring the police here!'

'My dear, we must,' said Aunt Hannah.

'But—the letter! You're not going to show them the letter?' All thought was gone but love for him, protection of him. I ran to Gereth and clutched him by the arm. 'You won't show them the letter, you won't tell them the rest? You'll just say that Dorion is dead?' But what did Aunt Hannah know of the letter—she or Lynn? I said: 'Well—you don't understand. But there was a—a letter . . .'

'*We* know of it. What do *you* know?' said Aunt Hannah.

'I read it. The day it arrived: day before yesterday, the day before we came down here.' I clung to Gereth, hysterically weeping. 'If the police see the letter, they'll think . . . They'll know . . .' All the terrors, all the long agony of dread was forgotten. Of course he's innocent, of course he wouldn't do anything to harm me; but if they see the letter, the police will think . . .

'What could they think?' said Aunt Hannah. 'Gereth could not even have read the letter. He can't read Welsh.'

He can't read Welsh. Long ago—long ago it seemed now, but it had been but a few brief weeks ago—I had recognised that he had not known what Aunt Blodwen was saying about me: he could not speak Welsh. I stammered: 'But then . . . ? But then . . . ?'

Gereth stood close to me, his left arm about me, holding me close. 'My dearest darling, what is this terror about?' He looked down into my tear-stained face, amazed, compassionate—kind. 'I am in no danger from the police. I've done nothing wrong. The letters were not even written to me.'

'Not written to you? But then who . . . ?'

Lynn stood as close to her mother's side as I to Gereth's; held tight to her mother's hand. She said: 'Laura—the letters were written to *me*.'

Men, women, children—even the beasts of the woods and the fields—they are all under her spell . . . Men, women and children; and this poor child . . .

Childhood playmates—Lynn so much nearer to Dorion's age than Gereth; childhood playmates, sharing the secret 'post office' in the wall, the dark-heightened terrors of the caves. Growing up together, Dorion with that voice that could tear at one's heartstrings, Lynn the 'genius' as a harpist. *We will wander the earth and all the world will be ablaze with our names* . . . I remembered the cool letter, beginning, true, with a common endearment, but so oddly without passion, a letter I had supposed written from a woman to the man she loved. I had thought even then that Dorion cared really only for the money: for the chance to fulfil her dream of fame. 'But Lynn—she put to you, a young girl like you, this terrible murder plot . . . ?' I did not stop then to wonder what good *my* death could bring about to them.

No plot at first, of course. Vague hints, vague longings, all sorts of plots and plans . . . 'I was a fool,' said Lynn. 'But you didn't know Dorion, Laura—not as I did; as *we* all do. You can't know how she could bring one under her spell. I thought how wonderful it would be, to roam the world with Dorion, as she said, with our music, making great names for ourselves; and whatever my talents might be, Dorion's singing would have done that for us. Who outside Wales knows of a Welsh voice singing with only the harp to accompany it? We would dress in the old style with tall hats, striped petticoats, bright scarves . . . We had it all worked out, I believed in it all. But then . . .'

'But then,' said Aunt Hannah, 'the plotting began. And with the very first hint of it, Lynn told me everything. But then suddenly—something happened, some letter came from an impresario in Milan, everything must come to a head much sooner than they had planned. And so she wrote off to Lynn . . .' She shook her head. 'The recklessness of the girl!'

'She didn't understand,' I said. 'She didn't recognise—wickedness. She thought that what you wanted, you should simply take by whatever means. I suppose she could not understand that others might not feel the same.'

'Of course, that letter,' said Aunt Hannah, 'Lynn sent straight to me; warning me of the danger that threatened me, asking what she should do.'

The danger that threatened *her*—that threatened Aunt Hannah Morgan. I recalled again the letter, read with the help of the dictionary, in feverish haste lest Gereth come back and find me with it. The letter that had said: *The time has come for your wife to die.* But in Welsh the word for a wife is the same as the word merely for 'a woman'. *The time has come for her to die*—for Aunt Hannah to die. Dorion needed money for this ambition of hers so passionately desired; and what more simple than to propose that they murder a young girl's own mother and so set themselves free?

'Aunt Hannah sent the letter to me,' said Gereth, 'with a covering note. I got hold of Lynn and she translated the whole letter to me and we arranged to come down here and hold a family conference.'

'But why didn't you *tell* me—?'

'It was Lynn's secret, dearest, not mine. And perhaps I should ask you—why didn't you tell me that you had seen the letter?'

I explained rapidly the circumstances of my reading the letter. 'But as you say, it was—it was Lynn's secret. I'd found it out by mistake and I was so new in the family.' I improvised hastily: 'I didn't like to intrude, I thought it best just to pretend not to know.'

'I wouldn't have minded you knowing, Laura, not really,' said Lynn. 'Only—well, it would have been a rather strange introduction to your brand new in-laws. And—I'd behaved very stupidly, worse than stupidly, making all those secret plans with Dorion.' She said again, helplessly: 'You don't know what an effect Dorion could have on one. She was older than I; I thought she was so—magical.'

'I do understand that, Lynn. I know that myself—even I.'

'Of course,' she said, sad and ashamed. 'Dorion cared nothing for me really, she wasn't really my friend. She was older than I, and I was flattered; but it was only because she thought Mama was rich.' She added, still anxious to vindicate herself to me: 'And there was no danger to *you*, Laura; no *reason* to tell you.'

'Not until Dorion knew she'd seen the letter,' said Aunt Hannah. She shook her head. 'For Dorion, no one existed but Dorion. If Laura were a danger to her—then Laura must be disposed of. Only her plan went astray. She sent the boy with the message, saying that Brack had been seen near the gold mines. But the boy came too soon. We all rushed off, Lynn gave no thought to going to the "post office". But Gereth—waiting about for you—remembered what the first letter had said. He found the note in the wall; but once again it was in Welsh, he could not read what it said.'

'I got a word or two,' said Gereth. 'But I couldn't make out the gist of it—'

'And so of course he brought you down to the caves, Laura, as we'd left him to do; none of us ever dreaming of the danger, not connecting it at all with Dorion. For then we hadn't read the letter as we have now: the letter from the "post office" . . .'

They talked on; but I heard no more, listened no more—only, held fast in my husband's arms, gave myself up to happiness. Peace enfolded me: the terrible past already grew dim. At least, I thought, I did not fail him at the end; when danger of 'exposure' threatened him, I forgot my own danger If my trust faltered—at the end, after all, it stood firm. And no one need ever know what my fears had been.

A knock at the front door. 'I had best go,' said Aunt Hannah. In the hall, a man's voice said: 'Mrs Morgan—good evening. You sent for me?'

'Yes,' said Aunt Hannah. 'Come in, Owen.' He followed her in, a large, ponderous young policeman. 'You know my nephew, Gereth Morgan, of course. He has something to show you.'

He skimmed through the two letters, tchk-tchking. 'Dorion y Gwrach! Dorion the Witch! What wickedness, Mrs Morgan, in that heart of hers! And yet . . .' He stood looking down at his big, red hands.

'You too?' She leaned forward and gently touched the rough, serge sleeve. 'Well—you're spared a great deal, Owen, boy. You won't have to see her hunted and caught and locked up in a cage.' She looked away from him, staring directly ahead of her into nothingness. 'We were just sitting there, Lynn and I. She lay very still as though she were asleep. After a little while, she raised her head up from the pillow. She cried out, as though someone had called her: "I answer!" Then she lay back; and when I looked close at her again, she had gone. I couldn't even tell you what moment she died.'

'I could, Mrs Morgan,' said Owen. 'At just before ten, her pony passed the police station, galloping, riderless. A few minutes later, Sir Ivor rang up to ask if there'd been an accident. Broomstick has come back to his old home.'

And at just before ten, Bracken also had been set free and

had left Dorion's side and come quietly downstairs alone. La Belle Dame sans Merci had surrendered up her powers.

'Well—better be getting on with it.' Owen fished out his notebook. 'If you could tell me, Mrs Morgan, just what happened?'

Aunt Hannah sat looking into the fire for a moment and made no reply, and I saw again upon her face that look it had worn when she had come into the room and told them that Dorion was dead. Finally she said: 'Laura—give me the amulet.'

She held it tightly while she spoke. 'With this ring, Owen, Dorion's face was accidentally scratched. She believed, you know, that if her blood were shed, she would die. She became hysterical. I thought she should lie down and take some sedative draught. She had...' She paused infinitesimally and her knuckles were white with the unconscious strength of her clutch upon the amulet ring. 'She had in her possession two white tablets which looked like something of the sort; you know that her father had been skilled in such matters, I thought that she would be accustomed to use only such medicines as he would have compounded for her. So—I gave her those.' She lifted her head and for the first time since she had started her recital looked directly into hie face. 'I think you will agree—a very natural mistake.'

The dog got up and went over and sat by her, his head against her hand. Otherwise, nothing moved, nobody spoke. 'I see,' said Owen, heavily, at last. 'So, Mrs Morgan, it was by your hand that ...' He broke off, pondering it. He was very young, very anxious, and in his eyes lay still the memory of Dorion Rhos. 'So, Mrs Morgan, it was your hand that—set Dorion free.' He glanced down at the letters, still held clutched in his hand. 'You forget, no doubt, in the stress of the moment that two pills are mentioned here ... ?

'Yes, said Aunt Hannah. 'In the stress of the moment—I forgot.'

'That's right,' he said. 'You forgot. *I* understand that. But in case others may not—?' He met her eyes, questioning; and then quietly let the two letters drop into the heart of the fire. 'You mistook the two tablets for sedatives,' he said. 'Under the circumstances, everyone will agree—a very natural mistake.'

And he was gone: painfully climbing up the stairs to the room where she lay in all her wild, pale beauty, the white lids closed for ever upon the strange secrets of the smoky grey eyes. Dorion the Witch was dead; and in the room below, I stood safe in the radiance of hope and love again—and Aunt Hannah put out her hand and wordlessly gave me back the amulet.

CHRISTIANNA BRAND

Mary Christianna Milne was born on 17 December 1907 in Malaya where her father was working as a tea planter. She lost her mother at an early age and was brought by her father to England, where she was schooled at a convent in Berkshire. At the age of seventeen she was effectively abandoned by her father and drifted in and out of various jobs before meeting a young surgeon called Roland Lewis, whom she would go on to marry in 1936, somewhat to his amazement. One of her many jobs around this time was a spell selling kitchen appliances, which brought the future prize-winning crime writer into contact with a woman so loathsome that she was memorialized as the victim in *Death in High Heels* (1941). This was the first of many mystery novels published by Mary Lewis as 'Christianna Brand', a soubriquet that combined her grandmother's 'catch-penny' surname with the first name of her beloved mother.

Brand's second novel was written during the London Blitz and for this mystery, *Heads You Lose* (1941), Brand created Inspector Cockrill of the Kent police. 'Cockie' was based on her beloved father-in-law and the book sold well. Her third book, *Green for Danger* (1944), was an even greater success and was filmed with the great character actor Alastair Sim playing Cockrill. A further five novels appeared before, for family reasons, Brand abandoned detective fiction for twenty long years. But, a writer to her soul,

Brand did not abandon writing altogether, working on film scripts and producing more short stories and a series of novellas for women's magazines, as well as playing an active part in the Detection Club and the Crime Writers' Association. Between 1964 and 1974 she also a trio of children's books featuring the redoubtable Nurse Matilda, latterly known as Nanny McPhee in a pair of films written by and starring Dame Emma Thompson. She also published novels under several other pseudonyms. She made a welcome return to writing detective fiction in the late 1970s, but her health was poor and she died on 11 March 1988 while working on 'Death on the Day', a final case for her best-known detective, Inspector 'Cockie' Cockrill.

'The Witch' was first published in *Woman's Journal* in August 1962.

DEATH IN A DREAM

Laurence Meynell

I'm 45, thin and intelligent. I'm not a tragic loser in life, but I'm certainly not one of the big winners. I get by. I've never had much success with women. As a child I remember a period when I was intensely—precociously—interested in mathematics, especially in the particular time theory of the moment; but I've forgotten all about that now, and I doubt whether that can have much to do with it.

And during the war (still looking for a possible explanation of this thing I've got—would you call it a gift or a curse?) I was crossing the suspension bridge at Marlow just by *The Compleat Angler* while a German aeroplane, beaten off from London, was dropping its load nearby.

An A.A. battery opened up and I got hit on the head by a fragment of falling shell. The only real touch of warfare I ever saw. Quite enough for me, too. I was badly concussed and was unconscious for five days in Marlow hospital.

When they discharged me the surgeon asked: 'No ill effects? No dual visions? No dual thought?' He seemed quite interested in me: but at the time anxious, of course, to get rid of me and to get on with the next case.

I didn't have any of the things he was asking about—then; but I have since wondered if that wasn't the start of it in some way.

The first time it happened to me was in June of 1961.

I thought I was listening to the eight o'clock news (I have a radio by my bed) and the announcer was saying in the ordinary way 'The Derby was won this afternoon by Psidium'—and then the details about the prices, distances, owners and so on.

A few seconds later I was awake and realised (a) that I had been dreaming and (b) that the Derby wasn't due to be run until 3 o'clock that afternoon.

I have never bet on a horse in my life (I don't know how to), but I looked at the runners in the paper, and saw that a horse called Psidium was among them and told the hall porter at my club that it would win.

It did.

The next occasion when the wheel of time slipped a cog for me was six months later. I don't want to use the word 'dream'. (What are dreams anyway?) Let's say that while I was what we agree to call 'asleep' I saw an air crash. A horrible business. Twisted red hot metal in a forest on a hillside. The trees crackling in the flames, passengers screaming with fear and agony and among them the face, momentarily but unmistakably glimpsed, of a woman I knew.

I was shaken.

After two hours debate with myself I rang her up.

'Funny you should ring me,' she said. 'I was just going to ring you, to say goodbye.'

'You're off somewhere?'

'Tom sent me a cable four days ago to go out and join him. I've been running round like a scalded cat. It's all been hectic and marvellous. I'm flying tomorrow.'

All right, you tell me what I should have done. I did nothing and the news of the crash was headline stuff. No survivors.

I was finding out that seeing round the corner can be uncomfortable. And my third experience has made me very conscious of the fact.

I'm not telling you what my job is; you might possibly work out who I am; but I will tell you one of my hobbies—music. Not playing, but the history of it. Out of the way and rather recondite stuff. I've reached the stage when I am called an 'expert' on it. Which means that all sorts of societies that want something on the cheap get me to lecture to them occasionally.

Three months ago I went on this sort of job.

I was invited to give a talk. Medieval church music. A bit highbrow, but that's how they like it at these festivals.

They were doing me proud. I was to stay at —— Hall, the seat of Sir X and Lady Y (wild horses won't drag any closer description from me!). So I packed a dinner jacket and set off.

At —— station, and I didn't know that such toylike places still existed, I was met as promised. But not by my host or hostess. The housekeeper Mrs Bedford, an intelligent and obviously extremely capable woman, was there with the station wagon.

Every sort of apology: Sir X and Lady X were in Verona; they should have been back that very day, but the flight was delayed by bad weather and now they couldn't make it till tea-time on the morrow.

Meanwhile I was to make myself entirely at home and Mrs Bedford would look after me.

After dinner I watched a play on TV, had a final nightcap, told myself that I would rub up my lecture notes next day, and went to bed.

I say that at two o'clock or thereabouts I woke up in a sweat and saw something happening in the room; you say that I was dreaming.

O.K., then I was dreaming. And what I dreamed was this:

I was looking at the room, at the very bed in which I was lying, but I wasn't lying in it any more: a middle-aged woman was.

She was obviously ill. The room was a sick room. Bottles—

medicines and tablets—by the bed and all the usual paraphernalia of illness about. I could feel the hot sweat pouring out of her forehead. I knew how desperately hard it was for her to get each breath. She was on the slope of living and might, or might not, come up to the top of it again.

Within seconds as I watched, horrified yet fascinated, it was decided for her.

The door opened and a nurse came in. Young, hard-looking in a way, yet attractive; very definitely attractive.

She picked up a pillow, forced it down over the head of the woman who was already fighting for every breath and held it there with all her might.

I screamed, but it was a dream scream; nobody heard it.

The good-looking young nurse held the pillow down grimly. She had a job because when people fight for life they fight hard. But she was young and fit, the woman in the bed (my bed) was middle-aged and already ill.

Presently the nurse threw the pillow away and looked closely down at her victim.

She was satisfied. She smiled.

I had seen murder done; but had it been committed or was it going to be committed? Which way had the cogs of time's wheel slipped for me—backwards or forwards?

My host and hostess arrived, full of apologies and amiability, during the morning. I was on the terrace to meet them. Sir X, a distinguished 65; his wife, 30 years younger I would say.

No stranger to me, of course. I had seen her in my dream. The nurse. No possible doubt of it. I knew her instantly. She was the murderess. She smiled at me delightfully. I think she was pleased to have another man in the house. A man 20 years younger than her husband.

Afterwards at the wine and cheese party (which is how these festivals are run) a woman who had enjoyed my talk told me about Sir X and his lady.

She was his second wife; the first had died three years ago and after rather a short interval Sir X had married the nurse. Romantic, wasn't it? she said.

So I came back rather more thoughtful than I had gone there. I have been sitting in my study thinking it all out; in fact, I have only just put down the telephone. Lady Y rang me up from a London hotel.

She is up in town on her own for a few days shopping and would so like to renew our too brief acquaintance. Is there any chance of our meeting?

Life can be complicated, can't it? Like I said earlier on. All right, you tell me what to do.

LAURENCE MEYNELL

Laurence Walter Meynell was born on 9 August 1899 at Eagle House in Eagle Street, Penn Fields, Wolverhampton. He was the youngest child of Agnes and Herbert Meynell, chairman of a local brass-foundry and, at the age of nine, he was sent away to St Edmund's, the oldest Catholic school in England, at which his brothers also boarded. Meynell was a keen sportsman and he was made the school's captain of cricket in 1917; in later years he would turn out for the Author's Club in their annual match against a publishers' eleven. In 1917, he enlisted and served in the Honourable Artillery Company, serving first in the reserve battery and later at the cadet school of the Royal Field Artillery.

After the Armistice, Meynell worked in advertising and as an estate agent, an experience he drew on for the smuggling mystery *Watch the Wall* (1934). He also taught at St Edmunds for six months between 1919 and 1920, where his roles included commanding the cadet corps. While teaching, Meynell became great friends with one of the visiting lecturers, Monsignor Ronald Knox, well-known to crime fiction fans for his Decalogue of rules for detective stories and as a commentator on Sherlock Holmes and the author of a few—too few—detective stories of his own. Meynell and Ronnie Knox shared a love of canoeing and long hikes, which they would meet up to undertake in later years. Encouraged by Knox, Meynell decided to enter a competition to find the best first novel, run by

George E. Harrap & Co. Selected as one of six on a shortlist put to a public vote, *Mockbeggar* (1924) concerns the loves and lives of a tiresomely witty 'insufferable but desirable' young Mayfair couple, Rachel Massinger and her husband Chickie whose life ends in tragedy. While his novel was not placed first, Meynell had found his vocation. *Lois* (1927) also deals with bright young things but is more bitingly satirical in tone. The central characters are super-ficial and rich, utterly oblivious to the kinds of pressures that had led in real life to the General Strike of 1926, and like the Bourbons and the Romanovs they end up on the wrong side of history.

To supplement his income while working on a novel, Meynell wrote short stories and he also wrote what would appear to be his only poetic work, *The Ballad of Penn Fields with a Plan of the Battlefield* (1927). His third novel, the horribly dated *Death's Eye* (1929), has a similar plot to *Lois* but the cast is divided on racial lines rather than socioeconomic ones. The novel ends not in revo-lution but in triumph for the British Secret Service, which would feature in several of his later books including *Bluefeather* (1928) and its sequel *Odds on Bluefeather* (1934).

In 1932 Meynell married Shirley Darbyshire, an Australian journalist and food-writer, who preferred to be known as Ruth. Initially the couple lived in London where they hosted networking evenings for young writers, and in 1934 they made a grand tour of Australia which provided him with ideas—and characters—for several books. On their return, they left the capital, which Meynell hated, for Buckinghamshire. Between 1941 and 1945, he served with the Royal Air Force Volunteer Reserve. After a spell at the rank of Flying Officer, dealing largely with administration, he was promoted to Squadron Leader and served as adjutant at three Bomber Command stations, for which he was mentioned in despatches in 1944.

In the early 1950s, the Meynells bought the former parsonage at Coleshill, Waller's Oak, and they both settled down to writing, Ruth having written her first novel shortly before her marriage.

With *Danger Round the Corner* (1952), Meynell created the character for which he is best known, the ageless private investigator Hooky Hefferman, who appears in 20 novel-length detective stories, the last being *Hooky Hooked* (1988), published just a year before Meynell's death. The Hefferman mysteries are a delightful blend of Wodehousian romance and light-hearted investigations, similar in some ways to the *Lovejoy* novels of Jonathan Gash.

By 1953, the couple were estranged and Meynell was living in London. After Ruth's death in 1955, he married Joan Henley, an actress and BBC presenter. It seems likely that they met through the BBC as Meynell had written—and read on air—several short stories in the 1930s, and in the late 1940s he had hosted a regular radio review of new films. After their marriage, the couple moved to Buckinghamshire, living initially at Folly Meadow in Penn, formerly the home of one of Queen Victoria's goddaughters. While continuing to write, he worked as literary editor of *Time and Tide* magazine from 1958 to 1960, and he was active in literary circles. He chaired the Authors Club and in 1954 served as President of the Johnson Society, a body set up to promote the life and legacy of Samuel Johnson, Meynell's great literary hero about whom he wrote an excellent profile, 'The Lonely Giant', for *The Listener* in 1946. In the 1960s, Meynell and Joan moved to High Firs in Hyde End, Great Missenden, and later they made their final move to the Sussex coast.

Over 60 years, Meynell wrote more than 150 books. As well as crime fiction under his own name, his output includes ten non-genre novels as 'Robert Eton' and *Inside Out! Or Mad as a Hatter* (1934) and *Women Had to Do It!* (1936), comedies written as 'Geoffrey Ludlow'. There are also biographies, for example of the cricketer *Plum Warner* (1951) and several *Great Men of Staffordshire* (1955) as well as the fictional *Bessie Scudd* (1968), 'the impregnable virgin'. His non-fiction includes a popular profile of the county of *Bedfordshire* (1950), *Famous Cricket Grounds* (1951) and numerous factional 'career stories' such as *Animal Doctor* (1956), *Jane: Young*

Author (1954) and *Shirley: Young Bookseller* (1956), the latter two being among four written as 'Valerie Baxter'. He also wrote fiction for younger readers, including historical thrillers and two series about adventurous children; these appeared as by 'A. Stephen Tring', a pseudonym chosen because Meynell happened to be toying with a length of string while trying to think of one.

Laurence Meynell died at Hove on 18 April 1989.

'Death in a Dream' was published in the *Liverpool Echo* on 29 November 1963.

THE HAUNTED GRANGE OF GORESTHORPE

Arthur Conan Doyle

Looking back now at the events of my life that one dreadful night looms out like some great landmark. Even now, after the lapse of so many years, I cannot think of it without a shudder. All minor incidents and events I mentally classify as occurring before or after the time when I saw a Ghost.

Yes, saw a ghost. Don't be incredulous, reader, don't sneer at the phrase; though I can't blame you for I was incredulous enough myself once. However, hear the facts of my story before you pass a judgment.

The old Grange used to stand on my estate of Goresthorpe in Norfolk. It has been pulled down now, but it stood there when Tom Hulton came to visit me in 184-. It was a tumble-down old pile at the meeting of the Morsely and Alton roads where the new turnpike stands now. The garden round had long been choked up by a rank growth of weeds, while pools of stagnant water and the accumulated garbage of the whole village poisoned the air around. It was a dreary place by day and an eerie one by night, for strange stories were told of the Grange, sounds were said to have come from those weather-beaten walls, such as mortal lips never uttered, and the elders of the village still spoke of one, Job Garston by name, who thirty years before had had the temerity to sleep inside, and who had been led out in the morning, a whitehaired broken man.

I used, I remember, to ascribe all this to the influence of the weird gaunt old building upon their untutored minds, and moralized upon the effects of a liberal education in removing such mental weaknesses. I alone knew however that the Grange had certainly, as far as foul crime was concerned, as orthodox a title to be haunted as any building on record. The last tenant as I discovered from my family papers was a certain Godfrey Marsden, a villain of the first water. He lived there about the middle of last century and was a byword of ferocity and brutality throughout the whole countryside. Finally, he consummated his many crimes by horribly hacking his two young children to death and strangling their mother. In the confusion of the Pretender's march into England, justice was laxly administered, and Marsden succeeded in escaping to the continent where all trace of him was lost. There was a rumour indeed among his creditors, the only ones who regretted him, that remorse had led him to commit suicide, and that his body had been washed up on the French Coast, but those who knew him best laughed at the idea of anything so intangible having an effect upon so hardened a ruffian. Since his day the Grange had been untenanted and had been suffered to fall into the state of disrepair in which it then was.

Tom Hulton was an old college chum of mine, and right glad I was to see his honest face beneath my roof. He brightened the whole house, Tom did, for a more good-humoured hearty reckless fellow never breathed. His only fault was that he had acquired a strange speculative way of thinking from his German education, and this led to continual arguments between us, for I had been trained as a medical student and looked at things therefore from an eminently practical point of view. That evening, I remember, the first after his arrival, we glided from one argument into another but all with the greatest good humour and invariably without coming to any conclusion.

I forget how the question of ghosts arose; at any rate there we were, Tom Hulton and I, at midnight in the depths of a debate about spirits and spiritualism. Tom, when he argued was wont to produce a certain large briar root pipe of his, and by this time he was surrounded by a dense wreath of smoke, from the midst of which his voice issued like the oracle of Delphi, while his stalwart figure loomed through the haze.

'I tell you, Jack,' he was saying, 'that mankind may be divided into two classes, the men who profess not to believe in Ghosts and are mortally afraid of them, and the men who admit at least the possibility of their existence and would go out of their way to see one. Now I don't scruple to acknowledge that I am one of the latter school. Of course, Jack, I know that you are one of these *credo-quod-tango* medicals, who walk in the narrow path of certain fact, and quite right too in such a profession as yours; but I have always had a strange leaning towards the unseen and supernatural, especially in this matter of the existence of ghosts. Don't think though that I am such a fool as to believe in the orthodox spectre with his curse, and his chain warranted to rattle, and his shady retreat down some back stairs, or in the cellar; no, nothing of that sort.'

'Well, Tom, let's hear your idea of a creditable ghost.'

'It's not such an easy matter, you see, to explain it to another, even though I can define it in my own mind well enough. You and I both hold, Jack, that when a man dies he has done with all the cares and troubles of this world, and is for the future, be it one of joy or sorrow, a pure and ethereal spirit. Well now, what I feel is that it is possible for a man to be hurried out of this world with a soul as impregnated with some one all-absorbing passion, that it clings to him even after he has passed the portals of the grave. Now,' continued Tom, impressively waving his pipe from side to side through the cloud that surrounded him, 'love or patriotism or some other pure and elevating passion, might well be entertained by one who is but a spirit, but it is different, I fancy, with such grosser feelings as hatred or revenge. These one could imagine, even after death, clogging the poor soul so that it must still inhabit that coarse clay which is most fitted to the coarse passions which absorb it; and thus I would account for the unexplained and unexplainable things which have happened even in our own time, and for the deeply rooted belief in ghosts which exists, smother it as we may, in every breast, and which has existed in every age.'

'You may be right, Tom,' said I, 'but, as you say, *quod tango credo*, and as I never saw any of your "impregnated spirits" I must beg leave to doubt their existence.'

'It's very easy to laugh at the matter,' answered Tom, 'but there are few facts in this world which have not been laughed at, sometime or another. Tell me this, Jack, did you ever try to see a ghost? Did you ever go upon a ghost hunt, my boy?'

'Well, I can't say I ever did,' said I, 'did you?'

'I'm on one just now, Jack,' said he, and then sat puffing at his pipe for some time. 'Look here,' he continued, 'I've heard you talk of some old manor or Grange you have down here, which is said to be haunted. Now I want you to lend me the key of that, and I'll take up my quarters there tomorrow night. How long is it since anyone slept in it, Jack?'

'For heaven's sake, don't think of doing such a foolhardy thing,' I exclaimed. 'Why only one man has slept in Goresthorpe Grange during a hundred years, and he went mad to my certain knowledge!'

'Ha! that sounds promising, very promising,' cried Tom in high delight. 'Now just observe the thick headedness of the British public, yourself included, Jack. You won't believe in ghosts, and you won't go and look where a ghost is said to be found. Now suppose there was said to be white crows or some other natural curiosity in Yorkshire, and someone assured you that there was not, because he had been all through Wales without seeing one, you would naturally consider the man an idiot. Well, doesn't the same apply to you if you refuse to go to the Grange and settle the question for yourself once for all?'

'If you go tomorrow, I shall certainly go too,' I returned, 'if only to prevent your coming home with some cock and bull story about an impregnated spirit, so good night, Tom,' and with that we separated.

I confess that in the morning I began to feel that I had been slightly imprudent in aiding and abetting Tom in his ridiculous expedition. 'It's that confounded Irish whisky,' thought I. 'I always put my foot into it after the third glass, however perhaps Tom has thought better of it too by this time.' In that expectation however I was woefully disappointed, for Tom swore he had been awake all night, planning and preparing everything for the evening.

'We're bound to take pistols you know, old boy; those are always taken; then there are our pipes and a couple of ounces of bird's-eye, and our rugs, and a bottle of whisky, nothing else, I think. By Jove, I do believe we'll unearth a ghost tonight!'

'Heaven forbid!' I mentally ejaculated but as there was no way out of it I pretended to be as enthusiastic in the business as Tom himself.

All day Tom was in a state of the wildest excitement, and as evening fell we both walked over to the old Grange of Goresthorpe. There it stood cold, bleak and desolate as ever with the wind howling past it. Great strips of ivy which had lost their hold upon the walls swayed and tossed in the wind like the plumes of a hearse. How comfortable the lights in the village seemed to my eyes as we turned the key in the rusty lock, and having lit a candle began to walk down the stone-flagged dusty hall!

'Here we are!' said Tom, throwing a door open and disclosing a large dingy room.

'Not there for Goodness' sake,' said I, 'let's find a small room where we can light a fire and be sure at a glance that we are the only people in it.'

'All right, old fellow,' answered Tom laughing. 'I did a little exploring today on my own hook and know the place pretty well. I've got just the article to suit you at the other end of the house.'

He took up the candle again as he spoke, and having shut the door he led me from one passage to another through the rambling old building. We came at last to a long corridor running the whole length of one wing of the house, which certainly had a very ghostly appearance. One wall was entirely solid, while the other had openings for windows let in at every three or four paces, so that when the moon shone in the dark passage was flecked every here and there with patches of white light. Near the end of it was a door which led into a small room, cleaner and more modern looking than the rest of the house, and with a large fireplace opposite the entrance. It was hung with dark red curtains, and when we had got our fire ablaze it certainly looked more comfortable than I had ever dared to expect. Tom seemed unutterably disgusted and discontented by the result; 'Call this a haunted house,' he said, 'why we might as well sit up in a hotel and expect to see a ghost! This isn't by any means the sort of thing I have been looking forward to.' It was not until the briar had been twice replenished that he began to recover his usual equanimity of temper.

Perhaps it was our curious surroundings which flavoured the bird's-eye and mellowed the whisky, and our own suppressed excitement which gave zest to the conversation. Certainly a pleasanter evening neither of us ever spent.

Outside the wind was howling and screaming, tossing the trailing ivy in the air. The moon shone out fitfully from between the dark clouds which drifted across the sky, and the measured patter of the rain was heard upon the slates above us.

'The roof may leak, but it can't get at us,' said Tom, 'for there's a little bedroom above our heads with a very good floor too. Shouldn't be surprised if it's the very room where those youngsters were cut up by that model father of theirs. Well, it's nearly twelve o'clock, and if we are going to see anything at all, we ought to see it before very long. By Jove, what a chill wind comes through that door! I remember feeling like this when I was waiting outside before going in for my oral exam at college. You look excited too, old boy.'

'Hush, Tom, didn't you hear a noise in the corridor?'

'Hang the noise,' said Tom, 'pass me the bottle, old boy.'

'I'll swear I heard a heavy door slamming,' I insisted. 'I'll tell you what, Tom, I feel as if your ambition was going to be realized tonight and I'm not ashamed to say that I'm heartily sorry I came with you on such a foolhardy errand.'

'Dash it all,' said Tom, 'it's no use funking it now — By Jove, what's that?'

It was a gentle pit pat pit pat in the room and close to Tom's elbow. We both sprang to our feet, and then Tom burst into a roar of laughter. 'Why, Jack,' he said, 'you're making a regular old woman of me; it's only the rain that has got in after all and is dropping on that bit of loose paper on the wall yonder. What fools we were to be frightened! Why here's the very place it dropped-'

'Good God!' I cried, 'what is the matter with you, Tom?' His face had changed to a livid hue, his eyes were fixed and staring, and his lips parted in horror and astonishment.

'Look!' he almost screamed, 'look!' and he held up the piece of paper which had been hanging from the mildewed wall. Great heaven! it was all freckled and spotted with gouts of still liquid blood. Even as we stood gazing at it, another drop fell upon the floor with a dull splash. Both our pale faces were turned upwards tracing the course of this horrible shower. We could discern a small crack in the cornice, and through this as through

a wound in human flesh the blood seemed to well. Another
drop fell, and yet another, as we stood gazing spellbound.

'Come away, Tom, come away!' I cried at last, unable to bear
it longer. 'Come! God's curse is on the place.' I seized him by
the shoulder as I spoke and turned towards the door.

'By God, I won't,' cried Tom fiercely, shaking off my grasp,
'come up with me, Jack, and get to the bottom of the matter.
There may be some villainy here. Hang it, man, don't be cowed
by a drop or two of blood! Don't try to stop me! I shall go'; and
he pushed past me and dashed into the corridor.

What a moment that was! If I should live to be a hundred I
could never shake off my vivid remembrance of it. Outside the
wind was still howling past the windows, while an occasional
flash of lightning illuminated the old Grange. Within there was
no sound save the creaking of the door as it was thrown back
and the gentle pit pat of that ghastly shower from above. Then
Tom tottered back into the room and grasped me by the arm.
'Let us stick together, Jack,' he said in an awestruck whisper.
'There's something coming up the corridor!'

A horrible fascination led us to the door, and we peered
together down the long and dark passage. One side was, as I
have said, pierced by numerous openings through which the
moonlight streamed throwing little patches of light upon the
dark floor. Far down the passage we could see that something
was obscuring first one of these bright spots, then the next, then
another. It vanished in the gloom, then it reappeared where the
next window cast its light, then it vanished again. It was coming
rapidly towards us. Now it was only four windows from us, now
three, now two, one, and then the figure of a man emerged into
the glare of light which burst from our open door. He was
running rapidly and vanished into the gloom on the other side
of us. His dress was old fashioned and dishevelled, what seemed
to be long dark ribbons hung down among his hair, on each
side of his swarthy face. But that face itself — when shall I ever

forget it? As he ran he kept it half turned back, as if expecting some pursuer, and his countenance expressed such a degree of hopeless despair, and of dreadful fear, that, frightened as I was, my heart bled for him. As we followed the direction of his horror stricken gaze we saw that he had indeed a pursuer. As before we could trace the dark shadow flitting over the white flecks of moonlight, as before it emerged into the circle of light thrown by our candles and fire. It was a beautiful and stately lady, a woman perhaps eight and twenty years of age, with the low dress and gorgeous train of last century. Beneath her lovely chin we both remarked upon one side of the neck four small dark spots, and on the other side one larger one. She swept by us, looking neither to the right nor left, but with her stony gaze bent upon the spot where the fugitive had vanished. Then she too was lost in the darkness. A minute later as we stood there, still gazing, a horrible shriek, a scream of awful agony, rang out high above the wind and the thunder, and then all was still inside the house.

I don't know how long we both stood there, spellbound, holding on to each other's arms. It must have been some time for the fresh candle was flickering in the socket when Tom, with a shudder, walked rapidly down the passage, still grasping my hand. Without a word we passed out through the mouldering hall door, out into the storm and the rain, over the garden wall, through the silent village and up the avenue. It was not until we were in my comfortable little smoking room, and Tom from sheer force of habit had lit a cigar, that he seemed to recover his equanimity at all.

'Well, Jack,' were the first words he said, 'what do you think of ghosts now?' His next remark was 'Confound it, I've lost the best briar root pipe I ever had, for I'll be hanged before I go back there to fetch it.'

'We have seen a horrible sight,' said I. 'What a face he had, Tom! And those ghastly ribbons hanging from his hair, what were those, Tom?'

'Ribbons! Why, Jack, don't you know seaweed when you see it? And I've seen those dark marks that were on the woman's neck before now, and so have you in your medical studies I have little doubt.'

'Yes,' said I, 'those were the marks of four fingers and a thumb. It was the strangled woman, Tom. God preserve us from ever seeing such a sight again!'

'Amen,' said Tom, and those were the last words we interchanged that night.

In the morning Tom, his mission ended, went down to London, and soon afterwards set sail for the coffee estates of his father in Ceylon. Since then I have lost sight of him. I do not know whether he is alive or dead, but of one thing I am very sure, that if alive he never thinks without a shudder of our terrible night in the haunted Grange of Goresthorpe.

ARTHUR CONAN DOYLE

Arthur Conan Doyle, the most influential figure in the history of crime and mystery literature, was born in Edinburgh, Scotland, on 22 May 1859. His parents were Mary Josephine Foley and Charles Altamont Doyle, an artist and illustrator. From the age of eleven, Doyle studied at a Catholic school, Stonyhurst College, where as well as playing a full part in school sports he founded, edited and largely authored a single issue of a magazine, *The Stonyhurst Figaro*. Doyle also studied at Stella Matutina, a Jesuit school in Austria. However, rather than inspire him, these religious educational establishments convinced him to become an agnostic. At Edinburgh University, he underwent five years of 'drudgery' as he studied for his intended future profession as a doctor, and he would later immortalise two of his tutors, Professor William Rutherford and Doctor Joseph Bell, as the rumbustious explorer George Challenger and Sherlock Holmes respectively.

While studying, Doyle wrote fiction and his first short story, 'The Mystery of Sasassa Valley', was published in *Chamber's Journal* in September 1879. A few months before his 21st birthday he took up a position as doctor on the *Hope*, a whaling ship, but this gave him little opportunity to hone his developing skills as a physician. On returning to Edinburgh he completed his degree and in 1881 enlisted for a four-month tour of duty as a surgeon on the *SS Mayumba*, a passenger ship sailing between England and the West

Coast of Africa. Doyle next moved to Southsea where he established himself as a general practitioner while playing a full part in the social and sporting life of the town. He was a keen footballer and a strong cricketer, although he was once bowled out for 15 by the great W. G. Grace. He was also a founder member of the Portsmouth Literary and Scientific Society; at its first meeting in November 1883, Major-General George Evatt lectured on his life as an army doctor in the second Anglo-Afghan war, which would later inspire the creation of Dr John Watson. At the Society's second meeting, Doyle spoke on 'The Arctic Seas' and at a later meeting on the life and work of Thomas Carlyle.

In 1885, Doyle married Louisa Hawkins, a widow whose brother was one of his patients. He and Louisa, whom he called 'Touie', had two children: a daughter Mary and a son known by his middle name, Kingsley. Doyle also continued to write. In the late 1880s, one of his near neighbours in Shaftesbury Road, Southsea, was a Mrs Sherlock of Holm Leigh, and she may have provided part of the inspiration for the name of Sherlock Holmes, whose first 'adventure', *A Study in Scarlet*, would be published in *Beeton's Annual* in November 1887. This was followed by *Micah Clarke* (1889), *The Sign of Four* (1890) and *The White Company* (1891); and he also secured publication of an earlier manuscript, *The Firm of Girdlestone* (1890).

Increasingly specialising in the eye, Doyle undertook further studies in Vienna in 1891 and on his return he and Touie moved to London where they eventually settled at 12 Tennison Road, Upper Norwood. He took rooms in Wimpole Street as an oculist, dealing with patients in the morning and working at a hospital in the afternoon, leaving only part of the evening for writing. Eventually something had to give and in 1892 Doyle resolved 'to throw physic to the dogs' and become a professional writer, juggling the commercially advantageous adventures of Sherlock Holmes with historical novels, writing at a mahogany desk surrounded by his father's drawings and souvenirs of his own youthful adventures, including a bear's skull and a seal's paw brought back from the Arctic. His work appeared in countless newspapers and magazines—from *London Society* to *The Boy's Own Paper*. He also supported novel literary endeavours: together with Bram Stoker, Grant Allen and others, he co-authored a round-robin novel, *The Fate of Fenella* (1891) and in 1892 his story 'The Major's Card' was published in the first issue of *Sword and Chatelaine*, a new but short-lived Southsea literary magazine for the forces.

In 1893, Doyle decided to kill off Sherlock Holmes after 23 successful short stories, in 'The Adventure of the Final Problem', a case set in Switzerland which the author Silas Hocking had identified as the ideal resting place for the detective. In the same year, Touie was diagnosed with tuberculosis and Doyle decided that the family should move away from London and settle in Hindhead, Surrey. While Touie recuperated in Switzerland, he oversaw the building of their new home, 'Undershaw', completed in the late autumn of 1897. While Doyle had killed off his creation, Holmes was uneasy in his grave. Pressured by his publisher and mindful of the financial benefits, Doyle produced *The Hound of the Baskervilles* (1901), before reviving him properly in 'The Adventure of the Empty House'. Much as he regretted the fact, Holmes is unquestionably Doyle's greatest achievement. Excluding ephemera, the character appears in 58 short stories, four novels and one stage play by Doyle, but his fame can be measured in the innumerable pastiche adventures authored by hundreds of writers including Agatha Christie, J. M. Barrie, P. G. Wodehouse and even John Lennon.

As well as writing fiction, Doyle served briefly as a war correspondent and as a doctor in the Second Boer War which he chronicled. He also became interested in politics and over 20 years campaigned on many issues. He was in favour of a Channel tunnel but against free trade and uncontrolled immigration. He also joined the Liberal Unionist Party and stood for Parliament, losing to a Liberal Party candidate for the seat of Edinburgh Central in 1900 and again in 1906 at Hawick Burghs. In 1902 Doyle was knighted by King Edward VII, an honour declined by Sherlock Holmes in a later story.

After Touie's death in 1906, Doyle married Jean Leckie, with whom he had maintained a platonic relationship since their first meeting in 1897. They had three children together, their second son Adrian later collaborating with his father's biographer, John Dickson Carr, to produce *The Exploits of Sherlock Holmes* (1954). Over the next ten years he also published two of his most popular books: *The Lost World* (1912), forerunner of Michael Crichton's *Jurassic Park*, and *The Valley of Fear* (1914), the last of Sherlock Holmes' four novel-length adventures.

After the death of his first son in the 'flu pandemic of 1918, and the death of his mother two years later, Doyle began to display signs of the mental health issues that had affected his father and other members of his family. He published outlandish theories on the existence of fairies and made extravagant claims about spiritualism. But he also published his autobiography, *Memories and Adventures* (1924) and in March 1927 'The Adventure of Shoscombe Old Place', Sherlock Holmes's final 'final problem'.

Prodigiously active to the end, Arthur Conan Doyle suffered a heart attack and died at home on 7 July 1930.

Unpublished in the author's lifetime and very likely his first short story, 'The Haunted Grange of Goresthorpe' was first published in 2000 by Ash Tree Press in a limited edition of 500 copies.

MISLEADING LADY

Margery Allingham

'Lucille, you look beautiful.'

I'm afraid I may have sounded envious. In the days when Lucille and I shared a little bachelor-girl flat in Russell Square and we were both very glad of any small parts the London managers had to offer us, mink coats and thirty-guinea hats had not come our way. They hadn't come mine yet, but I am still Miss Genevieve Rupert, 'aunt to the heroine', or 'loquacious lady from next door', or sometimes, when I am very lucky, 'the heroine's friend'; but for Lucille, who is Mrs Raymond Asche, wife of the one and only Raymond, hero of two continents of film fans, the 'man with the smile you can't forget', thirty-guinea hats were just all right for shopping in and visiting one's poorer friends.

Yet she did not look particularly happy, I was astonished to see. She stood hesitating on the doorstep of our old flat looking like a shadow of her former self, a pathetic little shadow all wrapped up in money.

She is very pretty, and, even then, with her wide eyes dark and worried and her little mouth pursed, she looked charming. She is very small, with a divine figure and genuine ash-blonde hair, the sort they haven't learnt how to make yet. It curls round her face in tight little rings, which are merely arranged by the greatest coiffeuse on earth, not made by her.

'Oh, let me come in and sit down,' she said, and, hurrying into our old room, she pulled off the hat and hurled it sinfully into a corner and slipped out of the coat, allowing its silky folds to drop on to my dusty old carpet. I picked it up and, because I know her very well, told her what I thought of her. She grimaced at me.

'I wish I was back,' she said. 'I wish I hadn't married. I wish I was playing the ingenue to that beastly little cat—' Here she mentioned the name of a very famous actress. 'I wish I was dead.'

'You'd look very sweet anywhere, dear—even in your coffin,' I said cheerfully, eyeing her exquisitely tailored little frock with the big revers and the silly sleeves that were so cunning you couldn't take your eyes off them. 'What's the matter? One of the great man's fans getting difficult?'

'Oh, no!' she said, eyeing me seriously. 'It's nothing like that. He's still crazy about me and I adore him, Jeannie, really I do. He's just like he is on the films.'

I began to laugh, but I stopped when tears came into her eyes.

'I'm sorry,' I said. 'I know what you mean. What's the excitement?'

'I'm jealous.'

'Jealous?' I pricked up my ears. I'd always thought that by marrying the dream hero of some forty million earnest females Lucille was taking on a bit of a proposition. Still, she had said that none of his fans was difficult, and my suspicious mind leapt involuntarily to the thought of the exotic Irma Patchouka— Gladys May she was when I knew her—the co-star of his last film.

'If that woman—' I began.

'Oh, it's not that,' she said. 'It's him. I'm jealous of *him*. There's the house, too. It's haunted. It's a prison. It's haunted by the spirit of imprisonment.'

Then she began to cry.

'Look here,' I said, 'you want a psycho-analyst, or a fortune-teller might do. I might even put on a red wig and tell you one or two things myself. If you're yearning for the "bright lights" and the "romance of the stage", and all the other guff, then you're off your head. Do you remember what it was like, saving up to buy the odd pair of stockings, trudging home when the last bus had gone? Don't be silly.'

'It's not that.' She interrupted me with one of those pretty little gestures which might have made her famous had she had a strong enough personality to get across the footlights. 'It's something quite different. I want you to come down and see the new house. We're having a party there over Christmas. We've only just bought it, you know, and it's beautiful—it really is—and wonderful for Ray's publicity. His American people are simply hysterical over the photographs we've sent them. But it's haunted, and not by any usual sort of ghost. I noticed it as soon as we looked over the place, and I thought, like a fool, that I should be too strong for it. But I'm not. It's crushing me. Oh, what shall I do, what shall I do?'

She was in such a state and so genuinely upset that I began to take her seriously. I made her a cup of tea. I wouldn't let her talk until she had drunk it, and then I sat down on the hearthrug and looked up at her where she lay curled up on the sofa. I had got it in my head by that time that she was suffering from some sort of nervous fixation—they say rich women often get them—although I did think that, considering she'd only been married a year, Lucille was taking to the habit rather soon.

I decided to treat her very gently. You can't share the same flat with a girl for four or five years without getting fond of her in a sisterly sort of way, and I had always had a soft spot in my heart for Lucille.

'Atmosphere of the place oppressive?' I inquired.

'Oh, no, it's more than that,' she said. 'There's something there, something quite real. It doesn't howl about the place, but it opens doors and rustles curtains and that sort of thing.'

I felt my eyebrows rising into my hair. The poor old thing had got it badly. But I let her talk, and she seemed very grateful to do so, which made her look rather queer, curled up there in my shabby room, her beautiful clothes strewn about her.

'Ray and I are desperately fond of one another,' she went on unexpectedly. 'I know it sounds silly to say so, but it's one of those absurd idyllic marriages. I really do trust him, and although I know what he's going to say next he doesn't bore me. That's why I'm so frightened of this—this thing.'

'I haven't got the hang of it yet,' I said.

'I'll try to explain,' said Lucille. 'The house we bought used to belong to a sort of local tyrant. He was a very important man in the district, squire of the village, M.P., public bigwig, and so on. He went there when he was very young and didn't die till a year or two ago, when he was about a hundred. He adored the place, and it sort of soaked up his personality. That wouldn't matter so much, but he was a beast. He was very important, you see, locally—quite a little tin god, in fact—and about sixty years ago he married a very beautiful girl. They lived together for thirty years, and then she died. This part is really beside the point, but as soon as I heard the local stories I began to understand what it was that so terrified me about the place.'

'What did he do—beat her?' I inquired.

Lucille looked at me with round eyes.

'No. Worse than that; he imprisoned her. He turned her into a slave. He absorbed her personality. She never went out anywhere, she didn't have any friends round about. *He* was the big noise. People came to see *him*.'

She paused for breath, and I could see that the stories, whatever they were, had got on her nerves.

'When she wanted a new dress he used to buy her one in town and bring it down. They had no children, and she had nothing to do except potter about the place and wait for him to come home in the evenings. Now do you see what I mean?'

'No,' I said. I did not mean to be particularly dense, but there didn't seem to me to be anything in the story to get unduly excited about.

Lucille closed her eyes.

'He was a tyrant,' she said, 'and his personality is still there. And the awful thing is that it's beginning to affect us. Don't you see, Jeannie, I'm beginning to lead the same life. Ray is the big noise. People come to see Ray. I can go out if I want to, but Ray's been different lately. He seems to like to see me about the house. Suggested I might like to learn to make the local quince jelly.

'Oh, I know these are little things,' she went on, stretching out her hand to me, 'but it's something about the place, something uncanny. There's a great wall round the garden and I begin to feel I don't want to go out. When I make up my mind I'll run up to town and do some shopping there's a sort of influence which advises me to do it by telephone.'

She paused helplessly.

'This is silly,' she said. 'I can't make you understand. But he's there, Jeannie, he's there. I can hear him. One day I know I shall see him, imprisoning me, making me into the same sort of slave that his own wife was.'

I was silent. My own thoughts, I felt, erred on the practical side. I was thinking of diets and two hours' walking exercise every day and a course of the right reading. But I held my tongue because I knew, with a burst of intuition rather rare in me, that they would not be received with any great enthusiasm.

'Anyway, you'll come to the party, won't you? It's going to be hard work for me.' There were tears in Lucille's eyes. 'There'll be a lot of people, nearly all of them connected with Ray's business, people who have to be soothed and managed and treated properly.'

It sounded rather fun, but I did not say so.

'Oh, I'll come,' I said. 'I'd like to. We end next week to make way for the Boxing Night pantomime. Pull yourself together, old girl. It's probably all nerves.'

'Oh, it's not,' she said so wistfully that I felt sorry for her. 'He's there, bullying me, trying to make me interested in his garden, his rockery, his beastly little cupboards, his kitchens, his kennels, trying to tie me down to them. Oh, Jeannie, if I see him I shall go mad!'

I helped her on with her coat, and it was not until I went down to the street with her that I realised she'd had a great Buick and a chauffeur waiting the whole time.

I went back to the flat to boil myself an egg before going down to the theatre. I did not believe in ghosts, but I was worried about Lucille.

As soon as I entered Friars Cross, climbing out of Ray's Rolls-Royce at the front door and trying to look as though I was used to having a liveried footman to carry my portmanteau, I fell for the place.

It is enormous and not a bit Hollywood—that is to say, there is nothing at all fake about it. It is late Elizabethan, with gables and little carved bits over the windows, and is made of the sort of brick which some people call 'rose-coloured' but which is really the peculiar rusty pink of a very good strawberry ice when it has begun to melt.

There certainly was a wall all round the grounds. I had come in through the wrought-iron gates about a quarter of a mile down the drive, but what is a high wall if it encloses seven or eight acres of one's own property?

Just for a moment, as I entered the wide hall with the stone floor and the roaring fire on the enormous hearth, I did feel a slight qualm. It was not ghostly—at least, not exactly. I didn't expect to hear rustling chains or piercing shrieks, but I knew what Lucille meant when she said there was a sort of influence.

The place rather held out its arms and grabbed you, if you know what I mean. I felt I knew it, and it didn't surprise me at all when the incredibly smart maid, the silk of whose dress was a good deal better quality than mine, took me into an enormous lounge with great windows looking out over a grassy slope dotted with trees, a great beamed ceiling festooned with holly and laurels, and the walls partly panelled with authentic sixteenth-century carving.

I knew it was going to be like that, although I had certainly never been anywhere quite so palatial in my life.

Lucille gave a little squeak of joy and came running towards me.

'Darling, you're the first,' she said. 'I'm so glad to see you. Ray is upstairs changing; he's been shooting. Oh, Jeannie, do you feel it?'

I knew what she meant, but I chose to ignore it just then. I'm afraid the sight of her magnificent jade velvet hostess gown was making me wonder if my old yellow outfit was going to look too creased and mouldy for any self-respecting girl to be seen in.

But it was impossible to deny her for long. She was clinging to me as though I were the proverbial spar floating about after the wreck.

'My good girl,' I said, 'it's stupendous! I feel I've come to the baron's castle. D'you roast your own oxen, bake your own bread, and keep up your own army? It feels like that.'

To my alarm she turned pale.

'It does feel like that, doesn't it?' she said. 'That's the sort of feeling you get. It grows on you. You feel you've got to live up to it, satisfy it, feed it. Oh, Jeannie, if only I didn't love him so!'

'Where's my room?' I said. The old oak was beginning to make my rather towny greatcoat feel cheaper and cheaper every minute.

'I'll take you.'

As we went upstairs she apologised.

'I've had to put you in a little room,' she said, 'and you'll have to share my bathroom. There are such hordes and hordes of beastly businesspeople coming that even this great place gets filled up. It's quite the smallest bedroom of them all, but I knew you wouldn't mind.'

I didn't mind. I was enchanted. Anything larger would have made me feel I'd camped out in a church. Certainly the ceiling did slope on one side, but there were two dear little windows with casements and diamond panes, all genuine, which looked out over the south side of the house and made even the midwinter view of the garden adorable.

Lucille sat on the chintz-covered bed and watched me change.

'This—this was her room,' she said. 'His wife's. Not her bedroom, of course, but her own little room where she used to sit and sew and write letters. Wasn't it tragic? There she was with all this great house given over to his things, his friends, his guns, his dogs, and her tucked away in this tiny little room, poor pet, hiding and probably darning the linen.'

'Not a bad life.' The words were on the tip of my tongue but I didn't say them. I don't think I had begun to catch Lucille's resentment then, but I was beginning rather dimly to see what she was talking about.

Instead, I mentioned another sneaking idea which had crept into my mind. I am the least psychic, least impressionable person I have ever met, but the tales about the doors opening and shutting, the curtains moving, had stuck in my head, and it certainly was a very big place, and there were a lot of nooks and corners, it was incredibly old and I was going to sleep alone on Christmas Eve.

I said hesitantly:

'You haven't seen anything?'

'No,' said Lucille huskily, and her small face was drawn. 'Not yet.'

'Any—er—doors opening?' I ventured.

She nodded. Her eyes were round and frightened.

'Um—and sighs and things,' she said vaguely.

'Aren't the servants scared?'

'Oh, no. That's the dreadful part. It's—it's me he haunts. Only me. He wants to do the same thing to me as he did to her.'

It was fortunate, I suppose, or we might have frightened each other into fits, that a maid tapped on the door just then to announce that Mr and Mrs Dacre had just arrived and that Miss Irma Patchouka had 'phoned to say she was coming by a later train.

Lucille dismissed the girl and stood for a moment hesitating in the doorway,

'*His* business, *his* friends,' she said, and turned and fled before I could answer her.

I settled down to my make-up and tried to feel sympathetic. I was, but all the time my thoughts would wander in a most idiotic way. I found myself going all domestic. My mind drifted on to absurd things like the curing of bacon, the care of dogs, and I found myself in quite a fluster as I tried to remember whether I had heard that starched white tablecloths were coming back or if the best people were still using dinner mats.

The extraordinary thing was that I was quite happy. I went downstairs feeling placid and content and rather womanly. I put it down to the fact that it was Christmas.

I suppose they were stewing up for it all the evening, but the storm, such as it was, did not break until after dinner, when we were all sitting round in the huge lounge, sleepy after an enormous meal, listening to carol singers from the village, and all of us feeling, I suppose, rich and comfortable and very much at home.

There were, as Lucille had prophesied, hordes of people, quite a jolly crowd. Since Ray is at the head of his profession he can choose his own friends but, even if Theodore Dacre is a very famous director, it doesn't alter the fact that he is a very charming person.

Telfer, the comedian, was there; little Phelps, Ray's publicity man; and Bobby Jackson, all with attendant womenfolk.

There was a rather nice young man who sang, invited for my benefit, and one or two other people I did not know. It was all very confusing because some of the locals dropped in after dinner and, with the punchbowl flowing and everyone calling everyone else by their Christian names, you couldn't possibly keep tab of every single person.

It was Lucille's fault; honesty compels me to say that. Ray is one of those incredibly handsome people who have just that added something besides their good looks which makes them completely irresistible. Apart from this gift, which is just person-ality, he is a simple, kindly, sentimental soul with a flair for home life and, in fact, is really just the sort of person that the publicity man describes every film star to be. The only difference about Ray is that it's true.

He was enjoying himself. He had forgotten films and was being the popular country gentleman entertaining his friends on a Christmas night. And Lucille would not play.

More than that, she was definitely rude. When Telfer would refer to her as 'mine hostess' she snapped at him, and I saw Ray take her into a corner and remonstrate. She said something, and he reddened and looked at her with that helpless expression which must be worth about ten thousand a year to him, and said: 'Sweetheart, do make it home.'

I heard that last bit and felt quite embarrassed.

They went on all through the evening like that. Lucille delib-erately presented herself as the neglected, downtrodden wife, confined to the precincts of the house—a domestic slave, in fact. Somebody mentioned the words 'servant problem', and when Ray appealed to her for her opinion, she said quite waspishly:

'I suppose I ought to know something about it, dear. After

all, I have nothing else to worry about, have I? But I'm afraid I can't tell you anything. I'm so frightfully incapable.'

It made a nasty little gap in the lazy conversation, and not unnaturally people did leave her alone. She ought to have been the centre of the gathering, the very life and soul of it, but instead she somehow drifted into the background and That Woman—I won't call her Irma Patchouka, and she won't let me call her Gladys May—took her place. She's a born actress, and she just slipped into the part. I sat there feeling quite livid while she played the country hostess, the dear, domestic chatelaine, and saw Ray fall for it.

It was most annoying. Lucille was jealous—you couldn't blame her—and That Woman, who can't see a home without wanting to break it up, enjoyed herself thoroughly.

It was while I was sitting watching the performance, neglecting my little boy friend whose name I've forgotten and who only wanted to talk about his voice anyway, that I first saw the girl in the plaid dress. We were all scattered about the room, and she was in a corner by the fire. It did not occur to me that she was staying in the house; I thought she was one of the party that had come over with Sir Charles Parnham from Sedgewick Towers.

She was a funny little creature, very fashionable, almost Chelsea-ish in the stiff silk plaid dress, with her yellow hair dressed up on the top of her head and her big blue eyes, not a shade less intense than Lucille's own, fixed upon the scene.

I wondered who she was. She struck me as being intelligent— at least it was quite evident that she could appreciate the little tragi-comedy going on under her nose.

I don't think anyone else did, or at least not very much. Neither Ray nor Lucille are the people to quarrel in public, but the girl in the plaid dress saw all there was to see, and I caught her looking at Lucille rather wistfully once or twice.

There was a funny thing I noticed, too. The fire was burning low, and she bent down to put a log on it, but evidently changed her mind and sat up again, looking rather uncomfortable.

It was a trivial little incident, but I put it down as another piece of evidence to prove how that house did make one feel at home.

In the end That Woman rather overplayed the part, as she always does, and I saw Ray look at Lucille, who scowled at him furiously, with very much the same sort of expression as had lingered on the face of the yellow-haired girl.

I decided to have it out with her in the morning, although I didn't know what I could say with this 'haunting' idea in her head.

My mind having reverted to the question of haunting, it obstinately refused to leave it again. It was getting late, and gradually the company broke up. I did not see the girl in the plaid dress leave, and I thought she went when Sir Charles and his crowd drifted off about midnight.

I admit I hung about in front of the blazing fire for as long as I decently could. The dark corridors and ghostly carvings just did not appeal to me at that time of night. But That Woman was being so disgustingly domestic with Ray, and Lucille had already excused herself abruptly and gone to bed, so that in the end I was forced to go up.

Although the house has electricity Ray had kept the lighting subdued, so that the great hall was ghostly enough in all conscience with its hanging candelabra and wall sconces. It wasn't cold, in spite of the thin powdering of snow outside, and it wasn't draughty, because of the heavy curtains over every door, but I was shivering when I got into my pretty little room.

Somehow there I felt safe. There was a bright little fire in the grate, the big candle-shaped lights on my dressing-table were burning, and although the bed and the far corners of the room were in the shadow there was nothing ghostly about it; only warmth and comfort and homeliness, rather like a nursery.

I sat down at the dressing-table and looked at my distinctive rather than handsome face in the mirror. I could not get Lucille and her problem out of my mind. That she was very soon going to have a much bigger problem I was certain; if ever I had seen That Woman on the warpath I had seen her tonight. I had seen her great grey-green eyes travelling over the furniture and coming to rest on Ray's face with the good old-fashioned never-to-be-mistaken predatory gleam. She was after him all right, and she was going to get him unless Lucille gave him something better—and she certainly wasn't making any offers this evening.

I was still thinking when the door curtain rustled behind me and I turned my head just in time to see the girl in the plaid dress come quietly into the room. She smiled at me and I smiled back. I don't take to strange women as a rule and always make a point of not making friends with them. When you've been on the stage as long as I have—but that's another story. Anyway, I did smile, and whether it was the influence of the friendly intimacy of the party or the odd comfortableness of the house, I cannot say, but when she addressed me as an old friend I accepted her.

'I thought you wouldn't mind me coming in just before you go to bed,' she said. 'How do you like the house?'

'I love it,' I said.

'It's wonderful, isn't it?'

She spoke with such a warmth of feeling, such an indescribable fondness, that I stared at her.

'Do you know it well?'

'Every inch and corner and hole of it,' she said. 'I've known it for years and years.'

'Oh, you knew it before Lucille came?' I said. 'In the old man's time?'

She nodded.

'I've known it all my life, practically,' she said. 'You haven't been all over it, have you? You must. There are wonderful kitchens, great stone places with enormous cupboards and coppers, and hooks to hang the hams on, and places for the herbs. There's an apple store, too, lined with cedar. And down at the bottom of the garden there's a dovecot that dates from Norman times. Thousands and thousands of doves!'

She quite carried me away with her description of the place, and I took it for granted from what she said that she'd lived there as a child. In her hands the place took on a sort of magical quality, and I began to understand why it was that one felt that odd sensation of homeliness. It was a home. Someone had loved it as a home with a passionate intensity, something transcending ordinary affection. I supposed it was the old man.

Suddenly she looked up and I saw how incredibly fragile she was. Her hands were tiny and had fine blue veins on them. They looked ridiculously attractive peeping out of those absurdly mannered cuffs.

'Tell me about Lucille,' she said. 'Will she love the house?'

It seemed such an idiotic question that I stared at her, I suppose, and she hurried on.

'It must be loved—oh, it must! She's a darling, I like her. But she doesn't understand yet. She will, of course, but she's frightened of it. She's frightened of giving herself up to it. She doesn't realise how much it can give her back.'

The remark was so very apt that I found myself doing a quite unpardonable thing. I had no faint idea who the girl was and here was I in Lucille's house discussing her with a perfect stranger.

'She thinks it's haunted,' I blurted out.

'Haunted?' There was despair in the little face. 'Oh—oh, how terrible! Oh, how *could* she think that?'

She was so concerned that before I knew what I was doing I was pouring out Lucille's troubles.

'She thinks it's the spirit of the old man,' I said. 'He was very cruel to his wife, you know. Wouldn't let her buy her own dresses or anything. Kept her shut up and sacrificed her and everything else to his own importance.' I broke off abruptly. 'I say, did you know them? I'm awfully sorry.'

She rose and I noticed incongruously that she was wearing openwork stockings. I thought that was carrying the 1890 motif a bit too far, but of course I did not say so.

'Oh, yes, I knew him,' she said softly. 'I knew him very, very well. He wasn't cruel to her. He loved her. He loved his home, and she *was* his home.'

'That doesn't seem to be the general idea,' I said with some vague idea of sticking to my guns. 'I don't think she ever went out.'

'Why should she?' she said with a calm surprise that took me completely off my balance. 'Look here, listen to me. I knew her well, terribly well, and she was happy, I tell you, happier than anybody else in the world. She was married to a very important man. But what would his importance and his prowess have been to him if it hadn't been for her? This was her domain, her castle. In it he was safe, he was protected. Do you see what I mean? Oh, do you see what I mean?'

'I do,' said Lucille's voice from the doorway.

How long she had been standing there I did not know; but now, as I swung round, I saw her framed by the dark velvet of the door curtain. She was looking at the girl in the plaid dress and there were tears on her cheeks. She held out her hands.

'I'm sorry,' she said. 'I'm so sorry. You're right. Oh, my dear, I—I didn't know it was *you*.'

And then I suppose I witnessed one of the most extraordinary scenes that anyone in the world can ever have seen. I sat in between them, as it were, and the girl in the plaid dress stretched out her hands to Lucille. They did not touch each other. Their fingers were the fraction of an inch apart. They stood quite still for a moment, those two beautiful fair-headed creatures, and then the girl in the plaid dress disappeared.

I do not use the word lightly. She disappeared before my eyes. One minute she was there and the next she was gone, and Lucille was sobbing in my arms.

I was not frightened. When I look back on it now my hair stands on end and I have a prickling sensation down my spine, but at the time I was not frightened. I was overwhelmed, carried away if you like, by the truth of it all.

'She's right,' said Lucille, dabbing her eyes furiously. 'I didn't know who you were talking to, and I stopped to listen. I realised who she was almost at once. Oh, Jeannie, how I must have hurt her! Don't you see, it was *her*, it was her all the time.'

That ridiculous plaid dress, the old-fashioned hairdressing, which I had thought was an affectation, the openwork stockings, these details flashed through my mind and I gasped.

'But she was there,' I said. 'She was there in the room this evening. I saw her sitting by the fire.'

'I didn't see her,' said Lucille. 'I didn't see her until tonight, in here. But she goes all over the house, of course, she loves it so. I don't suppose I shall ever see her again, but I shall know she's about and I shan't mind. Did you hear what she said about her husband? He was an important man, you see, like Ray. After she died he never married again.'

The truth was only just forcing itself upon my mind.

'Her husband?' I said unsteadily. 'Then she is—was—'

'His wife,' said Lucille. 'Oh, darling, I must go to Ray.'

Curiously, I slept that night and in the morning I met the new Lucille. It was amazing how, once she got the idea, she took to it. It was the best Christmas Day I have ever spent. It was Lucille's house, Lucille's castle, Lucille's domain, and Ray's home.

I never saw That Woman so completely routed. In any other circumstances her discomfort would have been comic. With Lucille in her right place, Irma's attempts to be domestic looked merely vulgar, and in the end she saw it herself and decided she had to get back to town that night. Nobody minded, not even me, although she got my little boy-friend-who-sang to drive her back, which was typical of her.

When I packed my things to go back to town on the day after Boxing Night. Lucille came and sat on my bed.

'D'you know, I like this room,' she said. 'It's got such a beautiful aspect. Ray and I were talking it over. We thought we might make it the nursery. What do you think?'

MARGERY ALLINGHAM

Margery Allingham (1904–1966), one of the so-called 'Big Four', remains one of the best known and most popular writers of crime fiction. She was born in Ealing, West London, and, as both her parents were writers and her grandfather an editor, it was not surprising that even as a child she should enjoy writing, producing at the age of seven a journal for her family entitled *The Wag-Tale*, which included serial stories, poetry, a recipe and even an advertisement—for 'sinite of potassium' . . .

Allingham's earliest short story, 'The Rescue of the Rainclouds', was published in April 1917 in *Mother and Home*, the sister magazine of *Women's Weekly*, which was run by her aunt. The author was thirteen years old. By the time she was seventeen, she had written countless poems as well as several monologues and plays, including a three-act drama *Dido and Aeneas*, which was performed at King George's Hall in central London. And the precocious young teenager also completed *Blackkerchief Dick* (1923), a story of pirates in Stuart times, which her father claimed his daughter had been inspired to write by a series of séances.

In 1927, Allingham married Philip Youngman Carter. At around the same time, she resumed her writing career with *The White Cottage Mystery* (1928). This novella was first published as a newspaper serial and, as an innovation in deceit, the solution stands up against other classics of the genre such as Christie's *The Murder of Roger Ackroyd*. Given the enormous popularity of crime fiction at the time, it was not surprising that the young writer would next try her hand at a full-length mystery and, in emulation of Dorothy L. Sayers and others, create a 'great detective'. That first book was *The Crime at Black Dudley* (1929) and Allingham's sleuth was the dilettante Albert Campion who may or may not have been a viscount or a baron . . . or even a King-in-waiting.

Campion would go on to appear in seventeen novels, numerous short stories, and another novella, *The Case of the Late Pig* (1937). At her death Allingham left an unfinished 18th novel, which her husband completed; he would go on to write two more Campion novels and to start a third, which was completed on his death by Mike Ripley, who has also produced four other Campion novels so far. If Campion is Wimseyesque, his manservant certainly has nothing in common with Wimsey's Bunter; the 'large and lugubrious' Magersfontein Lugg is a most original creation, 'graceful as a circus elephant'.

As well as the Campion stories, Allingham wrote many other short stories and novellas, as well as a romantic thriller *The Darings of the Red Rose* (1930), originally published anonymously, and the non-series mystery *Black Plumes* (1940). There is also the trio of thrillers that were originally published as magazine serials under her own name but, when published in book form, were credited to 'Maxwell March', whom Allingham described as 'a first class hack—he makes the cash' and went on to note that 'Margery Allingham thinks of her reputation'. That reputation rests not only on her ability, like Dickens, to create truly memorable characters and to capture the atmosphere of a place, but also on her considerable strengths as a writer and her clever and playful approach to the construction of a mystery.

However, Allingham's best book may be her least well-known. Written at the request of an American friend, *The Oaken Heart* (1941) is set in the Essex village of Auburn which, even when the book was published, was readily identified as a lightly disguised version of Tolleshunt D'Arcy, the village where Allingham made her home after leaving London with her husband. Her only published book-length work of non-fiction, the book was acclaimed by contemporary critics as an outstanding portrait of how the inhabitants of a typical English village reacted to events, from the slow burning summer before the Munich Conference through to the arrival of evacuees and the coming of the Luftwaffe. After the Second World War, Allingham would play her part in healing D'Arcy and she would go on to write more novels, including the book that many consider to be her best, the Campion thriller *Tiger in the Smoke* (1952) and the final novel to be published in her lifetime, *The Mind Readers* (1965), which sadly reads more like a children's thriller than a mystery.

'Misleading Lady' was first published in the Christmas anthology *The Picture Show Annual* for 1935, and I am grateful to Barry Pike, the authority on Allingham's work, for drawing it to my attention.

THE LEGEND OF
THE CANE IN THE DARK

John Dickson Carr

The whole thing begun when I read in a Pittsburgh newspaper the account of my own death. It gave me a start to see 'Mr Stoneman Wood, for a number of years a well-known journalist and freelance writer, died at his home on North Highland Avenue yesterday. A heart-stroke . . .' It continued, just as matter-of-fact as you please.

I had been on a hunting-trip in Canada (liquor, too) and I suppose I should have been used to shocks, after my guide almost plugged me for a moose. He was such a treacherous rat that I had to fire him, and without him it took me rather longer than I had expected to get back. It didn't matter, of course, for since I had come into my uncle's money I was taking things easy and letting my cousin handle the affairs. Lord, it was a relief, not having to hammer out a column every day for the *Gazette*!

Well, as I say, I loafed along, sending no wires, asking no questions, and assuming that Cousin Stephen was taking care of the money. I was comfortable, well-fed, and knew that I could draw a cheque whenever pleased. So I got to Pittsburgh in a pleasant frame of mind—I'd surprise 'em, because I doubt anybody knew I was away.

It was on one of those smoky oil-lit milk trains that I opened my first home newspaper and saw that crazy announcement. It gave me an uncanny feeling; a mistake, but an odd and uncomfortable mistake. My eye kept going back to the headlines of the story. 'Oh, what the devil!' says I, and then I would look at 'STONEMAN WOOD DIES—'

I left the train at East Liberty and started to walk out to the house on Highland Avenue. It was cool and had been raining; there was absolutely nobody to be seen, for the streets were very wide and deserted, with nothing except a few electric signs. I could see only occasional lights on Highland Avenue, which is long and windy. Now there was none of the usual atmosphere of Pittsburgh that night: I felt as though I were walking on completely foreign ground. Sometimes it took me minutes to recognize big houses set back behind their iron fences, and I had seen those houses every day for ten years.

Then I realised that somebody must be following me. The sky looked strangely *light*, but for a while I couldn't see the person behind me, though I thought I could hear him walking. I also thought I could hear his cane going tap-tap on the pavement, slowly. Finally, I turned around and saw a huge figure that looked as though it wore a high black coat. It had a cane. I began to grow afraid of that figure, though I didn't understand why. Never did it enter my head that it might be an ordinary pedestrian. I started walking faster, and it didn't walk faster—the cane tapped slowly, but every time I would look, there it was behind me.

When I reached the walk that led up to my house it was right behind me. I began to run. There was a low light behind the ground-glass door of the vestibule, the only illumination on a big rugged black house. Yet when I looked at that door (I had seen it every day for

more than ten years) I thought there was lettering on it. And it was *open*. Just when I got inside, under a light in the dark hall, the door opened behind me, and in blundered that figure following me. It was even huger, and as it stared straight at me I suddenly noticed that it was *blind*.

It grinned and said, '*Hello.*' Well, I leave it to you what I did. It would be cowardly to call out, yet I wanted to arouse the house; but my God! I thought, 'What if there's nobody here, and I'm alone with this person? I didn't even question it. I turned around and went towards the stairs; there was a revolver in my room. I stumbled up in the dark, and groped along the wall of the second floor, and I found my door. From the faint light in the hall, I saw the person right behind me when I got inside the room. He was standing by the door. I rushed across the room in the dark . . . Then I noticed that the place had a sickening heavy sweet smell. I touched something in the dark; it was a flower, banks of flowers. And the room was shut up.

I found a lamp at last, and when I pulled the cord so that it glowed dimly in the big room, there was the blind man beside me. He took hold of my arm, stared in my face, and said in a strange voice, 'Why didn't you tell me there was a dead man in your bed?'

Well, we were right beside the bed. It had smooth sheets, smooth and white except for a motionless bulge under them. There *was* a man in the bed. His eyes were closed and his face waxy. Against the white sheets it seemed as though I were looking in a mirror, for the man was an exact counterpart of me. Maybe I was about to faint, for the room assumed a dizzy appearance; I felt sick at the stomach.

'Why don't you open your eyes?' asked the blind man, grinning.

I rushed towards the door, collided with it, and left the blind man in the middle of the room. I gave a scream.

Lights began to go up in the house, cold lights. In that dark hallway, with the faded carpet, I stood with the lights beating on me. I saw my Aunt Miranda, in a dressing-gown, put her head out of one door; instead of shrieking, as she seemed about to do, she began to cry and blubber. Her head, hair in curlers, disappeared. Other relations looked out . . .

Somebody cried, 'Lock the door!—Stoneman—he's walking!—'

They shrank away, they banged their doors as I tried to speak to them. Was I dead, after all?

Then I saw the open door of my cousin Stephen's room. I went in, and there was the dapper black- haired Stephen sitting on his bed. As he raised his head, he had the face of a man who feels himself falling out at a ten-storey window.

'Damn you,' said Stephen, yanking open the drawer of a table by his bed and pulling out a gun. After that he looked sick, and began to cry.

'What's the matter with you?' I said. 'Look here, I am Stoneman—'

'No, you're not,' he answered, 'and you're not a ghost, either; you're an impostor. You can never prove you left this house and went to Canada. The real Stoneman Wood is lying in that other room.'

I think he was gazing over my shoulder. He dropped the pistol on the bed; I think he must have seen something behind me. It scared him so that he couldn't talk straight, but out tumbled the whole story. He had planned my trip to Canada and kept it secret from everybody. He had hired the guide who was to kill me. Then he had got a body that resembled me, and, since we lived alone in the house, it was easy to pretend that I had died from a heart attack; the family doctor had not been present, but a man of Stephen's procuring. Then he had assembled the relatives, knowing, of course, that my Uncle Stoneman's fortune would go to him. My only slip-up was that the guide had not killed me . . . My death in Canada, if killed by a guide, might cause comment, but the death of a man from heart failure never would, especially if a tearful cousin is around . . .

After it was finished I sat down on the bed and watched him.

I was beginning to feel better, but I was damp all over and nauseated. As I was about to ask him more questions, he shuddered, digging his face in the pillows . . . I heard the sound of a cane tapping on the front stairs.

'Look here,' I cried, 'who was the man that followed me?'

'Nobody followed you! I don't know!'

'Who was it that you saw behind me when I came in here— over my shoulder? You did see somebody, didn't you?'

'No!'

'Answer me!'

(In silence the front door banged.)

'Did you ever see . . . your uncle . . . that died?' Stephen asked chokingly.

'No!'

'He always . . . carried . . . a cane.'

JOHN DICKSON CARR

John Dickson Carr was born on 30 November 1906 in Uniontown, Pennsylvania, the son of Julia Kisinger and Wooda Carr, a prominent attorney and onetime Democratic Congressman. Carr Senior had edited the *Uniontown Daily Herald* where—not coincidentally—his son got his first break, writing regular columns and providing sporting and theatrical reviews. Carr Junior wrote in the evenings after school, where he excelled in the literary arts, finishing his first year's work with two distinctions: second prize in the school poetry competition and the gold medal in the countrywide Theodore Roosevelt competition conducted by the Colonial Dames of America.

When Carr moved to Haverford College he started writing for the college magazine, *The Haverfordian*, eventually becoming its editor. His juvenilia covers many genres but Carr most enjoyed writing—and reading—detective stories. At college he created Henri Bencolin, a Parisian investigator who would go on to appear in his first novel, *It Walks by Night* (1930), based on a story which had appeared a year earlier in *The Haverfordian* and can be found in *Bodies from the Library 3* (2020).

Carr's favourite kind of detective story involved the literary equivalent of a magic trick. They are commonly styled locked-room mysteries, an often misused term that is shorthand for a situation that seems impossible but for which there is a possible (if sometimes implausible) explanation; there may be a closed circle of suspects with respect to a locked-room murder, but the terms are not synonymous. Countless writers—from Arthur Conan Doyle and Agatha Christie to Soji Shimadi and Paul Halter—have written impossible crime stories. Many openly credit Carr as an influence, and it is also certain that without him there would have been no *Banacek*, no *Monk* and no *Death in Paradise*. He was, quite simply, *The Man Who Explained Miracles* (1995), to quote the title of the excellent biography by Douglas G. Greene, *the* authority on Carr's life and work.

Over 50 years, Carr presented almost every kind of impossible crime there is—from invisible assailants and vanishing murderers to cases that feature baffling clues and bizarre weapons—and he shares the distinction with Agatha Christie of creating *two* 'great detectives': as 'Carter Dickson' he wrote 22 novels with the rumbustious Sir Henry Merrivale, a barrister, spymaster and physician partially inspired by Carr's own father; and writing under his own name there is the gargantuan academic, Dr Gideon Fell, based on the creator of Father J. Paul Brown, G. K. Chesterton whose influence—and sometimes plots—can be seen throughout Carr's work.

As well as writing many books and short stories, Carr also produced dozens of radio plays, writing for the long-running CBS series *Suspense* and *Cabin B13* in the United States. After he moved to Britain in 1932, he worked for the BBC, for which he created the influential *Appointment with Fear* series. During the Second World War, he also played his part in the Allied war effort by writing semi-fictional propaganda plays. These aside, the majority of Carr's scripts are captivating and concise, pulling the listener in and playing with sound effects and dialogue to create atmosphere and intrigue, exemplified in *The Island of Coffins*, a collection of Carr's *Cabin B13* scripts published in 2021 by Crippen & Landru.

As well as the ability to create entrancing problems and memorable characters, Carr also developed the crime novel in two important ways. While he did not invent the historical detective story—that honour probably goes to Melville Davisson Post—Carr did much to popularise it after the Second World War, laying a trail for other writers like Anne Perry and Ellis Peters, as well as the modern master, Paul Doherty. Carr was also pioneering in his use of the supernatural and science fiction in novel-length detective stories like *Fire, Burn!* (1957), which features something very like time travel, and *The Burning Court* (1937), in which he provides a witchly solution as well as a rational one. Today Carr is recognised as a giant of the Golden Age of crime and detective fiction, and the only writer to have served as secretary of the Detection Club and president of the Mystery Writers of America, which awarded him Edgars in 1949 and 1962.

After suffering for some years from the legacy of heavy smoking, John Dickson Carr died from lung cancer at Greenville, South Carolina, on 27 February 1977.

'The Legend of the Cane in the Dark' was published in *The Haverfordian* in June 1926.

ST BARTHOLOMEW'S DAY

Edmund Crispin

The town of Clauvères stands to the north of Paris, about seven miles in the direct line from the Arc de Triomphe. Today the metropolis, expanding, has engulfed it and passed beyond, but until recently it could lay some claim to a separate and independent existence. The traveller, if he pauses there at all, will see streets of cobbles, small ugly cafés, a Nineteenth-Century church of no architectural interest, and beyond, the scattered peasant holdings on the low range of hills which rise from the banks of the Seine where it bends east towards St Nicholas. Only if he turns left by the greystone *mairie*, and makes his way beyond the shops and the marketplace, will he find anything to reward him; for a twenty minutes' walk in this direction, along a white, straight, dusty road, lined with tall elms, will bring him to the Château de l'Echarpe,

The Château has long been deserted, long been a museum relic of the *grand siècle*. The tall rooms with their painted ceilings and gilded chairs may be inspected on payment of five francs by anyone curious to recreate the manners of an earlier age. But few are thus curious; there are better Châteaux elsewhere, and Versailles itself can be reached in 25 minutes on the bus. For the rest, all that need be said of Clauvères for the purposes of this narrative is that it has one reasonably comfortable inn, the Coq d'Or.

To this inn, in the August of 1872, came an Englishman, a Mr Rotherham. He seems to have been a man of about 50, of independent means, and a dabbler in the obscure corners of historical research. Despite the rather ostentatious parade of erudition in his letters, he apparently published nothing—if, that is, the catalogue of the Bodleian is to be trusted; and one conceives that his scholarship was less a serious preoccupation than an excuse to the world, and perhaps to himself, for the aimless life of travel which he led. He was unmarried, and his nearest relation was a young nephew to whom he wrote frequently and at length.

Clauvères, though he neither knew nor intended it, was to be the terminus of his last journey. He had caught a particularly slow train from Rouen and was in no very good temper when he drove in a carriage from the station to the inn. The shortage of food and the other discomforts consequent upon the recently concluded Franco-Prussian war further exacerbated him.

'The inn,' he writes on the evening of his arrival, 'is a mediocre enough place, but the best to be found here; and the poverty which afflicts Paris itself, together with the fatigue and inconvenience of the daily journey here, have decided me to remain until my work is finished. My hostess is a dark, sallow, elderly woman, a widow, with one son, who is of an anarchical disposition, and a fanatical devotee of the new decadent "poetry" (so-called) represented by Baudelaire, Verlaine and others of that tribe. This much I gather from the copy of an advanced periodical which I discovered him reading.

'My room, on the first storey, has three tall windows looking out upon the street and a large four-poster bed, which appears, however, to be comfortable enough; though I have had removed from it that insanitary abomination so dear to the Gallic mind, the *feather-mattress*. Fortunately, the English currency is so valuable to these people in the present wretched plight of the country that I may count upon receiving every attention possible. The only disturbance which I am likely to encounter will be the noise of the market carts rattling over the cobbles in the early morning, and that I shall no doubt bear, since I do not anticipate being here more than a week at most.

'As you know, I am in hopes of completing here my investigations into the part played by the great family of Louvois in the religious wars of the Sixteenth Century, and I flatter myself that I shall have a number of fresh facts to offer to the Historical Research Society on my return. The immediate object of my interest is a relatively obscure collateral descendant of the great Charles de Louvois, one Raoul de Savigny who would not be in any way notable were it not for the fact that he was the only member of that staunchly Catholic family to join forces with the Huguenots, and that he was a victim of the great massacre of St Bartholomew's day. (It is a whimsical thought, is it not, that the 300th anniversary of that event takes place in only a few days' time? I must be on the watch for *spectres*!)

'The standard text-books say nothing of him beyond the bare fact of his death and the information—hardly to be wondered at in the circumstances—that he lived in strict solitude and seclusion. But since his abode was the Château de l'Echarpe, hardly three miles from the inn-door, I anticipate it may be possible to obtain locally those details in which the libraries are so peculiarly barren. In any event, I plan to visit the Château for the first time after breakfast tomorrow.'

This plan was duly put into effect. Mr Rotherham records that the day was unusually hot, even for August, and that there were a great many flies. Apart from these trials his walk to the Château was untroubled, and in his letter that evening he dilates at some length on his impressions of the countryside and his first view of the Château standing high above the slow-moving river.

He roused the caretaker (whom he describes as a 'surly, middle-aged peasant') from his cottage and was shown through the rooms. For the most part they bore witness to a period some 50 years later than that in which he was specially interested; but he was rewarded by discovering an authentic portrait of Viscount Raoul de Savigny hanging high above the fireplace in the great drawing-room. This he describes in some detail.

'It is a thin, weak, effeminate face, with narrow eyes and an unusually red mouth, at first appearance the face of a man about 30 years of age; a closer inspection, however, convinced me that the sitter must have been nearer 40 when the portrait was painted. He wears a rich dress of red silk and velvet, and the chain and medal of some insignia (I could not at the distance discern what) hangs about his neck. An hour glass, held horizontally so as to prevent the flow of sand from one end to the other, is in his right hand, and his left rests upon an open book, on one page of which some writing is discernible.

'Wishing to inspect the writing more closely, I asked our unamiable friend if a stepladder could be procured; but he made so great a fuss over the difficulties attendant upon this—as I had supposed—simple operation, that I had to resign myself to waiting until my return on the morrow for my curiosity to be satisfied.'

Evidently the caretaker proved unsatisfactory in other respects also. He knew nothing about the Château beyond information of the conventional guidebook variety, and that was concerned wholly with the family which succeeded the Savignys in occupancy. They had not remained there long, nor any subsequent tenants; and the place had been empty for the last 50 years.

'But if Monsieur wishes to know more, he should visit Monsieur le Curé, who understands about these things.'

'Really.' These priests were apt to fancy themselves as historians, Mr Rotherham reflected. 'Are there any documents connected with the Savignys to be seen locally?'

'Yes, Monsieur. They are in the possession of M. le Curé.' The man hesitated 'Perhaps—'

'Well?'

'I was going to say that if Monsieur is interested in le Vicomte Raoul de Savigny, he should perhaps see these documents before he proceeds further in the matter.'

'Certainly I must see them. If they are of historical importance, they should have been donated to one of the libraries. But I have noticed that the Church is apt to have no conscience in these matters.'

The tour of inspection over, they left the house and crossed the broad neglected lawn at the back. Rococo bowls and statuary were ranged beneath the windows. At its farthest extremity the lawn rose in a short precipitous slope to meet the first trees of the park. And among the trees something which winked in the morning sunlight caught Mr Rotherham's eye as he was turning to leave.

'What is that?' he asked, pointing.

'It is nothing, Monsieur.' The man's tone was guarded.

'Nonsense,' said Mr Rotherham. 'I distinctly caught the sun's reflection in a window.' He took a few steps. 'A building.'

'A mausoleum, Monsieur.'

'Great heavens, man'—Mr Rotherham was excited—'why didn't you tell me? What sort of place is it? Who is buried there? You must take me to it at once.'

'There is nothing of interest there, Monsieur.'

'Surely I may be allowed to judge—' Mr Rotherham hesitated, stopped, felt in his pocket, and produced a twenty-franc note. But the man shook his head.

'No, Monsieur, it is not that. If you insist, I will take you to it. But you cannot see the interior.'

'There is no key?'

'Yes, Monsieur, there is a key. I could wish there was not. I should like to see it destroyed. But the family has forbidden visitors entrance to the tomb. And I was never curious to go in myself.'

If these remarks struck Mr Rotherham as strange, he does not mention the fact. He merely asked again, 'And who is buried there?'

'Only one man: Monsieur Raoul de Savigny.'

'Raoul—! We must go there at once.'

And so the two set off.

The mausoleum stood—and still stands—at the top of a slight eminence, surrounded and overshadowed by the trees of the park. It is circular in shape and built in the neoclassical style which the renaissance made fashionable in France, with ornamental pillars surmounted by Ionic capitals all about it.

The roof is of copper and there is a stout oak door, carved with the arms of the de Savignys. The only unusual feature is the circlet of low elongated windows set below the roof about twelve feet from the ground, occupying very much the same position as clerestory windows in a church. Upon these Mr Rotherham gazed long and earnestly. Finally he asked if a ladder could be fetched.

'Monsieur wishes to look in at the windows? I should not advise it.'

Mr Rotherham was beginning to lose patience. 'What is all this nonsense?' he snapped. 'I trust you are not afraid of ghosts? In any case it is not you whom I am asking to ascend the ladder. For the last time will you get it for me or will you not?'

The caretaker shrugged. 'As Monsieur wishes.'

The ladder was brought and set against the side of the mausoleum, and Mr Rotherham began his climb. Halfway up he was assailed by a sudden misgiving: it would not be pleasant, on arriving at the window, to find someone looking out at you . . . But he braced himself and went on, and in fact no such eventuality occurred.

The windows were filthy, both inside and out, and it was

difficult to make out much of what lay within. He could discern, however, the stone sarcophagus in the centre, and on the east side some kind of altar, with a brass crucifix on it. A little disappointed, he had turned away and was beginning to descend, when he was startled by a violent clanging noise from within the tomb. And when, conquering an unexpected reluctance, he looked in again, he saw that the brass crucifix had fallen onto the stone floor.

The caretaker was awaiting him at the bottom of the ladder, his face a little paler than before. 'Monsieur heard?'

'Yes, of course,' said Mr Rotherham shortly. He was no doubt annoyed at having been so alarmed. 'I shall be returning tomorrow,' he went on quickly, 'to look more closely at the portrait.'

'If Monsieur could find it convenient to arrive before four o'clock—I shall be closing the grounds at that hour—'

Mr Rotherham tut-tutted his annoyance. 'Well, if it must be, it must be. It seems very early to have to leave.'

'I am going away, Monsieur. The day after tomorrow is August the 24th. I shall return on the 25th and shall be happy then to show Monsieur anything he pleases.'

'A not unsatisfactory day,' Mr Rotherham concludes his letter, 'and with promise of better to come tomorrow, when I visit the priest. The incident of the crucifix did, I confess, temporarily disturb me, but I think you know that I do not subscribe to the current superstitions on such subjects; and no doubt there is some perfectly natural explanation of the phenomenon.'

His second night at the Coq d'Or was not as tranquil as he had anticipated. Whether it was due to the bed, or to the unfamiliar surroundings, or to some other reason, he got but little sleep, and that little was troubled with dreams.

'One in particular,' he notes in his diary, 'kept recurring. I seemed to be running along a dark cobbled street, with the high gables of houses on either side. And all the time a voice was speaking rapidly and continuously in my ear, in a sort of high, thin monotone. *"Je ne suis pas encore prêt,"* it said, *"l'experience n'est pas complete."* ("I am not yet ready, the experiment is not complete.")

'At times it rose to a desolate wail which I do not, even now, like to think of. There were torches, I think, and a crowd of indistinct people who were trying to get hold of me. Then I was in a room, standing with my back to the wall, and there was a sudden sharp pain in my right side, and the people and the torches came up to me and were doing something to my mouth. The voice rose to a high, bubbling scream in the middle of a sentence, and then broke off, and I awoke.'

I conjecture that Mr Rotherham was a man not easily daunted, for he seems despite this to have been in high spirits when, after breakfast next morning, he set off to see the Curé, who proved to be a lean ascetic man, a very heavy smoker of yellow cigarettes which he rolled himself. He appeared oddly reluctant to further Mr Rotherham's business but was eventually persuaded to produce some faded sheets of yellow parchment, written in a crabbed sixteenth-century hand.

'You will find here an account,' he said, 'of the death of le Vicomte Raoul de Savigny in the massacre of St Bartholomew's day, 1572, together with other matters concerning him. It was written by one Jean de Tourcoing, at that time the priest of this parish, a few months after the events took place.'

This really was a find. Mr Rotherham took the parchment with hands which he could hardly prevent from trembling with excitement. 'I may have your permission to copy this?'

The priest nodded. 'But I would rather you copied it here, my son—it is not long. Please do not misunderstand me; I would of course trust you with the manuscript. But there are other reasons.' He hesitated. 'I must leave you now to say Compline. Please avail yourself of this room as much as you wish. And—'

Mr Rotherham looked up from the parchment sheets. 'Yes?'

'You will find something in those pages which may tempt you to a certain course of action. Resist that temptation, my son—resist it for your own good.' The priest's manner was intent.

'Of course, of course,' said Mr Rotherham, who wished to be left alone with the manuscript. 'Whatever you advise.'

It is improbable that the priest can have been deceived by this hurried acquiescence, for he added, more kindly, 'And remember, my son, at any time and in any emergency I am at your service.' Then he turned and went out.

The account of Jean de Tourcoing, brief though it was, was undoubtedly authentic and contemporary. Mr Rotherham found in it much to excite and a little to disturb him. It confirmed that Catherine de Medici was personally responsible for the massacre; it gave the number of victims in the Paris area as 13,000 (but this was probably guesswork and could not be relied on); and it repeated the legend—Mr Rotherham smiled a little at this—that Charles IX was thereafter haunted by the spirits of dead Huguenots.

The number of the murdered in Clauvères itself was not large, but some considerable space was given up to the death of Raoul de Savigny, as by far the most notable among them. One passage is worth transcribing here in full.

'De Savigny, torturer, murderer, magician and apostate, met his deserved end upon this same glorious night of August 24th. A man forever fearful of death, forever scheming by vile art to prolong his own wretched estate and keep earthbound his heretic soul in the middle career betwixt our Almighty Lord and His Adversary the Devil, and who, being cravenly terrified of both Heaven and Hell, sought to transgress and defy the inexorable decree of our going hence, he was hounded upon this same night like a dog through the streets, and struck to his own wall by a shaft in the right ribs.

'And the soldiers, being desirous of entertainment, were in mind—he being thus helpless—to torture him; in pursuance of which, his head, arms and legs being clamped to the wall, his teeth were first drawn, singly, and his mouth slit back from the corners to the cheek-bone; he crying out the while that he was not yet ready for death, and imploring the soldiers to spare him. Then his fingernails were torn out and the bones of his fingers separately broken. In all this he fainted often and was revived before the operation proceeded.

'At last, after five hours of continual mutilation, he was seen to be dead. And the parts of the body were assembled and embalmed in linen, and a tomb built in the park, and the remains placed there, and with them all the papers relating to his family and himself, and so at last he was left alone. All this I witnessed.

'Jean de Tourcoing *scripsit*,
'Ao 1573, in the month of February, A.M.D.G.'

When Mr Rotherham left the priest's house with his transcript of this document he was thoughtful, and the subject of his reflections is revealed in a letter which he wrote to his nephew immediately on returning to his room at the inn.

'You will think less hardly of my intent,' he says, 'if you consider the immense additions to historical knowledge which will almost certainly be derived from the papers in the mausoleum. To ask permission to go in there would, I know, be a fruitless endeavour; there is too much superstition against it, and the caretaker made it clear that on this score the family which owns the Château is adamant. But I believe I am competent to carry through the business without leaving any traces. All depends upon whether the key has been left behind in the caretaker's cottage.'

Mr Rotherham's plan, in brief, was as follows: during the

afternoon he would purchase in the town a length of rope and a good lantern, and when darkness fell he would leave the inn, giving as his excuse the desire for a moonlight walk, and make his way to the Château de l'Echarpe. There he would climb the wall, an operation which, from what he remembered, was likely to present few difficulties, search the cottage of the absent caretaker for the key to the mausoleum, make his way in there, take the documents referred to by Jean de Tourcoing, re-lock the tomb, restore the key carefully to the cottage, and return to the inn.

He anticipated no trouble in opening the sarcophagus, as he had noted that the lid was a light one of copper, and—a surprising feature—was not fastened down. Presumably the stout oak door was considered a sufficient safeguard against anyone's getting in or out.

Poor Mr Rotherham! One may admire his courage, if not his wisdom. Curiously enough, he does not appear to have remembered the priest's warning, or, if he did remember it, he was determined to ignore it. And when its full significance was at last borne in on him, it was far, far too late.

The story he was to tell subsequently was also prepared, for it would be impossible to conceal the fact that something criminal had been afoot, and after his visit to the Curé it was very likely that he would be connected with it. He would say that he had got into conversation with a stranger in a café (he would not, of course, know the stranger's name or be able to describe him minutely), and had chanced to mention to him the existence of the papers in the mausoleum and his own regret at being unable to see them; that on the following day the stranger had reappeared, in possession of those same papers and demanding payment for them; that, being incapable of dealing physically with the stranger, he had handed over the money; that the stranger had subsequently disappeared; and that, horrified by so flagrant a theft, he had hastened to return the papers to their owners—though not, he added to himself, before sufficient time had elapsed to allow him to make a copy of them. It is perhaps fortunate for Mr Rotherham's reputation that so threadbare an account was never put to the test.

Darkness fell with the moon three-quarters towards the full, and a small wind crept in sudden gusts round the corners of the house and over the cobbled streets, stirring the rich, dusty foliage in the trees which stood opposite the inn. Mr Rotherham set out at about half-past ten, carrying his lantern and his rope in a suitcase. He was relieved that no one was about when he left the inn, for he would have been hard put to account for so unusual a piece of equipment for a moonlight stroll.

The journey to the Château was accomplished without incident; the only people he saw were a pair of lovers, too engrossed in their own concerns to pay any attention to him. The tall iron gates leading into the grounds were locked, but a convenient beech tree which stood by the wall made it unnecessary for him to use his rope—Mr Rotherham, despite his 50 years, was an active, even an athletic, man.

The grounds were silent and deserted. A windowpane smashed gave him access to the caretaker's cottage, and after a short search he found what he wanted—a huge, ancient key, rusted and corroding. Then he was out in the night air again and making his way towards the mausoleum.

I can picture to myself his feelings as he stood before the tall oak door, the key in one hand, his lighted lantern in the other. It is not good, in the darkness, to be near places where dead people are. But whatever fears he may have had, he suppressed them and went on with the job in hand. The lock was rusty from long disuse and it was several minutes before the wards would turn. Then the door stood open and he was inside.

The sarcophagus, a tall black mass, was in front of him, its copper lid illuminated by the straggling beams of moonlight which filtered through the windows, and the air was almost unbearably foul. In the light of the lantern he could see the brass crucifix on the floor where it had fallen the day before.

He took two steps forward, hesitantly, and all at once was overwhelmed by a dreadful and irresistible feeling that he was not alone. Another two steps and with sudden violence the door of the mausoleum slammed to behind him, and he was conscious at the same moment of a voice gabbling softly and repeatedly in his left ear some such words as: '*Dorenavant tu seras assure de compagnie.*' ('From henceforth you may rest assured of having company.')

Blind with terror, he ran to the door, clawed it open, and somehow got outside. But the key was aged and rotten, and when he tried to turn it in the lock it broke off in his hand. Throwing everything aside, he made for the wall of the park, somehow scrambled over it, and dropped into the road beyond.

Of the journey back he afterwards remembered nothing but an aching misery. But he no longer had the terrible sense that someone or something was with him, and he heard the clocks of Clauvères strike half-past eleven. It still wanted half an hour to St Bartholomew's day.

Arrived at the inn, he drank some brandy, crept up to his room and, in a futile endeavour to compose his mind, wrote down in his diary the events of the evening. 'God have mercy on me,' the entry concludes, 'I did not know. I meant well. If only I could have locked the door after me . . .'

At this point the writing tails away. For now, at twenty-past midnight on the 24th of August, he knew again that he was not alone.

He turned, and saw what was in the big four-poster bed.

The rest shall be told in his own words. It is daylight again, and he is in another room of the inn, lying on the bed with a broken leg, and composing a letter—the last—to his nephew. The writing is that of an old man, and his fingers tremble so he can hardly hold the pen.

'... the doctors say that it would be dangerous for me to be moved, and nothing will persuade them. Yet I would suffer the most dreadful physical pain conceivable to get away from this place. In the name of heaven, come to me as fast as train and boat will carry you.

'After that renewed and terrible conviction that I was again in the presence of something malevolent and evil, I looked towards the bed. Conceive of my extreme terror when I saw some creature sit up in it. It was swathed about with soiled linen like a mummy, with the arms close against the sides. There was no face, only ragged black holes where the eyes and mouth should have been, and that of the mouth dirtied and caked about with dry blood.

'Then the arms came away from the sides with a ripping and dust of rotten cloth, and it crawled off the bed and started towards me. I screamed out and ran for the door. There was a violent pain in my left leg, and blackness.

'I can write no more. Even in the sunlight, and with another person in the room, the memory of these things fills me with a worse horror than in my nightmares I had ever thought possible. For God's sake, come to me! The prospect of the brief hours of darkness before next midnight is unbearable to me.'

On August 26th, Mr Rotherham's nephew arrived at the inn. What he saw there sent him after a few moments running to the bathroom, where he threw up long and violently.

I was in Clauvères myself during the August of 1939, just before the war. The then landlord of the Coq d'Or was a grandson of the 'anarchical young man' to whom Mr Rotherham refers, and it was over a glass of beer with him in the inn parlour that I heard what became of Mr Rotherham. He was reluctant to speak of it at first, but I scented some kind of mystery and was eventually able to persuade him.

'I can only tell you, Monsieur,' he said, 'what my grandfather told me. The Englishman, you understand, would not be left for a moment alone, and it fell to my grandfather to stay with him in the room. As darkness approached, his agitation greatly increased, but towards midnight he fell silent for a short while. Then my grandfather, who was dozing off in his corner, was startled to hear him cry out in a terrible voice, "Get the priest! For God's sake get the priest!"

'My grandfather hesitated, but so urgent was the request that he felt he must comply. As he left the room he was conscious of the smell of something that was decayed, and halfway down the passage he turned and saw that the door of the bedroom was opening slowly and he heard the Englishman's voice cease abruptly. He hesitated, but'—the landlord shrugged—'he had no desire to go back then, and he ran to the priest's house. They returned a little after midnight, but there was nothing to do except cover the Englishman's face.'

'How did he die?' I asked.

'That, Monsieur, my grandfather would never say.'

Obviously the matter could not be allowed to rest there. I happened to remember that a friend of mine knew someone of the name of Rotherham, and since the name is not altogether common I wrote asking if he could give me any information on the subject. A week later I was rewarded by the arrival of a bulky package.

The Rotherham my friend knew was a son of the nephew to whom our Mr Rotherham wrote, and enclosed were the letters, diary and documents from which the preceding narrative had been pieced together.

'B—— made no objection to lending them,' my friend wrote. 'All except the letters were returned to his father, as the nearest surviving relative, after his great-uncle's death. He says there was one thing among the personal effects which puzzled his father a good deal. It was found clutched in the unfortunate man's hand, and was a square gold medal, rather old and tarnished, with part of a heavy gold chain attached to it. On one side was an inverted crucifix, and on the other a clock face without hands, or from which the hands had been removed. B—— tells me that he got it out to look at some time ago, but took such a dislike to it that he had it destroyed.'

On the day following the arrival of this letter—it was August 23rd—I went out in the afternoon to the Château de l'Echarpe. The door of the mausoleum had been bricked up, but in other respects it was exactly as Mr Rotherham had described it. I found the present caretaker, a pleasant young man who wore a black beret and smoked a cigarette.

'I am sorry, Monsieur,' he said, 'but—'

'But you're going away,' I put in, 'and won't be back until the 25th.' And I explained my reasons for thinking that this would be so.

When I had finished, he nodded and looked at me shrewdly. 'There is still an hour before my train leaves,' he said. 'If Monsieur would like to see the portrait—?' Naturally enough, Monsieur was delighted.

My guide, who was more obliging than Mr Rotherham's, brought me a stepladder which enabled me to study the picture at close range. It was unsigned, probably the work of a clever amateur. The insignia round Viscount Raoul de Savigny's neck consisted of a square gold medal on a gold chain. The side which was not hidden showed (you will scarcely be surprised to hear it) a clock face from which the hands had been removed. And the writing in the book was a line from Ronsard: *J'éviterai plaisir et damnation.*' ('I shall avoid pleasure and damnation.')

The summer air was good after the musty uninhabited rooms of the Château.

'And now, Monsieur, I must leave,' said the caretaker. 'I was here once on St Bartholomew's day, and no money would induce me to be in this neighbourhood again. It is the talking, you understand, and the mindless laughter, and the soft feeble pawing at the doors and windows . . ' He smiled suddenly. 'If Monsieur will wait one moment, I will close my cottage and accompany him to the gates.'

He went off, whistling, and I strolled idly towards the mausoleum. There is a thornbush which stands near the door, and although the day was windless I saw that it was shaking violently. This induced me to change my plans and travel back to Paris on the evening train.

St Bartholomew's day was still eight hours ahead and, looking back on it, I am fairly sure that the disturbance in the thornbush was caused by a cat. But in matters of this sort I consider it foolish to take unnecessary risks.

EDMUND CRISPIN

Bruce Montgomery, who wrote detective fiction as 'Edmund Crispin', was born at Chesham Bois in Buckinghamshire on 2 October 1921. His Scottish mother, Marion Blackwood Jarvie, was an amateur musician and his Irish father, Robert Ernest Montgomery, a civil servant who in 1938 received the Order of the British Empire for his service in the India Department.

As a child, Montgomery excelled in music, painting and writing, but he was a shy child, whose deformity of the feet affected his ability to take part in physical activities at school, and a degree of reticence stayed with him all his life. At Merchant Taylors' School he developed as a musician and as a composer, and when he went up to Oxford, he blossomed. He was appointed organist and choirmaster at St John's College and, as well as playing music and attending choral evensong, he spent many hours in pubs in conversation with friends or solving the *Times* crossword, a life-long passion. He also read books and in his final year John Maxwell, then artistic director at the Oxford Playhouse, lent his friend a copy of John Dickson Carr's *The Crooked Hinge*. Montgomery stayed up all night to finish the book and so began a life-long passion for detective stories.

Montgomery's first detective novel, *The Case of the Gilded Fly* (1944), was written in only two weeks while he was still an undergraduate. His detective, Gervase Fen, is Professor of English

Language and Literature at Oxford, a breezy don with a love of hairy tweeds and fast cars, whose initials consciously replicated those of John Dickson Carr's best-known detective, Gideon Fell. Perhaps taking a cue from Carr's mysteries written as 'Carter Dickson', Montgomery's Fen novels—particularly the earlier titles—combine detection and madcap humour; and he also took from Carr the quirk of breaking the fourth wall from time to time to address the reader directly.

In September 1943, after coming down with a second-class degree in modern languages, Montgomery took up a position teaching English and Music at Shrewsbury School in Shropshire, where his favourite lesson was to read aloud the ghost stories of M. R. James. While at Shrewsbury, which would appear, thinly disguised, as Castrevenford School in *Love Lies Bleeding* (1948), he met regularly with another admirer of the work of John Dickson Carr, the poet Philip Larkin, whom Montgomery had met at Oxford. Together with Geoffrey Bush and others, Montgomery also formed The Carr Club, an informal society dedicated to the analysis of impossible crimes.

In 1945, Montgomery went to Devon, initially living with his mother at her home in Brixham and then in a bungalow near Dartington. In 1947, he became a member of the Detection Club, proposed by Carr himself, and often travelled up to London for the annual Detection Club dinner with his near neighbour Agatha Christie who, unlike most people, always called him Edmund.

Montgomery had continued to write detective novels throughout the 1940s, but by 1950 it was clear that music was a good deal more profitable than literature and what would for over twenty years appear to be the last of his 'Crispin' novels, *The Long Divorce*, was published in 1951.

As a musician and composer, Montgomery was largely self-taught. After moving to Devon, he performed regularly in local concerts and, in 1948, he and Geoffrey Bush conducted at London's Wigmore Hall. In a long career, Montgomery produced a major chorale, *The Oxford Requiem*, several songs and Shakespearean settings, as well as music for over 40 films, each of which would take him between four to six weeks to score. He composed the music for the first four of the *Doctor* comedies, based on the novels by Richard Gordon, and also for the first five *Carry On* films until he was sacked for missing a deadline. His favourite piece was another chorale, *Venus Praised*, but although his work was popular with audiences it was considered overly romantic by critics.

While composing music was his main occupation from the early 1950s, Montgomery did not abandon literature altogether. He reviewed books for the *Sunday Times* and edited anthologies. But he had always been a heavy drinker and by the mid 1960s his health was in decline. Alcohol was not his only problem: his right hand was gradually being crippled by Dupuytren's Contracture, which causes the fingers to turn inwards, eventually making him unable to play the piano and compose.

In 1976, Montgomery married his secretary Ann Clements who had worked for him since 1957. With her encouragement, he produced a final case for Gervase Fen, *The Glimpses of the Moon* (1977), but his health continued to deteriorate and he died at home on 15 September 1978.

'St Bartholomew's Day' was published in *Ellery Queen's Mystery Magazine* in February 1975.

MARTIN'S CLOSE

M. R. James

Some few years back I was staying with the rector of a parish in the West, where the society to which I belong owns property. I was to go over some of this land: and, on the first morning of my visit, soon after breakfast, the estate carpenter and general handyman, John Hill, was announced as in readiness to accompany us. The rector asked which part of the parish we were to visit that morning. The estate map was produced, and when we had showed him our round, he put his finger on a particular spot. 'Don't forget,' he said, 'to ask John Hill about Martin's Close when you get there. I should like to hear what he tells you.' 'What ought he to tell us?' I said. 'I haven't the slightest idea,' said the rector, 'or, if that is not exactly true, it will do till lunch-time.' And here he was called away.

We set out; John Hill is not a man to withhold such information as he possesses on any point, and you may gather from him much that is of interest about the people of the place and their talk. An unfamiliar word, or one that he thinks ought to be unfamiliar to you, he will usually spell—as c-o-b cob, and the like. It is not, however, relevant to my purpose to record his conversation before the moment when we reached Martin's Close. The bit of land is noticeable, for it is one of the smallest enclosures you are likely to see—a very few square yards, hedged in with quickset on all sides, and without any gate or gap leading into it. You might take it for a small cottage garden long deserted, but that it lies away from the village and bears no trace of cultivation. It is at no great distance from the road, and is part of what is there called a moor, in other words, a rough upland pasture cut up into largish fields.

'Why is this little bit hedged off so?' I asked, and John Hill (whose answer I cannot represent as perfectly as I should like) was not at fault. 'That's what we call Martin's Close, sir: 'tes a curious thing 'bout that bit of land, sir: goes by the name of Martin's Close, sir. M-a-r-t-i-n Martin. Beg pardon, sir, did Rector tell you to make inquiry of me 'bout that, sir?' 'Yes, he did.' 'Ah, I thought so much, sir. I was tell'n Rector 'bout that last week, and he was very much interested. It 'pears there's a murderer buried there, sir, by the name of Martin. Old Samuel Saunders, that formerly lived yurr at what we call South-town, sir, he had a long tale 'bout that, sir: terrible murder done 'pon a young woman, sir. Cut her throat and cast her in the water down yurr.' 'Was he hung for it?' 'Yes, sir, he was hung just up yurr on the roadway, by what I've 'eard, on the Holy Innocents' Day, many 'undred years ago, by the man that went by the name of the bloody judge: terrible red and bloody, I've 'eard.' 'Was his name Jeffreys, do you think?' 'Might be possible 'twas— Jeffreys—J-e-f—Jeffreys. I reckon 'twas, and the tale I've 'eard many times from Mr Saunders—how this young man Martin— George Martin—was troubled before his crule action come to light by the young woman's sperit.' 'How was that, do you know?' 'No, sir, I don't exactly know how 'twas with it: but by what I've 'eard he was fairly tormented; and rightly tu. Old Mr Saunders, he told a history regarding a cupboard down yurr in the New Inn. According to what he related, this young woman's sperit come out of this cupboard: but I don't racollact the matter.'

This was the sum of John Hill's information. We passed on, and in due time I reported what I had heard to the Rector. He was able to show me from the parish account-books that a gibbet had been paid for in 1684, and a grave dug in the following year, both for the benefit of George Martin; but he was unable to suggest anyone in the parish, Saunders being now gone, who was likely to throw any further light on the story.

Naturally, upon my return to the neighbourhood of libraries, I made search in the more obvious places. The trial seemed to be nowhere reported. A newspaper of the time, and one or more news-letters, however, had some short notices, from which I learnt that, on the ground of local prejudice against the prisoner (he was described as a young gentleman of a good estate), the venue had been moved from Exeter to London; that Jeffreys had been the judge, and death the sentence, and that there had been some 'singular passages' in the evidence. Nothing further transpired till September of this year. A friend who knew me to be interested in Jeffreys then sent me a leaf torn out of a second-hand bookseller's catalogue with the entry: JEFFREYS, JUDGE: *Interesting old MS. trial for murder*, and so forth, from which I gathered, to my delight, that I could become possessed, for a very few shillings, of what seemed to be a verbatim report, in shorthand, of the Martin trial. I telegraphed for the manuscript and got it. It was a thin bound volume, provided with a title written in longhand by someone in the eighteenth century, who had also added this note: 'My father, who took these notes in court, told me that the prisoner's friends had made interest with Judge Jeffreys that no report should be put out: he had intended doing this himself when times were better, and had shew'd it to the Revd Mr Glanvil, who incourag'd his design very warmly, but death surpriz'd them both before it could be brought to an accomplishment.'

The initials W. G. are appended; I am advised that the original reporter may have been T. Gurney, who appears in that capacity in more than one State trial.

This was all that I could read for myself. After no long delay I heard of someone who was capable of deciphering the shorthand of the seventeenth century, and a little time ago the typewritten copy of the whole manuscript was laid before me. The portions which I shall communicate here help to fill in the very imperfect outline which subsists in the memories of John Hill and, I suppose, one or two others who live on the scene of the events.

The report begins with a species of preface, the general effect of which is that the copy is not that actually taken in court, though it is a true copy in regard to the notes of what was said; but that the writer has added to it some 'remarkable passages' that took place during the trial, and has made this present fair copy of the whole, intending at some favourable time to publish it; but has not put it into longhand, lest it should fall into the possession of unauthorized persons, and he or his family be deprived of the profit.

The report then begins:

This case came on to be tried on Wednesday, the 19th of November, between our sovereign lord the King, and George Martin Esquire, of (I take leave to omit some of the place-names), at a sessions of oyer and terminer and gaol delivery, at the Old Bailey, and the prisoner, being in Newgate, was brought to the bar.

Clerk of the Crown. George Martin, hold up thy hand (which he did).

Then the indictment was read, which set forth that the prisoner, 'not having the fear of God before his eyes, but being moved and seduced by the instigation of the devil, upon the 15th day of May, in the 36th year of our sovereign lord King Charles the Second, with force and arms in the parish aforesaid, in and upon Ann Clark, spinster, of the same place, in the peace of God and of our said sovereign lord the King then and there being, feloniously, wilfully, and of your malice aforethought did make an assault and with a certain knife value a penny the throat of the said Ann Clark then and there did cut, of the which wound the said Ann Clark then and there did die, and the body of the said Ann Clark did cast into a certain pond of water situate in the same parish (with more that is not material to our purpose) against the peace of our sovereign lord the King, his crown and dignity.'

Then the prisoner prayed a copy of the indictment.

L.C.J. (Sir George Jeffreys). What is this? Sure you know that is never allowed. Besides, here is a plain indictment as ever I heard; you have nothing to do but to plead to it.

Pris. My lord, I apprehend there may be matter of law arising out of the indictment, and I would humbly beg the court to assign me counsel to consider of it. Besides, my lord, I believe it was done in another case: copy of the indictment was allowed.

L.C.J. What case was that?

Pris. Truly, my lord, I have been kept close prisoner ever since I came up from Exeter Castle, and no one allowed to come at me and no one to advise with.

L.C.J. But I say, what was that case you allege?

Pris. My lord, I cannot tell your lordship precisely the name of the case, but it is in my mind that there was such an one, and I would humbly desire—

L.C.J. All this is nothing. Name your case, and we will tell you whether there be any matter for you in it. God forbid but you should have anything that may be allowed you by law: but this is against law, and we must keep the course of the court.

Att.-Gen. (Sir Robert Sawyer). My lord, we pray for the King that he may be asked to plead.

Cl. of Ct. Are you guilty of the murder whereof you stand indicted, or not guilty?

Pris. My lord, I would humbly offer this to the court. If I plead now, shall I have an opportunity after to except against the indictment?

L.C.J. Yes, yes, that comes after verdict: that will be saved to you, and counsel assigned if there be matter of law: but that which you have now to do is to plead.

Then after some little parleying with the court (which seemed strange upon such a plain indictment) the prisoner pleaded *Not Guilty*.

Cl. of Ct. Culprit. How wilt thou be tried?

Pris. By God and my country.

Cl. of Ct. God send thee a good deliverance.

L.C.J. Why, how is this? Here has been a great to-do that you should not be tried at Exeter by your country, but be brought here to London, and now you ask to be tried by your country. Must we send you to Exeter again?

Pris. My lord, I understood it was the form.

L.C.J. So it is, man: we spoke only in the way of pleasantness. Well, go on and swear the jury.

So they were sworn. I omit the names. There was no challenging on the prisoner's part, for, as he said, he did not know any of the persons called. Thereupon the prisoner asked for the use of pen, ink, and paper, to which the L. C. J. replied: 'Ay, ay, in God's name let him have it.' Then the usual charge was delivered to the jury, and the case opened by the junior counsel for the King, Mr Dolben.

The Attorney-General followed:

May it please your lordship, and you gentlemen of the jury, I am of counsel for the King against the prisoner at the bar. You have heard that he stands indicted for a murder done upon the person of a young girl. Such crimes as this you may perhaps reckon to be not uncommon, and, indeed, in these times, I am sorry to say it, there is scarce any fact so barbarous and unnatural but what we may hear almost daily instances of it. But I must confess that in this murder that is charged upon the prisoner there are some particular features that mark it out to be such as I hope has but seldom if ever been perpetrated upon English ground. For as we shall make it appear, the person murdered was a poor country girl (whereas the prisoner is a gentleman of a proper estate) and, besides that, was one to whom Providence had not given the full use of her intellects, but was what is termed among us commonly an innocent or natural: such an one, therefore, as one would have supposed a gentleman of the prisoner's quality more likely to overlook, or, if he did notice her, to be moved to compassion for her unhappy condition, than to lift up his hand against her in the very horrid and barbarous manner which we shall show you he used.

Now to begin at the beginning and open the matter to you orderly: About Christmas of last year, that is the year 1683, this gentleman, Mr Martin, having newly come back into his own country from the University of Cambridge, some of his neighbours, to show him what civility they could (for his family is one that stands in very good repute all over that country), entertained him here and there at their Christmas merrymakings, so that he was constantly riding to and fro, from one house to another, and sometimes, when the place of his destination was distant, or for other reason, as the unsafeness of the roads, he would be constrained to lie the night at an inn. In this way it happened that he came, a day or two after the Christmas, to the place where this young girl lived with her parents, and put up at the inn there, called the New Inn, which is, as I am informed, a house of good repute. Here was some dancing going on among the people of the place, and Ann Clark had been brought in, it seems, by her elder sister to look on; but being, as I have said, of weak understanding, and, besides that, very uncomely in her appearance, it was not likely she should take much part in the merriment; and accordingly was but standing by in a corner of the room. The prisoner at the bar, seeing her, one must suppose by way of a jest, asked her would she dance with him. And in spite of what her sister and others could say to prevent it and to dissuade her—

L.C.J. Come, Mr Attorney, we are not set here to listen to tales of Christmas parties in taverns. I would not interrupt you, but sure you have more weighty matters than this. You will be telling us next what tune they danced to.

Att. My lord, I would not take up the time of the court with what is not material: but we reckon it to be material to show how this unlikely acquaintance begun: and as for the tune, I believe, indeed, our evidence will show that even that hath a bearing on the matter in hand.

L.C.J. Go on, go on, in God's name: but give us nothing that is impertinent.

Att. Indeed, my lord, I will keep to my matter. But, gentlemen, having now shown you, as I think, enough of this first meeting between the murdered person and the prisoner, I will shorten my tale so far as to say that from then on there were frequent meetings of the two: for the young woman was greatly tickled with having got hold (as she conceived it) of so likely a sweetheart, and he being once a week at least in the habit of passing through the street where she lived, she would be always on the watch for him; and it seems they had a signal arranged: he should whistle the tune that was played at the tavern: it is a tune, as I am informed, well known in that country, and has a burden, '*Madam, will you walk, will you talk with me?*'

L.C.J. Ay, I remember it in my own country, in Shropshire. It runs somehow thus, doth it not? [Here his lordship whistled a part of a tune, which was very observable, and seemed below the dignity of the court. And it appears he felt it so himself, for he said:] But this is by the mark, and I doubt it is the first time we have had dance-tunes in this court. The most part of the dancing we give occasion for is done at Tyburn. [Looking at the prisoner, who appeared very much disordered.] You said the tune was material to your case, Mr Attorney, and upon my life I think Mr Martin agrees with you. What ails you, man? staring like a player that sees a ghost!

Pris. My lord, I was amazed at hearing such trivial, foolish things as they bring against me.

L.C.J. Well, well, it lies upon Mr Attorney to show whether they be trivial or not: but I must say, if he has nothing worse than this he has said, you have no great cause to be in amaze. Doth it not lie something deeper? But go on, Mr Attorney.

Att. My lord and gentlemen—all that I have said so far you may indeed very reasonably reckon as having an appearance of triviality. And, to be sure, had the matter gone no further than the humouring of a poor silly girl by a young gentleman of quality, it had been very well. But to proceed. We shall make it appear that after three or four weeks the prisoner became contracted to a young gentlewoman of that country, one suitable every way to his own condition, and such an arrangement was on foot that seemed to promise him a happy and a reputable living. But within no very long time it seems that this young gentlewoman, hearing of the jest that was going about that countryside with regard to the prisoner and Ann Clark, conceived that it was not only an unworthy carriage on the part of her lover, but a derogation to herself that he should suffer his name to be sport for tavern company: and so without more ado she, with the consent of her parents, signified to the prisoner that the match between them was at an end. We shall show you that upon the receipt of this intelligence the prisoner was greatly enraged against Ann Clark as being the cause of his misfortune (though indeed there was nobody answerable for it but himself), and that he made use of many outrageous expressions and threatenings against her, and subsequently upon meeting with her both abused her and struck at her with his whip: but she, being but a poor innocent, could not be persuaded to desist from her attachment to him, but would often run after him testifying with gestures and broken words the affection she had to him: until she was become, as he said, the very plague of his life. Yet, being that affairs in which he was now engaged necessarily took him by the house in which she lived, he could not (as I am willing to believe he would otherwise have done) avoid meeting with her from time to time. We shall further show you that this was the posture of things up to the 15th day of May in this present year. Upon that day the prisoner comes riding through the village, as of custom, and met with the young woman: but in place of passing her by, as he had lately done, he stopped, and said some words to her with which she appeared wonderfully pleased, and so left her; and after that day she was nowhere to be found, notwithstanding a strict search was made for her. The next time of the prisoner's passing through the place, her relations inquired of him whether he should know anything of her whereabouts; which he totally denied. They expressed to him their fears lest her weak intellects should have been upset by the attention he had showed her, and so she might have committed some rash act against her own life, calling him to witness the same time how often they had beseeched him to desist from taking notice of her, as fearing trouble might come of it: but this, too, he easily laughed away. But in spite of this light behaviour, it was noticeable in him that about this time his carriage and demeanour changed, and it was said of him that he seemed a troubled man. And here I come to a passage to which I should not dare to ask your attention, but that it appears to me to be founded in truth, and is supported by testimony deserving of credit. And, gentlemen, to my judgement it doth afford a great instance of God's revenge against murder, and that He will require the blood of the innocent.

[Here Mr Attorney made a pause, and shifted with his papers: and it was thought remarkable by me and others, because he was a man not easily dashed.]

L.C.J. Well, Mr Attorney, what is your instance?

Att. My lord, it is a strange one, and the truth is that, of all the cases I have been concerned in, I cannot call to mind the like of it. But to be short, gentlemen, we shall bring you testimony that Ann Clark was seen after this 15th of May, and that, at such time as she was so seen, it was impossible she could have been a living person.

[Here the people made a hum, and a good deal of laughter, and the Court called for silence, and when it was made]—

L.C.J. Why, Mr Attorney, you might save up this tale for a week; it will be Christmas by that time, and you can frighten your cook-maids with it [at which the people laughed again, and the prisoner also, as it seemed]. God, man, what are you prating of—ghosts and Christmas jigs and tavern company—and here is a man's life at stake! [To the prisoner]: And you, sir, I would have you know there is not so much occasion for you to make merry neither. You were not brought here for that, and if I know Mr Attorney, he has more in his brief than he has shown yet. Go on, Mr Attorney. I need not, mayhap, have spoken so sharply, but you must confess your course is something unusual.

Att. Nobody knows it better than I, my lord: but I shall bring it to an end with a round turn. I shall show you, gentlemen, that Ann Clark's body was found in the month of June, in a pond of water, with the throat cut: that a knife belonging to the prisoner was found in the same water: that he made efforts to recover the said knife from the water: that the coroner's quest brought in a verdict against the prisoner at the bar, and that therefore he should by course have been tried at Exeter: but that, suit being made on his behalf, on account that an impartial jury could not be found to try him in his own country, he hath had that singular favour shown him that he should be tried here in London. And so we will proceed to call our evidence.

Then the facts of the acquaintance between the prisoner and Ann Clark were proved, and also the coroner's inquest. I pass over this portion of the trial, for it offers nothing of special interest.

Sarah Arscott was next called and sworn.

Att. What is your occupation?

S. I keep the New Inn at—.

Att. Do you know the prisoner at the bar?

S. Yes: he was often at our house since he come first at Christmas of last year.

Att. Did you know Ann Clark?

S. Yes, very well.

Att. Pray, what manner of person was she in her appearance?

S. She was a very short thick-made woman: I do not know what else you would have me say.

Att. Was she comely?

S. No, not by no manner of means: she was very uncomely, poor child! She had a great face and hanging chops and a very bad colour like a puddock.

L.C.J. What is that, mistress? What say you she was like?

S. My lord, I ask pardon; I heard Esquire Martin say she looked like a puddock in the face; and so she did.

L.C.J. Did you that? Can you interpret her, Mr Attorney?

Att. My lord, I apprehend it is the country word for a toad.

L.C.J. Oh, a hop-toad! Ay, go on.

Att. Will you give an account to the jury of what passed between you and the prisoner at the bar in May last?

S. Sir, it was this. It was about nine o'clock the evening after that Ann did not come home, and I was about my work in the house; there was no company there only Thomas Snell, and it was foul weather. Esquire Martin came in and called for some drink, and I, by way of pleasantry, I said to him, 'Squire, have you been looking after your sweetheart?' and he flew out at me in a passion and desired I would not use such expressions. I was amazed at that, because we were accustomed to joke with him about her.

L.C.J. Who, her?

S. Ann Clark, my lord. And we had not heard the news of his being contracted to a young gentlewoman elsewhere, or I am sure I should have used better manners. So I said nothing, but being I was a little put out, I begun singing, to myself as it were, the song they danced to the first time they met, for I thought it would prick him. It was the same that he was used to sing when he came down the street; I have heard it very often: '*Madam, will you walk, will you talk with me?*' And it fell out that I needed something that was in the kitchen. So I went out to get it, and all the time I went on singing, something louder and more bold-like. And as I was there all of a sudden I thought I heard someone answering outside the house, but I could not be sure because of the wind blowing so high. So then I stopped singing, and now I heard it plain, saying, '*Yes, sir, I will walk, I will talk with you,*' and I knew the voice for Ann Clark's voice.

Att. How did you know it to be her voice?

S. It was impossible I could be mistaken. She had a dreadful voice, a kind of a squalling voice, in particular if she tried to sing. And there was nobody in the village that could counterfeit it, for they often tried. So, hearing that, I was glad, because we were all in an anxiety to know what was gone with her: for though she was a natural, she had a good disposition and was very tractable: and says I to myself, 'What, child! are you returned, then?' and I ran into the front room, and said to Squire Martin as I passed by, 'Squire, here is your sweetheart back again: shall I call her in?' and with that I went to open the door; but Squire Martin he caught hold of me, and it seemed to me he was out of his wits, or near upon. 'Hold, woman,' says he, 'in God's name!' and I know not what else: he was all of a shake. Then I was angry, and said I, 'What! are you not glad that poor child is found?' and I called to Thomas Snell and said, 'If the Squire will not let me, do you open the door and call her in.' So Thomas Snell went and opened the door, and the wind setting that way blew in and overset the two candles that was all we had lighted: and Esquire Martin fell away from holding me; I think he fell down on the floor, but we were wholly in the dark, and it was a minute or two before I got a light again: and while I was feeling for the fire-box, I am not certain but I heard someone step 'cross the floor, and I am sure I heard the door of the great cupboard that stands in the room open and shut to. Then, when I had a light again, I see Esquire Martin on the settle, all white and sweaty as if he had swounded away, and his arms hanging down; and I was going to help him; but just then it caught my eye that there was something like a bit of a dress shut into the cupboard door, and it came to my mind I had heard that door shut. So I thought it might be some person had run in when the light was quenched, and was hiding in the cupboard. So I went up closer and looked: and there was a bit of a black stuff cloak, and just below it an edge of a brown stuff dress, both sticking out of the shut of the door: and both of them was low down, as if the person that had them on might be crouched down inside.

Att. What did you take it to be?

S. I took it to be a woman's dress.

Att. Could you make any guess whom it belonged to? Did you know anyone who wore such a dress?

S. It was a common stuff, by what I could see. I have seen many women wearing such a stuff in our parish.

Att. Was it like Ann Clark's dress?

S. She used to wear just such a dress: but I could not say on my oath it was hers.

Att. Did you observe anything else about it?

S. I did notice that it looked very wet: but it was foul weather outside.

L.C.J. Did you feel of it, mistress?

S. No, my lord, I did not like to touch it.

L.C.J. Not like? Why that? Are you so nice that you scruple to feel of a wet dress?

S. Indeed, my lord, I cannot very well tell why: only it had a nasty ugly look about it.

L.C.J. Well, go on.

S. Then I called again to Thomas Snell, and bid him come to me and catch anyone that come out when I should open the cupboard door, 'for,' says I, 'there is someone hiding within, and I would know what she wants.' And with that Squire Martin gave a sort of a cry or a shout and ran out of the house into the dark, and I felt the cupboard door pushed out against me while I held it, and Thomas Snell helped me: but for all we pressed to keep it shut as hard as we could, it was forced out against us, and we had to fall back.

L.C.J. And pray what came out—a mouse?

S. No, my lord, it was greater than a mouse, but I could not see what it was: it fleeted very swift over the floor and out at the door.

L.C.J. But come; what did it look like? Was it a person?

S. My lord, I cannot tell what it was, but it ran very low, and it was of a dark colour. We were both daunted by it, Thomas Snell and I, but we made all the haste we could after it to the door that stood open. And we looked out, but it was dark and we could see nothing.

L.C.J. Was there no tracks of it on the floor? What floor have you there?

S. It is a flagged floor and sanded, my lord, and there was an appearance of a wet track on the floor, but we could make nothing of it, neither Thomas Snell nor me, and besides, as I said, it was a foul night.

L.C.J. Well, for my part, I see not—though to be sure it is an odd tale she tells—what you would do with this evidence.

Att. My lord, we bring it to show the suspicious carriage of the prisoner immediately after the disappearance of the murdered person: and we ask the jury's consideration of that; and also to the matter of the voice heard without the house.

Then the prisoner asked some questions not very material, and Thomas Snell was next called, who gave evidence to the same effect as Mrs Arscott, and added the following:

Att. Did anything pass between you and the prisoner during the time Mrs Arscott was out of the room?

Th. I had a piece of twist in my pocket.

Att. Twist of what?

Th. Twist of tobacco, sir, and I felt a disposition to take a pipe of tobacco. So I found a pipe on the chimney-piece, and being it was twist, and in regard of me having by an oversight left my knife at my house, and me not having over many teeth to pluck at it, as your lordship or anyone else may have a view by their own eyesight—

L.C.J. What is the man talking about? Come to the matter, fellow! Do you think we sit here to look at your teeth?

Th. No, my lord, nor I would not you should do, God forbid! I know your honours have better employment, and better teeth, I would not wonder.

L.C.J. Good God, what a man is this! Yes, I *have* better teeth, and that you shall find if you keep not to the purpose.

Th. I humbly ask pardon, my lord, but so it was. And I took upon me, thinking no harm, to ask Squire Martin to lend me his knife to cut my tobacco. And he felt first of one pocket and then of another and it was not there at all. And says I, 'What! have you lost your knife, Squire?' And up he gets and feels again and he sat down, and such a groan as he gave. 'Good God!' he says, 'I must have left it there.' 'But,' says I, 'Squire, by all appearance it is *not* there. Did you set a value on it,' says I, 'you might have it cried.' But he sat there and put his head between his hands and seemed to take no notice to what I said. And then it was Mistress Arscott come tracking back out of the kitchen place.

Asked if he heard the voice singing outside the house, he said 'No,' but the door into the kitchen was shut, and there was a high wind: but says that no one could mistake Ann Clark's voice.

Then a boy, William Reddaway, about thirteen years of age,

was called, and by the usual questions, put by the Lord Chief Justice, it was ascertained that he knew the nature of an oath. And so he was sworn. His evidence referred to a time about a week later.

Att. Now, child, don't be frighted: there is no one here will hurt you if you speak the truth.

L.C.J. Ay, if he speak the truth. But remember, child, thou art in the presence of the great God of heaven and earth, that hath the keys of hell, and of us that are the king's officers, and have the keys of Newgate; and remember, too, there is a man's life in question; and if thou tellest a lie, and by that means he comes to an ill end, thou art no better than his murderer; and so speak the truth.

Att. Tell the jury what you know, and speak out. Where were you on the evening of the 23rd of May last?

L.C.J. Why, what does such a boy as this know of days. Can you mark the day, boy?

W. Yes, my lord, it was the day before our feast, and I was to spend sixpence there, and that falls a month before Midsummer Day.

One of the Jury. My lord, we cannot hear what he says.

L.C.J. He says he remembers the day because it was the day before the feast they had there, and he had sixpence to lay out. Set him up on the table there. Well, child, and where wast thou then?

W. Keeping cows on the moor, my lord.

But, the boy using the country speech, my lord could not well apprehend him, and so asked if there was anyone that could interpret him, and it was answered the parson of the parish was there, and he was accordingly sworn and so the evidence given. The boy said:

'I was on the moor about six o'clock, and sitting behind a bush of furze near a pond of water: and the prisoner came very cautiously and looking about him, having something like a long pole in his hand, and stopped a good while as if he would be listening, and then began to feel in the water with the pole: and I being very near the water—not above five yards—heard as if the pole struck up against something that made a wallowing sound, and the prisoner dropped the pole and threw himself on the ground, and rolled himself about very strangely with his hands to his ears, and so after a while got up and went creeping away.'

Asked if he had had any communication with the prisoner, 'Yes, a day or two before, the prisoner, hearing I was used to be on the moor, he asked me if I had seen a knife laying about, and said he would give sixpence to find it. And I said I had not seen any such thing, but I would ask about. Then he said he would give me sixpence to say nothing, and so he did.'

L.C.J. And was that the sixpence you were to lay out at the feast?

W. Yes, if you please, my lord.

Asked if he had observed anything particular as to the pond of water, he said, 'No, except that it begun to have a very ill smell and the cows would not drink of it for some days before.'

Asked if he had ever seen the prisoner and Ann Clark in company together, he began to cry very much, and it was a long time before they could get him to speak intelligibly. At last the parson of the parish, Mr Matthews, got him to be quiet, and the question being put to him again, he said he had seen Ann Clark waiting on the moor for the prisoner at some way off, several times since last Christmas.

Att. Did you see her close, so as to be sure it was she?

W. Yes, quite sure.

L.C.J. How quite sure, child?

W. Because she would stand and jump up and down and clap her arms like a goose [which he called by some country name: but the parson explained it to be a goose]. And then she was of such a shape that it could not be no one else.

Att. What was the last time that you so saw her?

Then the witness began to cry again and clung very much to Mr Matthews, who bid him not be frightened. And so at last he told this story: that on the day before their feast (being the same evening that he had before spoken of) after the prisoner had gone away, it being then twilight and he very desirous to get home, but afraid for the present to stir from where he was lest the prisoner should see him, remained some few minutes behind the bush, looking on the pond, and saw something dark come up out of the water at the edge of the pond farthest away from him, and so up the bank. And when it got to the top where he could see it plain against the sky, it stood up and flapped the arms up and down, and then run off very swiftly in the same direction the prisoner had taken: and being asked very strictly who he took it to be, he said upon his oath that it could be nobody but Ann Clark.

Thereafter his master was called, and gave evidence that the boy had come home very late that evening and been chided for it, and that he seemed very much amazed, but could give no account of the reason.

Att. My lord, we have done with our evidence for the King.

Then the Lord Chief Justice called upon the prisoner to make his defence; which he did, though at no great length, and in a very halting way, saying that he hoped the jury would not go about to take his life on the evidence of a parcel of country people and children that would believe any idle tale; and that he had been very much prejudiced in his trial; at which the L.C.J. interrupted him, saying that he had had singular favour shown to him in having his trial removed from Exeter, which the prisoner acknowledging, said that he meant rather that since he was brought to London there had not been care taken to keep him secured from interruption and disturbance. Upon which the L.C.J. ordered the Marshal to be called, and questioned him about the safe keeping of the prisoner, but could find nothing: except the Marshal said that he had been informed by the underkeeper that they had seen a person outside his door or going up the stairs to it: but there was no possibility the person should have got in. And it being inquired further what sort of person this might be, the Marshal could not speak to it save by hearsay, which was not allowed. And the prisoner, being asked if this was what he meant, said no, he knew nothing of that, but it was very hard that a man should not be suffered to be at quiet when his life stood on it. But it was observed he was very hasty in his denial. And so he said no more, and called no witnesses. Whereupon the Attorney-General spoke to the jury. [A full report of what he said is given, and, if time allowed, I would extract that portion in which he dwells on the alleged appearance of the murdered person: he quotes some authorities of ancient date, as St Augustine *de cura pro mortuis gerenda* (a favourite book of reference with the old writers on the supernatural) and also cites some cases which may be seen in Glanvill's, but more conveniently in Mr Lang's books. He does not, however, tell us more of those cases than is to be found in print.]

The Lord Chief Justice then summed up the evidence for the jury. His speech, again, contains nothing that I find worth copying out: but he was naturally impressed with the singular character of the evidence, saying that he had never heard such given in his experience; but that there was nothing in law to set it aside, and that the jury must consider whether they believed these witnesses or not.

And the jury after a very short consultation brought the prisoner in Guilty.

So he was asked whether he had anything to say in arrest of judgement, and pleaded that his name was spelt wrong in the indictment, being Martin with an I, whereas it should be with a Y. But this was overruled as not material, Mr Attorney saying, moreover, that he could bring evidence to show that the prisoner by times wrote it as it was laid in the indictment. And, the prisoner having nothing further to offer, sentence of death was passed upon him, and that he should be hanged in chains upon a gibbet near the place where the fact was committed, and that execution should take place upon the 28th December next ensuing, being Innocents' Day.

Thereafter the prisoner being to all appearance in a state of desperation, made shift to ask the L.C.J. that his relations might be allowed to come to him during the short time he had to live.

L.C.J. Ay, with all my heart, so it be in the presence of the keeper; and Ann Clark may come to you as well, for what I care.

At which the prisoner broke out and cried to his lordship not to use such words to him, and his lordship very angrily told him he deserved no tenderness at any man's hands for a cowardly butcherly murderer that had not the stomach to take the reward of his deeds: 'and I hope to God,' said he, 'that she *will* be with you by day and by night till an end is made of you.' Then the prisoner was removed, and, so far as I saw, he was in a swound, and the Court broke up.

I cannot refrain from observing that the prisoner during all the time of the trial seemed to be more uneasy than is commonly the case even in capital causes: that, for example, he was looking narrowly among the people and often turning round very sharply, as if some person might be at his ear. It was also very noticeable at this trial what a silence the people kept, and further (though this might not be otherwise than natural in that season of the year), what a darkness and obscurity there was in the court room, lights being brought in not long after two o'clock in the day, and yet no fog in the town.

It was not without interest that I heard lately from some young men who had been giving a concert in the village I speak of, that a very cold reception was accorded to the song which has been mentioned in this narrative: '*Madam, will you walk?*' It came out in some talk they had next morning with some of the local people that that song was regarded with an invincible repugnance; it was not so, they believed, at North Tawton, but here it was reckoned to be unlucky. However, why that view was taken no one had the shadow of an idea.

CODA TO THE LATE PROVOST'S GHOST STORY

Dorothy L. Sayers

To the Editor of the Eton College Chronicle.

DEAR SIR,—Lord Peter Wimsey (who, as you may possibly recollect, is an Old Etonian) has been greatly interested in the list of questions about the late Provost's *Ghost Stories*, published in your issue for November 12. He asks me to send you the enclosed copy of a letter from a member of the Wimsey family, which he acquired some time ago for the collection of family papers at Bredon Hall. It appears to shed some light upon the matter of Mr George Martin (question 2).

The writer of the letter was Lord Charles Wimsey, brother to the Duke of Denver of that period. He was at this time about twenty years of age, and appears to have been sent into Devon upon some matrimonial project. The letter is addressed to a Cambridge friend.

Trusting that you will find the account of interest.

I am,

Yours faithfully,

DOROTHY L. SAYERS.

24 Newland Street,

Witham, Essex.

December 28, 1936.

Exeter.

the 28th November 1684.

DEAR JACK,—Rat me! but I think my father is out of his mind to send me a-wooing at this time of the year. I came hither yesterday about dusk, after such a wintry pilgrimage across these damned inhospitable moors as my bones ache only to think on; befouled with mire, pierced through by the wind, and my horse near foundered with tumbling in and out of bog-holes a dozen times in an hour. I have little news to tell thee, save one trifling adventure, which, whether it be physical or metaphysical, I leave to our Cambridge philoso-phers to determine.

I lay last night at Mr Coffyn's. He received me kindly according to his lights, with a great supper of beef pasties and cyder; and when we were well stupefyed with this coarse entertainment proposed, by way of divertisement, that we should go forth to see a great sight; no less than a young 'squire of the neighbourhood, now waiting execution in the county gaol for the murder of his trollop. This looby, it seems, hath had the honour to be haled to London, to receive judge-ment at the hand of Jefferies himself; so that the mere whiff of the Town upon him hath lent him a kind of fashionable perfume in the nostrils of these Westcountry savages. Thinking I might as well do anything as sit in the parlour playing Ombre with mine host and his two plain-faced daughters, I consented. At the door of the prison we encountered the Ordinary, bound upon the same errand. We found the condemned man laid upon his bed in a little stone room, that smelt very unwhole-some—I wish I may not have catched the fever for my pains. At our first coming in, he lay huddled close against the wall muttering to himself; we took him to be light-headed. The keeper bade us observe that he was well lodged, with a hand-some bed and all things suitable to his condition. Very well (said I), but if you wish he shall live to be hanged you were best put him in a dryer place—at the same time feeling of his mattress, which indeed was wringing wet from the bedfoot. Mr Coffyn observed it, too, and chid the Keeper for his neglect. Nay (says the fellow) 'tis a good dry cell enough; if there is any damp on the mattress it is that he hath faln into a sweat with thinking on his latter end.—Why fool (said I) were he to sweat, that were the saving of him, but his skin is burning dry. With that, I put my hand upon his shoulder, when he lets out a great screech, crying, Ann Clark, Ann Clark, take your hand from my neck! Mr Coffyn started back, presently giving me to understand, this was the name of the young woman that was murdered. I then searched the bed further, and found in it a little patch of duckweed, about the bigness of a crown-piece, as fresh and green as tho' it had been that moment taken from pond of water—which seemed a strange thing, seeing this weed is green only in Summer. The Ordinary turning pale and crying, God bless us, we all beheld the wetness dry away from the bed before our eyes, very like an egg when it is taken from the pot, only without any vapour; and the sick man thereafter more quiet. We knew not what to make of it, except it might be the heat of the fever that dryed the place. Mr Coffyn told me, what I had not known before, that Ann Clark met her death by drowning in a pond, being about the middle of May last.

The weather showing signs of mending, I mean to push forward to-morrow. This is a barbarous dull town, with not an ounce of fine snuff to be had for love or money, and no object of interest but a Gothick Cathedral, for which I have no manner of use. If you love me, wish me safe back in Town before Christmas, whole and sound, and (by good Fortune) still a bachelor.

Ever, dear Jack, thine assured trusty friend,

C. WIMSEY.

M. R. JAMES & DOROTHY L. SAYERS

Montague Rhodes James was born on 1 August 1862 at Goodnestone Parsonage in Dover, Kent, the son of Mary Horton and the Reverend Herbert James. James was educated at a private school at East Sheen before, following in his father's footsteps in 1876, he went to Eton College as a King's Scholar. In 1882 he went up to Cambridge after winning the Newcastle Scholarship for Classics and Divinity, Eton's premier academic prize at that time, as well as the Prince Consort's prize for French. At King's College, he achieved the highest distinctions in classics and theology and was awarded a Fellowship. His achievements in teaching, researching and writing led to his being appointed Provost in 1905. James' many achievements at King's included being elected in 1906 as first President of the Cambridge Society for the Encouragement of Arts and Crafts, and the Vice Chancellorship between 1913 and 1915. He also played a prominent role in the life of the city, including in 1914 working jointly with the Mayor to raise funds for the acquisition of braille literature for the city's branch of the National Institute for the Blind.

In 1918, James returned to Eton as Provost, teaching and leading in his own inimitable way; in December 1919, together with colleague Allen Ramsey, James wrote a play—in Latin—entitled 'The Founder's Pageant and Play of St Nicholas', which recounted the raising to life of a trio of murdered schoolchildren. In a speech in 1921, James expressed the view that every teacher should be in love with their profession and have 'some special mental interest—literary, scientific, or artistic—of his or her own'. In his case, that interest was the writing—and telling—of ghost stories, at which James is peerless. A ghost story, he prescribed, should conform to two rules: the setting of the scene must be in ordinary life and the circumstances convincing so that the reader may say, 'This might happen now, and to me'; and the ghost *must* be malevolent.

In his lifetime, James was best-known as an authority on apocryphal and medieval literature, which led to his being awarded the Order of Merit by King George V in 1930. As well as ghost stories and a novel for children, *The Five Jars* (1922), he wrote numerous academic and other books, including *Old Testament Legends* (1913) and *Suffolk and Norfolk* (1930). His recreations were patience and piquet, and James once said that the best things in life were 'the Bible, Homer, Shakespeare, Handel and Dickens, the Elgin Marbles and Salisbury cathedral, the open country, the sea and the stars: and the knowledge that all these may be made to disclose'.

In January 1936, James fell ill and he died at The Lodge in Eton on 12 June 1936.

Dorothy Leigh Sayers was born on 13 June 1893 in Oxford, the daughter of Helen Leigh and the Reverend Henry Sayers, who was chaplain at the cathedral and headmaster of the Choristers' School. From 1909 to 1912 Sayers boarded at the Godolphin School in Salisbury, where she achieved the highest mark in the whole of England in the Cambridge Higher Local Examinations. She was awarded a scholarship in modern languages and medieval literature at Somerville College, Oxford, where she was awarded a first-class honours degree in 1915. In line with the antediluvian attitudes of the times, Sayers did not receive her university degrees formally until 1920, and one of the first women to do so.

While opinions vary as to how far Sayers can be regarded as a feminist, she was throughout her life a humanist, albeit one with strong religious beliefs. On coming down from Oxford, Sayers joined the London advertising agency, S. H. Benson, where she worked as a copywriter on campaigns for Guinness and Colman's mustard, authoring *The Recipe Book of the Mustard Club* (1926). It was while working for Bensons that Sayers wrote her first novel, *Whose Body?* (1923), featuring the Oxford-educated Lord Peter Wimsey, who would go on to become one of the best-loved detectives of the Golden Age. Wimsey appears in eleven novels by Sayers and 21 collected short stories, as well as 'The Locked Room', which was published for the first time in *Bodies from the Library 2* (2019) and a handful of unfinished stories. In addition to chronicling Wimsey's life and investigations, Sayers was an active member of the Detection Club, and she edited three superb volumes of *Great Stories of Mystery, Detection and Horror* (1928, 1931 and 1934).

Together with her prolific reviews for the *Sunday Times* and elsewhere, Sayers played a major part in countering the damage done to the reputation of crime writers by the tsunami of badly written and poorly plotted mysteries in the 1920s and 1930s. Dorothy L. Sayers—she never liked anyone forgetting the 'L.'—died on 17 December 1957 at 24 Newland Street in Witham, Essex. Today a fine statue of the author stands opposite the house; it was erected by the Dorothy L Sayers Society (www.sayers.org.uk).

'Martin's Close' was first published in the M. R. James collection *More Ghost Stories of an Antiquary* (1911). Sayers' coda appeared in the correspondence column of the *Eton College Chronicle* dated 4 February 1937. In the 12 November 1936 issue, Lieutenant-Colonel Edward Newman Mozley, D.S.O., an Old Etonian serving with the Royal Engineers, had posed various questions regarding James's ghost stories. These included a request for 'any unpublished records which may exist relative to the visits paid to Mr George Martin between his trial and execution', a request that Sayers was delighted to fulfil.

ACKNOWLEDGEMENTS

'The Red Balloon' by Q Patrick copyright © the Estate of Hugh Wheeler 1953.

'Terror' by Daphne du Maurier copyright © 1928 by Daphne du Maurier, reprinted with permission of Curtis Brown Group Ltd, London.

'The Green Dress' by Anthony Berkeley printed by permission of The Society of Authors as literary representative of the Estate of Anthony Berkeley Cox.

'Personal Call' by Agatha Christie copyright © 1954 Agatha Christie Limited. All rights reserved. Agatha Christie® is a registered trade mark of Agatha Christie Limited in the UK and elsewhere.

'The Woman Who Cried' by H.C. Bailey © the estate of H. C. Bailey 1912.

'The Witch' by Christianna Brand copyright © Christianna Brand 1962. Reprinted by permission of A M Heath & Co. Ltd Authors' Agents.

'Death in a Dream' by Laurence Meynell copyright © Laurence Meynell 1963.

'The Haunted Grange of Goresthorpe' by Sir Arthur Conan Doyle © Charles Foley, Georgina Doyle, Richard Doyle & Catherine Beggs 2000, reprinted by permission of The Conan Doyle Estate.

'Misleading Lady' by Margery Allingham (1935) reprinted by permission of Peters Fraser & Dunlop (www.petersfraserdunlop.com) on behalf of the Estate of Margery Allingham.

'The Legend of the Cane in the Dark' by John Dickson Carr copyright © John Dickson Carr 1926.

'St Bartholomew's Day' by Edmund Crispin copyright © Rights Ltd 1975.

'Coda to the Late Provost's Ghost Story' by Dorothy L. Sayers copyright © 1937 the Trustees of Anthony Fleming (deceased).

Every effort has been made to trace all owners of copyright. The editor and publishers apologise for any errors or omissions and would be grateful if notified of any corrections.

Also available

BODIES FROM THE LIBRARY 1

Lost tales of mystery and suspense
from the Golden Age of Detection

Selected and introduced by Tony Medawar

This anthology brings together 16 forgotten tales that have either been published only once before – perhaps in a newspaper or rare magazine – or have never before appeared in print. From a previously unpublished 1917 script featuring Ernest Bramah's blind detective Max Carrados, to early 1950s crime stories written for London's *Evening Standard* by Cyril Hare, Freeman Wills Crofts and A.A. Milne, it spans five decades of writing by masters of the Golden Age.

Most anticipated of all are the contributions by women writers: the first detective story by Georgette Heyer, *Linckes' Great Case*, unseen since 1923; the unpublished *The Rum Punch* by Christianna Brand, creator of Nanny McPhee; and Agatha Christie's *The Wife of the Kenite*, a dark tale of revenge published only in an Australian journal in 1922 during her 'Grand Tour' of the British Empire.

With other stories by Detection Club stalwarts Anthony Berkeley, H.C. Bailey, J.J. Connington, John Rhode and Nicholas Blake, plus Vincent Cornier, Leo Bruce, Roy Vickers and Arthur Upfield, this essential collection harks back to a time before forensic science – when murder was a complex business.

Also available

THE GOLDEN AGE OF MURDER

The Mystery of the Writers who Invented
the Modern Detective Story

By Martin Edwards

Detective stories of the Twenties and Thirties have long been stereotyped as cosily conventional. Nothing could be further from the truth.

The Golden Age of Murder tells for the first time the extraordinary story of British detective fiction between the two World Wars. A gripping real-life detective story, it investigates how Dorothy L. Sayers, Anthony Berkeley, Agatha Christie and their colleagues in the mysterious Detection Club transformed crime fiction. Their work cast new light on unsolved murders whilst hiding clues to their authors' darkest secrets, and their complex and sometimes bizarre private lives.

Crime novelist and current Detection Club President Martin Edwards rewrites the history of crime fiction with unique authority, transforming our understanding of detective stories, and the brilliant but tormented men and women who wrote them.

'Few, if any, books about crime fiction have provided so much information and insight so enthusiastically and, for the reader, so enjoyably.'   THE TIMES